"How can I help the prince find his princess?" His voice lowered to a caressing baritone. "He is so lonely, and the right woman is waiting for him, but how does he find her?"

He was doing it again, Celestine thought, glancing with dismay into the aristocrat's expressive eyes. As if he didn't have enough ladies to flirt with!

"I think you will find some way, my lord. If you will excuse me, I must find out if the girls are back from their walk yet." She rose to go.

Justin caught her hand. "Don't go yet." He pulled her back. He stood and held her hand, touching it gently. "How are your hands today. Are they any better?"

Celestine flushed with mortification. She wanted to snatch her hand away and hide it behind her, but he had a light but powerful grip on it. His long, strong fingers were curled around hers, and it wouldn't do to have a tug of war. His closeness was disconcerting—the warmth that radiated from his body, the scent of some hair pomade or cologne, the way his wide shoulders and sturdy body blocked everything else from her view. "They are a little better, my lord. Now I really must . . ." She tugged on her hand, but he didn't let go.

"Don't run, Celestine. Don't be afraid of me. I would never harm you."

His voice was a low murmur and she felt herself falling under his spell—felt her heart throbbing and swelling with desire. What was he doing to her with just a touch, just a word?

Then, before she could stop him, he turned her hand over and his lips caressed her palm in a lingering kiss. . . .

CELEBRATE THE NEW YEAR
WITH ZEBRA REGENCY ROMANCE AND
THESE TALENTED NEW AUTHORS

LORD
ST. CLAIRE'S
ANGEL

Donna Simpson

Zebra Books
Kensington Publishing Corp.
http://www.zebrabooks.com

ZEBRA BOOKS are published by

Kensington Publishing Corp.
850 Third Avenue
New York, NY 10022

Zebra and the Z logo Reg. U.S. Pat. & TM Off.

First Printing: December, 1999
10 9 8 7 6 5 4 3 2 1

Printed in the United States of America

This is for Mick, who believed in me before I believed in myself, and for Mom, Agnes Simpson

One

"Thank God she is so plain! We'll not have the same trouble this Christmas we had last year with your wretched brother!"

Celestine Simons stopped outside of her employers' drawing room, hesitating to intrude. The voice was that of her employer, Lady Elizabeth St. Claire, Marchioness of Ladymead. She was evidently speaking to her husband, and perhaps would not welcome an interruption.

"True, Elizabeth. Miss Simons is not at all the sort of female Justin prefers. She is satisfyingly homely—and aware of it, too, if I am not mistaken. It is her best protection from my brother."

Lord St. Claire had a rich, booming baritone from making many speeches in the House of Lords, and Celestine heard every word with humiliating clarity. She shrank back against the ivory-papered wall, knowing she could not now enter without the most mortifying sensibility that they were discussing her. She hung her head, too stunned by the cruel accuracy of the words to retreat.

"All too often governesses today seem to be pretty, pert little misses with ideas above their station," Lady St. Claire said, her light, feminine voice fading and strengthening as she evidently walked around the room. "And you cannot tell me Justin was alone in the flirtation. Miss Chambly had her eye on him from the moment he stepped across our threshold!"

"I blame Justin, though, my dear. Her very position as our governess should have protected her from his predations! I don't know what to do with that scalawag of a brother of mine! It is time he took a wife and stopped his alley-cat behavior."

"August! Language!"

"Really, my dear, I said alley-cat, not whoring . . ."

"August!"

There was a muffled shriek, then some whispering, the sound of a loud kiss, and then a rustle.

"*You*, husband, are a scamp, very much like your brother." Lady St. Claire's voice was breathless, but smugly pleased.

"Ah, but I confine my 'predations' to my lady wife," the marquess growled. More rustling and a low chuckle followed.

Celestine, her cheeks burning, hustled away from the door toward the great curved staircase and began to ascend, embarrassed at having lingered long enough to overhear such an intimate exchange between her employer and his wife.

Plain. She knew she was plain, but to know she owed her employment in the St. Claire household to that fact! She had never suspected their quick hiring of her had to do with anything more than her accomplishments: French, Latin, a little Greek, history, a fair knowledge of mathematics and science, household arts and accounts. And all along it was mostly because she was plain!

She paused on a landing, one hand on the smooth wood banister. Holding back the tears that welled in her eyes, she pressed one palm to her burning cheek. Then, as always, she dropped her hands, hiding them in the folds of her skirt, letting the cool gray fabric swirl over the gnarled knuckles and crooked fingers. Lord and Lady St. Claire had nothing to worry about. Their brother was safe this year, for he would surely not force his attentions on an aging, plain, arthritic spinster governess. She returned to the schoolroom and her duties.

* * *

Justin St. Claire, astride his magnificent hunter, Alphonse, rode to the front door of Ladymead Manor, hurled himself from the saddle and tossed the reins to a stablehand who had appeared at the sound of hoofbeats. His breath puffed out in steamy clouds as he raced up the stone steps and banged on the brass knocker.

The butler opened the door and bowed him in, taking the coat and scarf Justin tossed at him.

"Where's the family, Dobbs?"

"His lordship is in the library, and her ladyship is in the parlor with Lady Charlotte and Lady Gwenevere."

Without waiting for the butler to announce him, Justin raced down the hall, threw open the door, and knelt on the soft Oriental carpet. "Where are my favorite girls?" he cried.

Lottie and Gwen, seven and five years of age, respectively, looked up from the needlework their mother was showing them and shrieked with excitement. In a moment they had abandoned their mother and raced across the room, flinging themselves at their uncle in gleeful disarray.

"Charlotte! Gwenevere!" Lady St. Claire cried, striving to bring order.

She was drowned out by the tumultuous wrestling match that now took place as Justin dared the girls to find a treat. They diligently searched his coat pockets, crowing with delight as they found some paper-wrapped bonbons.

Justin, his dark curls tumbled across his high forehead, smiled over at his sister-in-law, who tried to look severe as he turned her daughters into tiny lunatics for a few moments. Finally Elizabeth laughed, too, and stood, crossing to his side. He rose from the carpet and planted an affectionate kiss on her pale, soft cheek.

He held her at arm's length, looking her over from the top of her lace-capped head to the dainty slippers that peeked out from beneath the skirts of her rose muslin morning dress.

"Sister, you look lovelier than ever! If my brother had not had the good sense to snatch you up . . ."

"You would have trifled with my affections and then shunned me like an Almack's tea cake once they were engaged. I know you, too well, Justin." Her tone was wry, but there was affection in it nonetheless.

Justin laughed and glanced over at the two little girls, who had retreated to a settee and were comparing and sharing out the treats in some mysterious fashion. They were remarkably like their mother, with fine blond hair and pale, perfect complexions, cherubic in their chubby, healthy good looks.

"And what are you doing looking after your own children, my lady?" Justin asked, a hint of sarcasm in his cultured voice. Dark thick brows rose above sparkling blue eyes.

"I am demonstrating some needlework for them that their governess is not adept at—*petit point.*" Lady St. Claire moved slightly and motioned to a chair near the hearth. Those who knew her well would have recognized the lift of her chin as a challenge. "This is the new governess, Miss Simons. Miss Simons, my brother, Lord Justin St. Claire."

Justin glanced over at the chair and saw a drab little creature in an ugly gray gown. She had brown hair pulled back in a heavy, severe bun, and her face was pink from some unidentifiable emotion, or perhaps just from proximity to the fire that blazed in the hearth. She rose, hastily curtseyed, then sat again and cast her eyes back down to the mending on her lap.

He gave his sister a quizzical glance. "What happened to the little charmer you had here last Christmas?" he asked quietly, a grin quirking his lips.

"You know very well what happened," Elizabeth said, her tone growing cold. "And I do *not* wish to discuss it." She retreated to the settee and took the bonbons from the two girls before they could eat the whole lot. "Miss Simons," she said, raising her voice, "could you take the girls up and have Elise wash their faces and hands? They are sticky from candies."

The governess stood, her eyes downcast, and moved to the children, taking their hands in her larger ones. That was when Justin noticed her hands were malformed, the knuckles swollen and red, the fingers crook'd in an awkward manner. He glanced in shock at her face and saw her eyes flutter to his, then widen as her cheeks flamed even more.

She had fine gray eyes, large, with luxuriant dark lashes. They were her best, or more accurately, her *only* good feature. The rest of her face was undistinguished— her mouth too large, her nose merely ordinary, and her complexion regrettably freckled under her eyes. She hurried from the room, the washed-out dress she was wearing making no sound as it dragged along the carpet.

As the door closed behind her, he gave his sister a knowing look. "Making sure I don't dally with the governess, Elizabeth?"

"Absolutely right," she said severely, sitting down on the green patterned sofa and folding her perfect, smooth hands in her lap. "We had to get rid of Miss Chambly after the butler caught the two of you under the kissing bough last year."

"What's a harmless kiss at Christmas?" he grinned, throwing himself in a chair and draping one long, lean leg over the arm.

"You know very well what is wrong with that! I will *not* have my girls' governess fluttering around trying to capture your hand!" she said, angrily, picking up the needlework she had abandoned and stabbing at it with the fine needle.

Then, in spite of her best intentions, Elizabeth's rosebud mouth quirked in a smile that held a trace of mockery. "Well, I believe we have outmaneuvered you this time, Justin. I defy you to flirt with Miss Simons!"

He gave a mock shudder. "She looks a most frightful sort, plain and spinsterish enough to freeze the most intrepid rake's marrow," he drawled. "Check, my dear sis."

Elizabeth nodded. "*And* she shows a becoming humility and a tendency towards piety. Check and mate, my dear brother. Now, let me tell you our plans for the seasonal festivities."

Celestine handed the two children over to Elise, their maid, and retreated to the schoolroom. It was a long, plain room on the third floor, but she had tried to make it comfortable with a worn carpet of uncertain pattern and some castoff furniture that the marquess had allowed her to relocate.

Her own bedroom, the children's room, their maid's room and the nursery shared the floor with sundry other rooms. Celestine's room was small but pleasant, with a few creature comforts considered adequate for the governess. Most of her time was spent in the schoolroom. That was where the fire was most often going, and it was cold in Cumbria in December—bitterly cold sometimes.

It wasn't just the heat that drew her to the schoolroom, though. The room was on the east side of the mansion, and there was a window on one wall that overlooked the fells above Ladymead, a sight she had come to love in the past year.

When she had first arrived at the mansion, she had been overwhelmed by the ruggedness of the landscape deep in Cumbria, the Lake District. It was wild, with low mountains, rushing streams, and flocks of Herdwick sheep everywhere. But Ladymead was very close to Ellerbeck, a pretty little town in the valley, and she settled in easier than she had anticipated. The people, unlike the landscape, were friendly and hospitable, and after a short while she felt at home.

Her life until then had been spent in gentle Devon, so the change in surroundings was complete, but she had come to appreciate and even love the wild landscape and the view of the fells, dark and brooding though they were, from the schoolroom window. There was something to be said for change, especially since her former life had nothing to offer her now except penury and hardship. How much better—to her mind, anyway—to be governess in a rich man's household than a poor spinster living on the charity of the parish. She sat down in the shabby armchair by the hearth, empty this time of the day, and curled her feet up underneath her. A wave of fatigue she had been fighting all afternoon swept over her, and she leaned her head back and closed her eyes. The thought she had been avoiding by concentrating on the fells and the scene outside the window now invaded her brain. So that was the infamous Justin St. Claire. He *was* devastatingly attractive, just as Elise had confessed to her, sighing with lovelorn pleasure when she described the younger brother of the marquess.

He was not nearly as tall as his brother, but he was as sturdily built, broad of shoulder, his torso tapering down to narrow hips. His hair was a little long for fashion, but it curled crisply, chestnut in color and glossy, and his eyes were a sparkling blue, like the midwinter sky in the Pennines. Had his eyes caused the curious tug in her breast? Or was it the smile that danced on his lips?

She didn't think she had seen any grown man who looked so mischievous. He looked as if he found life to be a grand joke, and he the only one who was in on it.

But he was shamefully irreverent, she had heard, and, from reports, a devil with the ladies, throwing even the housemaids in disarray by his mere presence. Mrs. Jacobs, the housekeeper, had a time of it keeping the maids from competing over who would take him his tea and open his curtains in the morning. Even the little tweeny seemed smitten, confessing to Celestine that she counted the moments when she tended his fireplace, cleaning the ashes and reblacking the grate, as the happiest of her day, just to be in the same room where her idol had slept!

But *she* was built along sterner lines, Celestine assured herself. She had been hired because she was plain and would not tempt his lordship into indiscretion, and she knew now her employment depended on it—not that she would ever have to worry about fending him off. She had seen his expression of veiled distaste as he looked her over, and then shock as his glance dropped to her hands.

She twisted them together, rubbing the knuckles of her right, feeling the familiar pain shoot through them. The inflammation was always worse with the arrival of the cooler weather in the autumn and winter. Until now she had suffered only intermittent episodes, and then the pain would gradually recede, along with the inflamed swelling. Most of the time her hands were as small and neat as any woman's.

But this winter was the worst she had suffered, and it had only started. Some mornings the pain was so bad her hands were almost crippled. Perhaps it was the strenuous work of taking care of two little girls or the colder weather of the Lakes District, but in just the few weeks since the inflammation started it had even become impossible to handle the fine, thin needle necessary for *petit point,* a form of needlecraft her ladyship was most adamant her girls learn. That was why she had taken them down to Lady St. Claire for a lesson in the delicate art and so had been there to witness the arrival of the infamous Lord Justin St. Claire, breaker of feminine hearts.

Sighing, Celestine sat up straighter, shaking off her sleepiness and pulling her needlework bag out from behind the chair to sort through her work. She might not be able to wield a *petit-point* needle, but she *would* get her presents for the girls done before Christmas. The soft cloth bodies of the dolls were done already; she had only the clothes to make and the features to do. That would have to wait for her hands to stop hurting, or for the pain to alleviate a little bit, because the expressions were very important.

Gwen was getting a nurse doll cradling a tiny baby doll,

and Lottie would receive a governess doll accompanied by a youthful student doll. The St. Claire seamstress had kindly donated some scraps of fabric, finer than anything Celestine had ever worn. The governess doll would be adorned in gray silk with a cap of white muslin trimmed in a bit of lace. The nurse doll would have a dark blue gown with a frilly apron over top.

As she worked on the nurse's dress, her mind wandered back to Lord Justin St. Claire. What would it be like to be a lady he was attracted to, she wondered. Was her involuntary reaction to him, the tug of attraction she felt when she looked up into his eyes, a result of his good looks? She supposed it was, which made her as silly as Elise.

But there was no harm in admiring a perfect form and beautiful eyes. One gazed at paintings to admire their beauty, so why not at a man? She gave a sharp little nod as she struggled to thread her needle, making several attempts before success was hers. That was true. She had merely an artistic appreciation for the symmetry of Justin St. Claire's perfect form and classic good looks. She could admire him as she would a Raphael painting or Michelangelo statue.

She paused to rub her aching joints. Her fingers were especially bad, and she quelled a spurt of fear that this time the pain and swelling would linger and become more debilitating. Thinking about the handsome young nobleman she had just met was preferable.

Had she ever felt that little tug before, the one deep in her breast that happened when she looked into the sparkling blue of his long-lashed eyes? No, never, she decided, but one did not expect to come face to face with a living work of art. That must be it. She bent back to her needlework.

Something rankled in Justin St. Claire's breast as he indulged in a cigar in his brother's billiards room. His

sister's cynical assessment of his lack of interest in the
new governess was somehow disturbing, but for what reason, he could not fathom. The gentlemen of his set were
all in favor of dalliances with the lower orders, if the girl
was pretty enough, but not one would have called Miss
Simons anything but a drab little field mouse. So Elizabeth knew that and took advantage of his taste in fe-
males—so what?

He knocked a couple of balls into the pockets of the
gorgeous mahogany table, then threw down the cue stick
and paced over to the maroon-velvet-shrouded window
that overlooked the terrace. This time of year nothing
adorned the low-walled terrace, which stretched the
whole length of the east side of the building, but he
stared out anyway, gazing at the leaden sky, the clouds a
solid wall over the deep purple-gray fells.

Did it bother him that Elizabeth knew him so well? Was
he annoyed his sister-in-law knew he had no restraint
where a pretty face was involved? He blew out a puff of
smoke and knocked the ash from his cigar into a dish
on the dark wood table. He hadn't ruined silly Miss
Chambly, for God's sake. He was not such a cad as that.
It really had been just a kiss—or, rather, a series of kisses
and some light caresses.

The chit had been aiming to catch herself an eligible
parti, and he had no intention of being caught in parson's
mousetrap. He was too old and wily a fox to be caught
in *any* trap, he chuckled to himself. Someday he would
marry, he supposed, but perhaps not until he was in his
forties. Then he would turn into a lecherous old man
and snag himself a wife of seventeen or eighteen.

He had no need to marry at all, as the succession of
Ladymead was assured. August had dutifully sired an heir,
his namesake the young Viscount Augustus, who was at
school at the moment, and a follow-up in little Lord Gilbert, the youngest child at two—Bertie to everyone who
loved the blue-eyed, blond-haired tyke.

He was glad to leave all the responsible work to August

so he could go on with his life of idle pleasure. Wasn't that the whole point of being an aristocrat? His brow clouded momentarily. His friends all lived their lives the same way. It wasn't as if he were the only one, damn it! He liked London, his clubs, and his pleasures.

But back to the problem of the governess. It was annoying Elizabeth should outmaneuver him like that, then crow about it. It would serve her right if he *did* make love to the new governess. As plain as she was, she would fall for him like a stone. Ripe for the plucking, no doubt. Wouldn't Lizzie be livid! He grinned and nodded to himself, turning away from the window and the bleak landscape. This Christmas might turn out to be even more entertaining than last year's.

Lovemaking was all very well, as pleasant a pastime as a man could wish for, but there might be more pleasure in tweaking his snobbish sister-in-law's nose—and he would be giving the plain little governess something pleasurable and romantic to look back on, too. He felt a little glow of satisfaction. Surely that was what the charity of Christmas was all about, giving to the less fortunate. He would give her her very own romantic Christmas Eve.

Two

"Lottie, watch out for Gwen, dear. She's little, and we don't want her falling into the river."

Celestine watched her young charges carefully as she walked along the road into Ellerbeck, carrying a parcel wrapped in crinkling paper and amber twine. The road descended the hill away from Ladymead, sloping down toward the town as it curved around a low fell. For a distance it followed the river, then crossed a bridge and meandered into the village. It was a long walk, but it did them all good to get exercise.

The old stone bridge that spanned the sparkling stream had no railing. Celestine had questioned its safety when she first arrived, but had been informed most bridges in the Pennines didn't have railings. This was to facilitate the wide packs horses often carried, laden with goods and wool. Some trails were impassable by cart or carriage, and much was conveyed by packhorses. Learning about her new home had been a constant pleasure and endlessly fascinating.

Gwen tripped to the edge of the bridge, and Celestine felt her heart lurch. Rushing to the girl's side, Celestine pulled her back. "You must be more careful, dear," she said, kneeling on the dry gravel in front of the child and holding her hands. She looked directly into Gwen's bright blue eyes, so big and so uncomprehending. "Listen to me. It could be dangerous to run to the edge like that, and you could end up in the river, very cold and *very* wet. Would you like that?"

The child shook her head no, then took her older sister's hand and walked sedately across the rest of the bridge. She was very young for five, Celestine thought. She did not understand much that went on around her, gazing at the world with big, blank, blue eyes that protruded slightly. And she rarely spoke—at least not in words anyone but her older sister understood.

Lottie was very protective of her little sister, and held on to Gwen's hand as a carriage went by so the child would not wander onto the road and get run down. Celestine breathed deeply, gazing around with some pleasure at the beautiful landscape.

Low mountains rose to the east, hazy and purple, the highest ones already shrouded in snow. In the valleys the air was clean, pure, and crisply cold on this early December day. There was no snow yet in the valley, but Celestine had already lived through most of one winter at Ladymead and knew the snow would come, deep and plentiful. That was one of the first differences she'd had to adjust to.

But it turned out to be one of the things she enjoyed most. The Lake District, as it was known for its long, narrow, glacier-carved lakes, was beautiful in all seasons, but if not for the painful inflammation of her arthritis at this time of year, winter would be her favorite. The other seasons were flamboyant in their radiant green and gold and crimson, but winter was subtle, clothed in melancholy hues of umber and sage and dark conifer-green.

Then would come the fresh contrast of snow drifting on the slate rooftops and lining the naked trees. Blue-gray shadows would settle in the hollows between the hills and even the bright winter sun would not take away the world's mellow tinge. It suited her, she thought as she walked down the sloping road, the girls ahead of her stopping to gather some dried weeds.

In a meadow near the base of the hill she could see a

flock of Herdwick, the sheep of the Lake District. They were hardy creatures, as were the people who lived and scrabbled their existence from the rocky soil of the Pennines. The marquess himself spent many hours talking to area farmers about sheep and pasturing. Even the parson had his animal flock, so much more easily guided than the human type.

"Ah, Miss Simons. Out for a rather lengthy walk?"

Celestine froze at the sound of a voice she had not been able to get out of her mind since the previous day. Long into the night she had heard its mocking tones in her mind.

She turned and gazed at Lord St. Claire, who strode up behind them, his cheeks pink from the cold air. "My lord." She nodded in acknowledgment of his greeting. "Yes. I remember as a child I always could settle down to schoolwork better if my energy was worked off in some way. I had some errands in Ellerbeck and the girls needed a walk." She was proud of herself. Her tone was cool, unengaged, and light.

He fell into step with her as they closed the distance between themselves and the girls.

"What a refreshingly sensible governess you are, to be sure. Most would say, 'Work before play!' I think play before work is infinitely more pleasant." He slanted her a sideways look.

She didn't know how to respond and, to her mortification, felt her cheeks burn. It seemed the moment she was in his company she began to blush. She *must* conquer that tendency. Luckily, at that moment Lottie and Gwen caught sight of their uncle and ran to his side, insisting on each taking a hand. Celestine felt they made an absurdly domestic picture strolling along the road into the village, as if they were a squire and his lady with their two children. How deceiving were appearances!

She searched for a neutral topic of conversation, something that should surely be easy to come up with, with a stranger. "I understand you visit Ladymead every Christmas, my lord. Do you visit only in the winter?"

"I generally make a visit in the summer, as well. This year I went to Brighton instead, or I would have had the pleasure of meeting you sooner."

Celestine caught his glance and was puzzled at the faint suggestion of heat as he let his gaze wander down her pelisse, over her body. Was something disarrayed about her clothing? She glanced swiftly down at the dark gray pelisse that covered her plain wool dress. No, all was buttoned as it should be, not a thing out of place.

She glanced back up into his blue eyes and her brow furrowed. What was different about his treatment of her today? The previous day he had dismissed her without a second glance, repulsed, as Lady St. Claire had intended him to be, by her plain face and swollen hands. She realized she was staring at him when she tripped over her own two feet, and he let go of Lottie's hand to grasp her arm.

"Whoops." He laughed.

"The . . . the road's a little uneven," she gasped, uncomfortably aware of the strength of his fingers searing her through the wool.

"Perhaps you grow a little tired," he suggested, smiling down at her and not letting go his hold.

She pulled away. Even though he was closer to the truth than she dared admit, she said, "No, not at all. I am fine."

They walked the rest of the way into town, past stone-walled, frozen gardens and a small orchard, with St. Claire making conversation with his nieces about Christmas. He seemed in no hurry to go on his own way. Celestine had no idea what his errands in town consisted of, nor did she dare ask. It would seem too much like she was interested.

They walked along the curved main street of Ellerbeck, past tidy stone cottages with shuttered windows and brightly painted doors, slowly approaching the commercial section of town where butcher and baker, draper and chandler huddled side by side, cheek by jowl, as if for warmth. The nobleman gazed about him with interest at the tidy homes, not having walked through the village much in recent years.

When their father died and his brother ascended to the title, Justin was a young man about town, spending most of his time in London, only visiting with his brother when he and Elizabeth made the long trip there from Ladymead for the Season. In recent years, with Elizabeth so occupied with bearing and caring for the children, August and Elizabeth had not ventured all the way to London together. August had come to London for the sitting of the House of Lords, but he lived a solitary existence in his Mayfair house. Justin had been forced to make a twice-annual foray to Cumbria himself if he wanted to see his sister-in-law and nieces and nephews, and he always enjoyed the visits. He was sincerely attached to his family, and the month he spent at Ladymead over Christmas and the two or three weeks in the summer sped by.

The buildings in Ellerbeck were constructed of glacial rock quarried or picked from the meadows and fields, and they huddled along roads that were curved, following the lay of the land. Early Cumbrians were wise enough to compromise with nature, rather than try to impose straight lines in country where there were none.

And so the houses and commercial buildings seemed almost a part of the landscape, the colors and materials blending into the surrounding fells and meadows. Justin compared them to the worker's cottages he had seen in London, most of them adrift in a sea of squalor and dirt, covered in the soot that was pandemic throughout the city. In the clean air and sweeping vistas, the modest homes looked fresh-scrubbed. The simplicity and honesty of construction was pleasing to the eye and warming to the heart. Curls of smoke puffed from chimneys and cheerful birds chirped from the barren trees.

For some reason he felt absurdly happy walking along the road into Ellerbeck, making dilatory conversation with the plain governess and accompanying his romping nieces. Miss Simons turned out to be an intelligent woman, with a surprising knowledge of the Lakes District for one so recently moved there.

"I have made it my business to learn about the area," she explained, gazing around with clear gray eyes. "Lottie has so many questions about everything from sheep to glaciation. I am ill-equipped to answer them, so I resort to books, which your brother is kind enough to allow me free access to."

"Kind!" Justin snorted. "It is hardly mere kindness. You are his daughters' governess. Surely the better informed you are, the better taught they will be."

"Ah, but that is where your brother differs from other men," Miss Simons said, glancing up at him around her bonnet, her unusually fine eyes bright from exercise and fresh air. "He *wants* his daughters to be well-taught and intelligent. So many gentlemen wish for their daughters to be taught only such social skills and accomplishments as are deemed necessary to catch a husband. Often they learn little more than the art of flirtation."

Justin cast a sly glance sideways. "And will you teach them that as well? The fine art of flirtation?"

"One cannot teach what one does not know," she replied softly.

"And will you resort to books for instruction, as you did for the history of this area? I would advise the penny novels for romance. They are filled with innocent young maids whose attractions drive noblemen to kidnap them and carry them off to Gretna."

"That kind of instruction would hardly be conducive to familial harmony, my lord," she said, dryly. "Nor would it facilitate an honorable and happy marriage when the girls are young ladies. If my task were to make them fit to occupy the scandal columns of the London newspapers, then certainly Mrs. Radcliffe and her ilk would be my resource material.''

He glanced at her in some surprise, but her face was hidden by her hideous bonnet. That she might have a sense of humor had never entered Justin's head. In his experience, governesses were either dry old sticks or meek, frightened girls, beaten down by life—or, in Miss Chambly's case, flirtatious, impertinent little chits. Miss Simons was none of those. He judged her to be in her twenties. Though her personality seemed retiring, she did not speak meekly, flirtatiously, nor even censoriously. She spoke to him as an equal would. How intriguing!

The little girls had run on ahead of them again, and as they entered the commercial heart of Ellerbeck, Miss Simons called them back and took them firmly in hand.

He accompanied them to the draper's shop, where the governess checked on an order of silk and lace Lady St. Claire was anxious for. Apparently she was having dresses made up for the little girls for Christmas, as well as new garments for herself. The shop assistant deferred to Mr. Ducroix, the owner, who bowed and smiled so much Justin thought his eyes would pop from his head. As they were leaving, the man slipped a wrapped bundle to Miss Simons and gave her a conspiratorial wink.

He wondered if there was some understanding between the governess and the draper. He was a mincing fellow with a faint French accent, he noted with disgust, for all he was kind to the little girls and deferential to Justin himself. Miss Simons was about to put the small package under her other arm, already being burdened as she was with her bulky, paper-wrapped parcel, but Justin insisted on taking charge of it.

He had the satisfaction of seeing her look startled, but she acquiesced with good grace, and they all proceeded to the subscription library to pick up some romances for Lady St. Claire and a book of receipts for the housekeeper, Mrs. Jacobs. The St. Claires had rather progressive ideas and provided usage of the subscription to any of their staff ambitious enough to want to read. Few of them took their employer up on that generosity, although Dobbs was known to have a not-too-secret addiction to the penny dreadfuls.

Justin took charge of the books, too, and the little girls giggled as he pretended to grunt and strain under the burden. Miss Simons turned a bright pink when he took her arm down the slippery step, even though he released her very quickly after.

She *was* ripe for the plucking, he thought with some satisfaction. He had known it would be this easy. A plain spinster against his practiced charms did not stand a chance. She would be eager for his touch, her fine gray eyes alight with passion and her ripe mouth slightly open in anticipation of his kiss . . . he halted himself in his thoughts.

Shaking his head as they strolled down the street, he wondered how much of his customary seduction was mere habit. He was allowing himself to get excited over a spinster, for God's sake!

He examined her critically, as another man might look over a painting he considered purchasing, or a horse he was bidding on at Tattersall's. Maybe her mouth *was* too wide for fashion, but it would be satisfying to kiss. And the curves under the worn pelisse were feminine and alluring enough to promise a comfortable tumble . . . a tumble? His eyes widened at the turn his thoughts had again taken.

Since when did he intend to take her to bed? He had no intention of disgracing the girl, just flirting enough that she would commit an indiscretion—just to show Elizabeth she could not thwart his holiday fun. Another kiss under the kissing bough or a cuddle in a dark corner, that was all. Then he would confess to Elizabeth he had done it just to spite her and promise not to look at the girl again, if she would just not fire her. That would be the end of it as far as he was concerned, and they would both have pleasant memories from a mild flirtation.

And to that end he must continue to charm her.

"And what does Miss Simons want for a special Christmas present?" he asked, harkening back to his conversation with the girls. They walked down a curved road by a low stone wall, the governess walking beside him and the two girls in front.

"Books," chirped Lottie, glancing over her shoulder at the two adults.

"A dolly," offered Gwen, one of her rare understandable utterances.

"She's too old for a dolly!" Lottie said scornfully. When her little sister's face became pinched with a hurt expression and Celestine gave her an admonishing look, the older girl put her arm over her shoulders and squeezed. "I'm sorry, Gwenny. A dolly then."

The two girls joined hands and ran down the walkway and up some steps into the confectioner's shop, where they knew Mrs. Gruett would have a sugarplum for them each. It was smack up against the baker, and when one door opened, an elderly, smiling woman nodding to them as she exited, and the fragrant scent of cinnamon and ginger assailed their nostrils.

"What is it to be? Books or a dolly?" Justin grinned.

Flustered, Miss Simons stared straight ahead. "I . . . I don't receive gifts . . . I mean . . ."

"Oh, come. Every lady likes gifts." Justin lowered his tone to a coaxing, seductive rasp. He took her arm as they prepared to enter the confectioner's to fetch the two girls. She started to pull away, but his arched brow and questioning expression confused her and she lowered her eyes. He retained her arm and murmured, "Some French perfume? Lace handkerchiefs?"

"I . . . I have little experience of gifts . . . I mean, since I was a girl."

"And that was when? Last year?"

"Many years ago, sir," she said quietly, withdrawing her arm from the crook of his elbow. "It has been many years since I was a girl."

He watched as she bustled forward through the door and exchanged a few pleasant words with Mrs. Gruett, then guided the girls back out into the winter sunshine. She hunched down to retie Gwen's bonnet, her gloved hands clumsy enough that it took a few tries. He wondered what was wrong with her hands and why they were so swollen. He had thought that kind of inflammation came only with age. It was not something he could ask about, and certainly nothing she would volunteer.

She was a puzzle, this plain, quiet, dignified little governess. She would not allow him to flirt with her, seeming to prefer real conversation to the teasing kind of talk he was used to having with women. In fact, when they conversed he forgot for long periods his intentions toward her, losing himself in intelligent, interesting discourse. It was a novelty to just *talk* to a woman, but he shrugged and decided if that was what she wanted, that was what she would get . . . for now.

They chatted and walked together as she discharged her duties one by one in the shops huddled along Ellerbeck's sloping streets. She must have asked everyone in the house if she could do something for them in town, he thought. She had been at Ladymead less than a year, but it seemed everyone in the town knew her, all muttering a pleasant good morning, nodding, or tipping a hat before making their more formal obeisance to him.

He knew the area was friendly, the people of Cumbria making up for the harshness of the landscape with an unusually high tolerance for strangers, but there was more than tolerance in their greetings to the governess. There were a few words exchanged, servants asked after, her own well-being questioned. One elderly lady took her aside and lectured her for a few minutes—perhaps about her hands, as she took the governess's hands in her own. At the end of the conversation, the old lady kissed Miss Simons's cheek and patted it too, before sending her on her way.

Finally they had rounded the bend and were on their

way back out of town. They were approaching the little stone church, its spire rising above the town like a finger pointing heavenward, offering all a chance for redemption. It was a pretty little church with a stone fence around it and a picturesque cemetery behind. Just as they were about to pass, a man came out a side door, closing it behind him.

"Ah, Miss Simons," he said, advancing down the path and coming out the gate set in the stone wall. "How delightful to see you, and of course Lady Charlotte and Lady Gwenevere!" He bent down to shake their hands solemnly, then straightened, swept back a dark lock of hair, and looked at Justin. "And Lord St. Claire, I believe? His lordship the marquess said he was expecting you. Delightful to meet you, my lord." He bowed, a graceful gesture.

The man was just too polite, Justin thought, but of course he was a vicar. Perhaps it went with the position. He was a handsome fellow, too, in a dark, square way. Justin would not normally have noticed that about another man, but there was something in his manner toward the governess that alerted him, and he looked the reverend over more carefully.

"Are you walking my way?" the vicar asked, turning his gaze back to Miss Simons.

She smiled, her lips curving in a delightful bow, and her gray eyes lit up, kindling from his. "We are, sir. In fact, I was on my way to drop this off at the vicarage!" She held out the wrapped parcel she carried—the one she had brought with her from Ladymead. "It is knitted stockings for Mother Gudge, and a few more dolls for the poor box. I do so want the poor children to have something for Christmas. Mr. Dougherty, his lordship's blacksmith, has promised some toys for the little boys, as well."

"Delightful!" the vicar said, offering her his arm. As she slipped her arm through his, he patted her gloved hand with a proprietary air. "You are so kind, Miss Simons, to busy yourself with making things for the poor with what little spare time you have. And you have an admirable way of rallying others to help, too. What a valuable talent that is, to be sure. But you must be tired, if you have walked all this way. May I offer my carriage and groom back to Ladymead?"

"That is not necessary," Justin interrupted, a little put out to find himself excluded from the conversation, along with a restive Gwen and Lottie. "I am carrying the lady's parcels, and it is not such a walk."

The vicar glanced at him, his expression serious. "Perhaps Miss Simons feels differently, my lord. She is not as strong as you, and we must cherish the ladies, do you not agree? Well, Miss Simons, may I offer my carriage? It would fit you all, I believe. It is elderly, but well-sprung."

"Thank you, Mr. Foster, but we will not need it today. It was very kind of you to offer, though."

Justin grimaced at the vicar's reproving look toward him, and gritted his teeth. "Miss Simons, if you are refusing the offer because of what I said, please do not . . ."

With a puzzled expression, the governess looked from one man to the other as if sensing the antagonism, faint but alive, between them. "Not at all. Mr. Foster, I merely came by to drop off the parcel and to ask about choir practice on Friday night. His lordship is sending Mrs. Jacobs, Elise, and me down in the carriage, and I wondered if anyone else needed a ride. We have room for another—perhaps even two, as Elise and I aren't that big!"

The vicar tore his gaze from the aristocrat and chuckled. He took both her hands in his own as they paused in front of a neat stone cottage that must be the new vicarage.

"I do not believe there is anyone else, Miss Simons, though it is kind of you to ask. But then you are always so thoughtful; it is in your nature, I believe. If I hear anything to the contrary, I shall send a message. This, I believe, is where we part company. Would that I could walk you back up to Ladymead myself! I would count it no small pleasure, but my duty lies elsewhere, I am afraid."

"You are too kind, Mr. Foster," Miss Simons said, with her eyes lowered. "I shall see you next at choir practice, then."

The vicar bowed over her hand, took the package from her and turned and made his bow to the brother of his patron. He then said good-bye to the children, who were restless to continue their walk. The foursome set off again, with Mr. Foster waving good-bye at his door, Celestine's package clutched securely under his arm.

"Pompous bootlicker!" Justin said.

Miss Simons glanced at him in some surprise. "I do not believe I detected any hint of obsequiousness, my lord!" she said, disapproval in her voice.

So that was how the wind blew, Justin thought. A match between the plain governess and the country vicar. And why not? Each could do worse. From his sister-in-law's conversation the previous evening, it was clear Miss Simons was of the untitled gentry—well-born, if not high-born. And the vicar seemed a harmless enough fellow, for all that the man grated on *his* nerves for some reason he couldn't quite name. "I believe" this, and "I believe" that!

But he would still have his flirtation, he decided. Even if Miss Simons's heart was engaged, he was a skilled master at stealing spoken-for hearts. In fact, it made the challenge all the more arousing. His blood was up for the hunt and the bugle had sounded.

The next few days passed without any opportunity for flirtation, though. Justin smacked balls around the table in the billiard room and brooded. The drab governess seemed to sense when he was nearing her and, if she was alone, she retreated every time. It was three weeks until Christmas, and he had set himself the unofficial deadline of Christmas Eve for his stolen kiss.

It was all the more difficult as Miss Simons did not dine

with the family and of course did not socialize. Elizabeth declared a holiday from the schoolroom for her girls, but that did not mean an end to the governess's duties. She seemed to be even busier, if that were possible.

Miss Simons gave the nurse a break from Bertie almost every day, taking him and the two girls out of doors for romps in the garden. He had joined them a few times, but the children occupied her time and demanded his full attention, as well. Still, he found himself enjoying the governess's company, even if he had to share her with his nieces and nephew.

At other times, she helped the housekeeper with household mending when she was in the sitting room with the girls. He joined them and sometimes read to his nieces from the adventure stories he had enjoyed as a lad. He knew Miss Simons was listening, too, from the smile that lifted her soft lips and her involuntary laughter when he embroidered the tales with his own humorous additions. Most times, though, she was not to be found. Presumably she was caring for her charges, but never was she seen when she did not have some occupation.

She was not at all like Miss Chambly. Last year's governess had dressed simply, as befitted her station, but she suddenly bloomed into a coquette when Justin looked her way and smiled. She had flirted and batted her eyes, giving him languishing glances no man could have ignored. But Miss Simons kept her eyes steadfastly turned away and her hands safely busy. It was annoying and not a little unsettling to find nothing—not flirtation, not kindness, not even trickery—could capture her attention.

And so he knocked the ivory balls around the billiards table in bored contemplation of his failure.

Elizabeth, her eyes flashing, stormed into the billiards room. She was a dainty, frivolous note in a very dark, masculine room. Her pale lemon dress seemed to glow in the setting of dark wood paneling, maroon carpet, and dull gold furniture.

"Justin, I will not have it!"

"Whatever do you mean, dear sister?" Laconically, he knocked the balls into pockets one by one, occasional puffs on a cigar his only break. His words were punctuated by the smack of ball against ball.

"I will not have you seducing this governess! The children love her, and I do not want to have to send her away!"

He glanced up at her. She stood, arms akimbo, her lips set in a grim line.

"Whatever has set you off this time, my dear sister?"

"Do not take me for a fool, Justin. I have seen your peculiar attentiveness toward Miss Simons. You spend hours every day in her company, and . . ."

"Cut line, Elizabeth! You exaggerate. I am here to visit with my nieces and nephews. If they happen to be with their drab little governess, what fault is that of mine?"

The marchioness was not to be put off so easily. As Justin stooped to return to his game, she grasped the cue stick and would not let go. He straightened and she glared up at him. "I am not blind, nor am I stupid. I have been debating whether to say something to you for two days, and now I have had a most disturbing visit. Just this afternoon the vicar was here. He was concerned, he said, as a man of God, to see your . . ." She frowned and glanced down for a moment: "How did he put it?" She nodded sharply and looked back up at him. "Ah, yes; he was concerned, he said, to see your dangerously overt attentions to someone so clearly below your touch. As Miss Simons's vicar, he felt duty-bound to question your motives."

"That pompous busybody!" Justin jerked the pool cue from Elizabeth's grasp and threw it on the table, the clatter echoing in the dim recesses of the room. "I merely happened to be going to Ellerbeck for some Christmas shopping and Miss Simons and I met by accident; that is when the vicar saw us together. In all courtesy, what did you expect me to do? Ignore her? Disregard the fact that she had more packages than she could carry? I am not such a cad as that."

Elizabeth's narrowed eyes spoke more than any words that she was not convinced.

It was vital that she be put from the scent or she would spoil everything. Justin quirked a grin, pouring all of his charm and considerable experience into his voice. He took Elizabeth's hands in his and kissed each one. "I would not dream of disturbing your peace, my dear, so set your mind at ease. You will not have to discharge Miss Simons."

Elizabeth looked up into his eyes for a moment. Finally she sighed and said, "Thank you, Justin. I was not looking forward to having to toss one of you out on your ear. It just might have been *you* I discharged this time." She whirled and was gone in swirl of silk skirts and sandalwood perfume.

"I said you wouldn't have to discharge her, not that I would not dally," Justin said to the empty room. He picked up his cue stick, leaned over again and stroked carefully, pocketing the ball he was aiming for. His determination increased. Little Miss Simons *would* take notice of him, or he would have to resign his honorary spot in the Seducers Club, an unofficial band of like-minded young men bent on romantic conquest. He had never failed yet, and would not now. And Elizabeth would get her comeuppance.

Three

Only four more weeks! Elise had assured her Lord Justin St. Claire was always back in London by the New Year, so she would have to endure his unwanted gallantries and seductive ways for only twenty-eight more days at the most—six hundred and sixty-eight hours. Forty thousand minutes, more or less.

She adjusted herself to a more comfortable position on the low chair by the hearth in the morning parlor, but did not often raise her eyes from her mending. Whenever she did, Lord St. Claire, who sat with his sister-in-law and her guests, would catch her eye and smile or do whatever it was he did with those amazing blue eyes of his. Somehow, with just a glance he could take her breath away.

Why did he insist on singling her out for his subtle flirtation? Celestine fumed, presenting an outwardly calm demeanor as she stitched a tablecloth hem. Though she sat in the parlor with the family, she had purposely put distance between herself and the others. She knew Lady St. Claire was a stickler for rigidly observed partition between the classes, and as a governess she had descended from her born position as a lady of gentility. Lady St. Claire was a snob, in other words, though she would surely not describe herself that way, nor would society. Those of her own position would say she knew her place and expected others to as well.

Celestine brooded on about the brother of her employer. The only place she had been safe from his flattery and smiles was the schoolroom, but as it was the holiday season, Lady St. Claire liked to see her little girls, dressed prettily and on their best behavior, down in the drawing room for company and she wanted Miss Simons there as well.

Her only salvation was Mr. Foster, the vicar, who was kind and gentle and would sit beside her and make pleasant, unthreatening conversation. He didn't flirt, and he didn't say inappropriate things or embarrass her. But the vicar visited only occasionally, twice since Lord St. Claire had arrived, and only stayed a half hour when he came.

If she had not been dependent on her position in the household for her livelihood, she would have had no compunction about putting the nobleman in his place. As it was, all she could do was retreat, try to avoid him, and wonder why he plagued her so.

Gwen was getting tired, Celestine thought, hearing the familiar whine in the child's voice as her mother attempted to coax a song from her youngest daughter. There were two neighborhood ladies visiting and Lottie was having a wonderful time being plied with attention and sweetmeats. But Gwen was tired and not behaving as well as she sometimes could.

"Perhaps I should take Gwen upstairs, my lady. She might be sleepy." Celestine swallowed determinedly and stood, coming out of the shadows as she spoke. Attracting anyone's attention was far from her mind, but she was aware St. Claire's gaze had swiveled toward her at the sound of her quiet voice.

"That may be best, Miss Simons." Lady St. Claire gratefully handed Gwen over to the governess. She was a good and indulgent mother, but not the most patient person in the world. She was occasionally harder on Gwen than necessary, especially concerning what she considered the girl's stubborn refusal to learn more quickly. She refused to acknowledge Gwen was not as quick mentally as Lottie

and should not be judged by the other child's precocious-
ness.

The little girl was, indeed, sleepy, and held her arms
up to be carried, so Celestine picked her up, staggering
under the little girl's dead weight. Either the child was
growing heavier, or she was not as strong as she used to
be. The wear and tear on her muscles was excruciating
and her fingers ached where the weight of the plump
child strained them. A moment later she felt the child
being pulled from her arms and found his lordship was
taking his niece from her.

"Let me carry her for you. She is too heavy and you
are not overly strong, I think." St. Claire gazed down at
her with some concern.

To Celestine's surprise, his expression seemed genuine,
and it was accompanied by a smile—not a flirtatious
smile, just a friendly one. Lady St. Claire cast a suspicious
look their way, and Celestine blanched. Her ladyship's
suspicions must not be aroused, or her position was in
danger. She had learned that much from the marchioness's own mouth. If Miss Chambly had been dismissed,
she was in danger from the aristocrat's gallantry, too.

"Nonsense! I can carry her perfectly well, my lord!"
She tried to take Gwen back into her arms. "Please, I am
used to it. I . . ."

"Don't be ridiculous!" he said, brusquely. "Lead the
way, Miss Simons. I only want to be of service to you, you
know."

"Oh, very well," she sighed. She dared not catch a
glimpse of Lady St. Claire's face, and she hastened to
precede her tormentor from the room and up the long
staircase. Her cheeks burned and her movements felt
jerky and inelegant, so very aware was she that he was
behind her and watching her progress, no doubt. When
they got to the third floor and then the room Gwen
shared with Lottie, Celestine turned, one hand on the
porcelain knob. "I'll take her now, my lord. I'll put her
to bed for a little nap and make sure Elise knows."

His blue eyes sparkling, he put one finger to his lips. "Shhh. She's already asleep, and transferring her would just wake her up. Open the door, if you please."

He was right, of course. Gwen *was* asleep on his shoulder, one thumb in her mouth. Celestine did as she was bid and followed him in as he glanced back at her. The room was decorated in pastel shades of green with cream accents, a pretty, restful room with a small chamber off of it for Elise, the children's maid.

"Which bed?" he asked.

"Which . . . oh, which bed is Gwen's!" She flushed guiltily, aware she had been too conscious of his strong form and masculine scent to remember he wouldn't know which bed was the little girl's. Such inattentiveness was unlike her, and she couldn't imagine what had gotten into her. She was normally so sensible. She pointed to the one near the wall and rushed over to it, pulling down the heavy brocade cover.

St. Claire, with a gentleness astounding in such a normally careless man, laid his niece down on the bed, and Celestine pulled up the covers. The governess then tucked the little girl in, smoothed back an errant curl, and kissed Gwen's forehead.

She rose to find St. Claire's eyes on her. She straightened and started to move past him.

"Wait," he whispered, laying one hand on her arm. "Why do you always run away from me?"

"I don't . . . run." She gazed toward the door with longing. The warmth of his hand burned through the light fabric of her sleeve. Why did she suddenly feel so breathless?

"Yes, you do. You run. And avoid me whenever I come near you. Am I so hideous?"

The question caught her by surprise and she looked him full in the face, straight into his glinting eyes, bright with humor and warmth. He moved closer to her, and she felt her free hand creep to her bosom over her pounding heart. "Hideous? Of course not, you are exceptionally . . . you know you are very . . ."

"And you stammer in my presence." His voice was deep, with a seductive timbre. "Am I so frightening, my dear?" he continued.

Every sense in her body was alert, aware of him. He was warm and strong and smelled of spice and tobacco, with a hint of fresh outdoors. She was so close that when she glanced up, she could see the faint dark shadow of whiskers along his strong jaw. She didn't think she had ever been this close to a man in all her years—or maybe it only felt that way—and it was arousing disturbing sensations. Her heart pounded, her blood coursed hot through her veins, and her breath was coming in short gasps.

"No, of course not, it's just . . ." She sighed, pulled her arm from his grasp, and moved past him out to the hall. He was impossible. And impossible to hate, although she had tried, knowing his actions could lose her her position. Why did he have such a profound effect on her when she knew him for what he was, a heartless flirt who had cost the last poor girl her position with the St. Claires and apparently did not care?

He caught up with her, gently closed the door behind him and took her hand in his. She gasped and pulled it away, hiding it behind her with the other, twisting them together in her skirt.

"I . . . I must go," she said, and ran down the hall to her own room, closing the door.

Justin heard the faint scratch of her latch being fastened and chuckled to himself. She tried to pretend indifference to him, but she was not indifferent. Far from it. It was like Eve and the serpent, he thought. She was sorely tempted by him, and he had only to name the time and place for her to succumb completely. Women were so very predictable.

* * *

It was her evening off at last, and Celestine dressed carefully for choir practice in the village church. She donned her second-best dress, a lavender muslin with a fine lawn tucker and pale green ribbons. Then she slipped on her best gloves and fit her bonnet, hideous as it was, on her neat brown hair. Mr. Foster would be there, and she liked to look her best. She flushed faintly at the turn her mind had taken. It had not escaped her notice that the vicar was uncommonly polite to her and went out of his way to secure her company if he was able.

Was she hoping for marriage, perhaps? Yes, she supposed she was. Marriage, a home, and a family to look after would be the pinnacle of her dreams. Was it too high to look, to think the vicar of Ellerbeck might choose her in marriage? Not at all, she told herself stoutly, as she was of very good family, landed gentry of probably higher rank than Mr. Foster. She had nothing to be ashamed of in her background, even if she had sunk to paid employment. She stood in front of the scarred mirror, straightened her bonnet, and caught sight of her large, gray eyes.

"Oh, Papa," she whispered, caught as she always was by her resemblance to him, at least in the eyes. Poor Papa. Toward the end he had seemed to be all eyes, large and gray and luminous, as he lay, wizened and emaciated, in his bed of pain. And then on that last day, in his fevered agony, his eyes had looked sunken but, oh, so peaceful when at last he said, "Celestine, I see the angels!" and had expired.

Brushing an errant tear from her freckled cheek, she did the one thing that always cheered her and took out the fine gold locket with the two miniatures, one of her mother and one of her father, and pinned it to her dress. She couldn't afford a chain for it, but it would be pinned over her heart, where it belonged.

With a deep breath, she straightened her sleeves, donned her gray pelisse, worn at the cuffs but still serviceable, and descended to the front hall to await Elise and Mrs. Jacobs, the housekeeper. Their one weekly indulgence was choir practice, and going out the front to the carriage was a concession to practicality, that being the easiest place for the coachman to pull up.

Albert, one of the footmen, bowed to her. "The rest are already in the carriage, miss. Coachman said to hurry; he don't like the cattle to stand in this cold weather."

Celestine bustled out, down the front steps, and took the groom's arm as he helped her up into the coach. Inside were Elise, Mrs. Jacobs, and . . . Lord St. Claire!

"My lord," she breathed, forced to take the seat beside him, as the housekeeper and maid shared the other seat with their backs to the horses.

His wicked grin in the dim confines of the carriage rattled her nerves. What was he doing? Why was he there?

"Miss Simons. I felt a desire to hear the choir at practice for the Yuletide festivities I have heard are the highlight of the year in Ellerbeck."

Elise giggled and the housekeeper beamed beneficently on the younger brother of her employer. Such condescension on his part was an enormous compliment.

"Surely you have seen the Christmas pageant before. I am informed it is performed every year," Celestine said, her voice sharper than she had intended.

"Ah, but you are wrong, Miss Simons. Oh, perhaps in my youth, but I did not spend much time here as a child. My father received the title when I was thirteen and already in school. We often traveled to my maternal grandmother's for Christmas, so no, I have not seen the Ellerbeck festival."

"But do you not spend every Christmas here?"

"Almost every one," he admitted. "But I have not attended the Christmas pageant in years."

"We are honored by your presence, my lord," Mrs. Jacobs said, ponderously.

"Surely our little choir is not worth your notice, sir, not when you have no doubt been in boxes in London

and heard the best sopranos, the most accomplished of
tenors . . ."

"I think our little choir is quite fine," the housekeeper
said, bridling at the implied criticism. She had picked up
an elaborately genteel accent from Lady St. Claire's maid,
though she didn't always remember to use it, so she pro-
nounced 'quite' as 'quaite' and 'fine' as 'fane'. She
dropped it as her defense of the local choir became more
boisterous. "Mr. Jenks, the choirmaster, why he's bin to
London himself and heard some o' that foreign rubbish
and says give him an honest English voice any day!"

Celestine flushed. "I did not mean to insult our intrepid band of singers, Mrs. Jacobs."

After that, Celestine stayed silent, gazing out the window at the darkened landscape touched by faint moonlight, listening to the nobleman's fulsome praise and
Elise's giggled responses offered as counterpoint to Mrs.
Jacobs's heavy courtesy. She pondered the man's actions
in accompanying them. What could he be about? Was he
so starved for something to do that he considered a choir
practice entertainment?

They all disembarked at the church, their male companion helping each down from the carriage. He held
Celestine's gloved hand just a fraction longer than necessary, and his warmth penetrated through the material.

She turned to him, undecided about his motives, and
gazed up at his smiling face. "No matter what Mrs. Jacobs
says, you must know our little group is nothing special to
hear." She glanced up the dark walk, where Elise and the
housekeeper were already entering the vestibule of the
church. She must not hang back too long with Lord St.
Claire, or it would surely be noted. "You would have been
better off staying at Ladymead and asking Lady St. Claire
to favor you with a tune on the piano. She has a lovely
voice."

"Ah, but this evening jaunt has other joys Ladymead
doesn't boast," he said, pulling her closer to him.

Celestine could not make out his meaning, nor the

teasing tone in his voice. She was sharply aware of the heat that emanated from him and the spicy scent of his hair pomade. He smelled and looked absolutely delicious, and she was sure he knew it. Though she could not summon the energy or desire to pull away from him, she attempted to ignore the way he squeezed her fingers gently and then put his hand in the middle of her back as they moved toward the church. She was horribly conscious of it, though, the warm pressure causing a flood of pink in her pale cheeks.

She had never thought herself susceptible to masculine good looks, but it seemed she was as silly as the greenest girl. *Was* it just his looks that made him so desperately attractive, or was there something more she was sensing? Was that why women everywhere fell for a handsome rogue, because they convinced themselves there was something more under the attractive *façade?* Or did handsome men learn early how to use their appearance to influence and seduce women?

They followed the others in through the side entrance, through the dark, echoing hall, to find the rest of the choir already assembled. Murmurs and a rustling of dresses greeted the marquess's brother, but the choirmaster, a rotund little martinet, called for order and immediately told them the program of rehearsal. Celestine forgot everything but the music, the best part of the evening for her.

She mounted to her position, closing out all other thoughts but the program. At least in this she could find peace. The whispering died down, and Mr. Jenks brought the little choir to order. Then they started.

Justin sat in the chill darkness in the family seat, a high-walled box that allowed him to see the choir, illuminated by smoking tallow candles only, but not the rest of the church behind him. Soon, the assembled voices filled the air and he sat back to listen. The governess had been right. The choir was not any different than a hundred country choirs in a hundred country churches.

Celestine. That was her name, though it didn't really suit her. It should be appended to some gloriously angelic little creature with flaxen hair, rosebud lips, and heavenly blue eyes. She was not that, nor would she ever be.

She would suit Jane or Mary or Ellen, plain, honest names to go along with her looks and personality. Why was he expending so much effort and so much time to awaken her interest? Boredom? Pique? It seemed the more she put him off, the harder he tried. It was no longer just to spite his sister-in-law, but for the challenge the governess represented.

He gazed up at the choir, housed in an intricately carved section of seats to the right of the altar. Just then, the chorus of voices hushed to a gentle croon. A clear soprano solo took over, and Justin was amazed to see it was Celestine who sang, her high voice fluting through the darkened chapel and soaring to the heights, echoing in the empty church. Her face was a study of rapture, eyes closed and mouth mobile with the angelic tones she was creating.

Celestial. At least her voice was that, if her appearance wasn't. He closed his eyes and rested his head back against the heavy English oak of the St. Claire box. With a voice like that she belonged in a chorus of angels, and there he was, trying like the dark angel, Lucifer, to pull down that delicate, fluttering creature for his own needs.

He would enslave her heart, seduce her into acquiescing to caresses that could possibly lose her position, though such was not his intent. He didn't *want* Elizabeth to let the girl go. But that was what had happened to the Chambly chit. Just for that one moment he sickened himself. Why could he not leave the poor creature in peace?

The words of her song, an ode to the Christ child, faded from his consciousness, leaving only the light, clear tones soaring to the heights of the vaulted ceiling, tugging his long-fallen heart along. As it followed Celestine's glorious voice to the upper reaches of the church, his heart opened to questions long suppressed. Where was

he going in life? What did he really want from an existence that often bored him with its endless social round?

He waited for an answer, clear and lucid, to flutter into
his heart and nestle there like a trusting dove. He *wanted*
an answer, *needed* an answer, but the only one that came
was that he had absolutely no idea what he wanted from
life. He had never given it a second's thought in all his
misspent years. Beyond the moment, which consisted of
seducing a new mistress, attaining a young girl's trust,
winning a bet or a game of cards, or downing a fine bottle
of Bordeaux, he didn't know if there *was* anything he
wanted from life.

There was certainly no need for him to have a purpose.
His brother filled the post of marquess with great dignity,
intelligence, and stolid worth. August had an heir in Gus
and a spare in Bertie, making Justin a useless adjunct to
the family—an unneeded twig on the family tree. Oh, he
had his own estate, Questmere, only fifty or so miles from
Ladymead, as a matter of fact, but it was capably looked
after by a bailiff and would descend to Bertie if anything
should happen to him. He visited it only occasionally on
his way to or from Ladymead to make sure everyone was
happy and healthy, which they always were.

He could go his own merry way for the rest of his life
and it would affect absolutely no one. He knew that August was getting impatient with his dilettante's life and
was pressuring him to find a young lady from the *ton* to
grace his table and his bed and start producing little St.
Claires, even though he was already doing a splendid job
of that himself. But it seemed a useless sort of time filler
to find a young lady for whom any husband of sufficient
birth would do and start siring more tiny aristocrats to
populate the *ton*.

He frowned, impatient with himself. But his mind
toiled on as the beautiful voice soared and swooped,
echoing against the high, vaulted ceiling. Questions with
no answers. Questions with unsatisfactory answers. Had
anyone in his whole life ever *needed* him? The young ladies

he squired during the Season needed him to lend them countenance as they gracefully swayed to the waltz. They needed him to collect their fans for them when they forgot them in the box after the opera. They needed him to court them so they could marry well and not disgrace their families. Needed *him?* Any other man of sufficient birth would do.

It was all so much refuse—litter on the winding roadway of a long and boring life. The years ahead stretched out into one long, intolerable highway of tedium and forgotten dreams, years spent frantically playing at being busy as he moved from house party to London Season to country gathering, with or without a family of his own.

He sighed and stretched out his long legs, the organ music filling the quaint church with seasonal carols. For some reason he thought of Celestine, her luminous gray eyes gazing at him with a tormented expression on her sweet, serious countenance.

Luminous? Sweet? Yes, she had those qualities, and likely more. He was doing her a disservice by trying to engage her interest when there could be no ending for it but hurt feelings on her part and empty triumph on his. Somehow in the sacred atmosphere of St. George's, his heart, that long-silent organ of feeling, whispered he was being thoughtless and cruel, callous to a young woman who must need her position very much. For a young woman of birth and breeding to descend to the rank of a governess, there must be a certain amount of desperation.

It would not do. He must not torture her. She was vulnerable to him; he felt it in the very marrow of his bones, and he had been a seducer long enough to know. He felt a trembling deep in his chest as Celestine's lovely voice filled the cool darkness once more. It occurred to him he held her very fate in his large hands. Tears sprang to his eyes. Horrified by his weakness, he pulled a handkerchief from his pocket and swiftly wiped away the telltale moisture. He was becoming maudlin.

But for those few minutes in the dark, it almost seemed he could hear the sound of angels in her voice, the sweet celestial sounds of heaven, the world beyond St. Peter's jealously guarded gate. The imagery was irresistible. He was a supplicant outside that gate, on his knees, begging for entrance. A stern man in white robes asked him the dreaded question: "What have you done in your life that is worthy of entrance here?"

If he never added anything to the plus side of his ledger, at least he would not add this one thing to the negative side. If he did not do another good thing in his life, at least he could say to himself he had left Celestine Simons, virtuous governess, heart-whole. He would leave her virgin heart in peace to find happiness with the vicar, perhaps, or some other worthy, dull, honest man who would make her a good husband.

Celestine lagged behind a chattering Elise and a smugly satisfied Mrs. Jacobs as they walked down the short hall to the great gothic-arched wooden doors. Even her conversation with Mr. Foster, brief as it was, had been carried out in a distracted state, not with her usual calm serenity, and the vicar had felt her distraction. He had frowned and bid her good evening coolly.

But another long ride back to Ladymead with Lord St. Claire loomed, and she was in no state for it. She always felt fragile, like glass, after a practice in which her solo parts were rehearsed. Singing the holy songs in the sacred confines of St. George's left her weak and trembling, with a heart so open and full she was always afraid she would weep—or be shattered by an unkind word.

But when she joined the two ladies, it was to find a gravely attentive Lord St. Claire. He handed each of them into the carriage in turn with no lingering pressure or teasing words and was quietly deferential, treating each woman exactly alike. Her heart flooded with gratitude and relief as he politely turned his remarks to the maid and housekeeper after one questioning glance at Celestine's drained, pale face.

She had a few moments to gather her wits as Mrs. Jacobs prosed on about the rehearsal, ending with an arch question to the man sitting opposite her.

"And *now* what do you think of our choir, my lord?" Her double chins quivered in expectation of his answer, as her beady eyes glared through the dimness.

"Quite extraordinary, Mrs. Jacobs, just as you said." His voice was quiet and serious.

Celestine stole a glance at him in the semidarkness. His noble profile was absolutely still for once, with no laughter or teasing looks being tossed this way and that, and no trace of sarcasm in his low, melodious voice. He was handsomer than any man she had ever seen—even more so, she thought, in his quiet reflection. His nose was straight, his chin firm, his lips . . . best not to think too much about his lips. She often found herself watching them when he spoke, relishing the fullness of the bottom one and the even white teeth behind it.

"I . . . I was especially moved by Miss Simons's solos," he continued, gazing straight ahead. "They were . . ."

"Ever so nice she sings, don't she? Though her voice is so very high, ain't it?" That was Elise, buoyed enough by the practice that she ventured an opinion even in such exalted company.

Lord St. Claire sat in silence for a moment before he spoke again. "I have heard many vocal performances; Miss Simons was right when she said that earlier. But there was something about her singing that left me breathless. It was sublime. I was—transported. That is the only word I can think of to describe my feelings. I felt like the gates of heaven had opened and I was chosen to hear an angel sing. The moment will live in my heart for a long time."

His voice was absolutely serious. Celestine, in her vulnerable state, felt her tears well up and a lump form in her throat. She choked them back. Not now! she fiercely told herself. But they would come and she must ignore them. They flowed down her face, dripping off her chin and onto her gloved hands, which were twisted together over her reticule. She cloaked her sob with a quiet cough. Then, in the dimness, she felt a touch on her hand and a square of fabric, a man's large handkerchief, being pressed there. One swift glance told her it was Lord St. Claire, though he was not drawing anyone's attention to her emotionally fragile state.

What a puzzle he was, she thought, as she pressed the deliciously scented square to her eyes. The pressure on her fingers ceased and he left her to her recovery, engaging the other two in a conversation that needed no contribution from her.

She wept silently, he thought, withdrawing his hand after putting his handkerchief in hers. It seemed his one weak compliment had burst some dam of reserve and her tears had flowed just as his had in the still, resonant reaches of the church. He was touched beyond belief that mere words, a trifling commendation from him, could break her reserve.

Had he ever touched a woman that way? He was awed by the powerful sensation he had of holding her living, beating heart in his hands and keeping it safe.

He wished he could be of more comfort. If only he could put an arm around her shoulder and draw her head down to rest on his chest, she could weep unrestrainedly while he soothed her. He felt an odd tug in the region under his breastbone, as if someone had tied a string to his heart and pulled it gently. Was he ill? Was this awkward emotionalism the precursor to a bout of the grippe?

He wished to offer Miss Simons aid, and all he could do was keep the chattering maid and the self-satisfied housekeeper busy so they would not inquire after Miss Simon's silence. He *would* give her time to recover. And he *would* leave off his pursuit of her. She was worthy of his respect and self-control, at the very least. She would suffer no more at his hands.

Four

Justin rose earlier than usual the next morning and actually whistled while his man, Dooley, dressed him and tied his cravat. He felt cleansed, somehow, and had an earnest desire to see Miss Simons again so he could prove to her in the light of day that he knew exactly how to treat her and would embarrass her with his attentions no more.

It was too bad the little governess did not breakfast with the family, but of course that would be unheard of. Why was that, he wondered. She was obviously of good family, and if her fortunes had not been depressed she would have been an honored guest. Though not of elevated rank, her birth was sufficiently genteel for a marquess's table. But because she had somehow fallen on bad times and had been forced to the extremity of educating a gentleman's brats in his home, she was now beyond the pale.

He shrugged as he strolled down the wide stairs. Society's dictates were not for such as he to defy, they just *were*. Little Miss Chambly, last year's governess, had obviously not seen any impediment to attaching the younger brother of a marquess, but then she was a foolish little widgeon, blessed with more hair than wit. Whatever had possessed his sister-in-law to engage her for the education of her daughters he did not know. Perhaps she was doing a favor for someone in taking the girl on, or repaying a favor bestowed.

He was not the first aristocrat to entertain himself with a little dalliance with the hired help. His own father had on more than one occasion lifted the skirts of his staff. In fact, of Justin's own knowledge there was at least one child sired on the wrong side of the blanket. Somewhere out there, he had a half-brother or -sister.

He had never gone so far as his father, finding his lusty entertainment in the arms of willing widows and bored wives. He had only ever stolen kisses from the serving class, but for Celestine's sake, this time he would refrain from inflicting his gallantries. Justin paused in his descent. Since when had his favors been a penance to be endured? Yet the girl acted as though she was being martyred on the cross of his attentions. Justin shrugged off the faint feeling of ill-use and entered the breakfast room, a pretty little dining room decorated in yellow and peach.

Elizabeth was alone, her husband having already eaten and started on his day's business. The present marquess was one aristocrat who would not bed his hirelings, no doubt. August was too aware of his elevated position and had a stern morality that made Justin want to twit him all the more. He didn't know what it was about goodness that made him so wicked, but there it was.

"Good morning, my dear," he said before cheerily bestowing a salute on his sister-in-law's presented cheek. He pulled out the chair beside her and glanced at the newspapers neatly piled on the table for perusal, selecting one and taking his seat.

A footman glided silently into the room with more tea and served the nobleman unobtrusively, while Lady St. Claire made small talk about the cold weather and the possibility of snow before Christmas. When Justin had been served and had a full plate of eggs, kippers, and kedgeree in front of him, she nodded regally for Albert, the footman, to absent himself.

Her fixed smile changed to a scowl, and she turned

and glared at Justin. "Now, you unprincipled bounder, I want a word with you." In her agitation she pointed her fork at him and jabbed it with each word, an unforgivable breach of etiquette and unlike Elizabeth to commit.

"And what have I done to deserve my sister's wrath?" Justin asked lightly, one elegant brow arched in surprise.

"You know very well! Maude, my dresser, could hardly wait to tell me what Mrs. Jacobs has been saying in the kitchen. She was all atwitter because his lordship had deigned to go to choir practice with them. *Choir* practice? Really, Justin, what is your game? Is it Elise or . . ." Her lovely face twisted in a frown. "But it couldn't be Celestine! You promised not to pursue a flirtation there. Out with it! Who are you trying to bed?"

Justin did not have to pretend to be offended. He was—and justly so, he thought. Did his sister think he could do nothing without an ulterior motive? And when had he ever *bedded* her servants? "You've already stated it can't be Miss Simons, so it must be Elise, eh? Maybe I lifted her skirts and had her right there in the carriage in front of the governess and the housekeeper, as I am such a bounder! I invited them to join in but they *declined*."

"Don't be vulgar, Justin!"

"Then don't be insolent." He threw down his fork and tossed his napkin on the table, then stood and strode to the door of the breakfast room. "I shall do what I want with whom I want, and I will not be hen-led like my dear, saintly brother! From now on, keep your elegant little nose out of my affairs, amorous or otherwise!" He slammed the door and headed for the stable, stopping only to have his man called to provide him with his crop and coat. He needed a good long ride to work off this latest indignity.

"Lottie, help Gwen with the paste. That's a good girl."

"Shall we do our play for all the comp'ny, Miss Simons?" Lottie asked, helping her little sister firm her tiny hands around the *papier-mâché* figure she was making.

"That will be up to your mama, my dear." Celestine watched the child and her younger sister, their hands white with flour paste, as they formed the paper into balls.

She knelt beside them for a moment and showed them how to give the ball a suggestion of a nose and chin, how to press in their tiny thumbs to make indentations for the eyes. She winced as she struggled back to her feet. It always took a few hours in the morning before her body would do as she commanded easily and without pain. This morning had been particularly difficult, and the cold of her room seemed to have seeped into her very bones. But she owed it to the girls to do her best not to let her physical limitations affect her work.

Gwenevere's round face was screwed up in concentration, and her tongue was pushed out through her teeth. Gwen was a special child, slower than Lottie had ever been, but with a sunny disposition and cherubic smile that melted the heart. Celestine smiled down at her as she wiped her hands off on her apron, giving her swollen knuckles a surreptitious rub to soothe their aching. If only there were something to take the pain away!

Lottie glanced at her, her expression serious. "Do your hands hurt you, Miss Simons?"

"Sometimes. But not always."

"What's wrong with you?"

Celestine smiled at the candor of youth. It was so much better than the sneaking side glances or disdain of adulthood. "It started when I was a child. My joints ache occasionally, and they get swollen. Not always. In the summer, you remember, they were fine. But the cold makes them ache, and there is nothing I can do about it." She looked down at her inflamed knuckles and slightly crook'd fingers, so ungainly looking, and remembered Lord St. Claire's gentle touch the night before.

What had happened to him between the time the choir started and the time they were finished? She had sensed

a difference in his manner. It had none of his gallant
raillery and more true gentility of spirit. He was more
dangerous to her in that moment than he had been with
all his teasing before then, for he became truly what she
had dreamed of in a man—in those rare moments she
allowed herself to dream of impossibilities.

And she had. She had been a young girl once, a girl
with air castles and fairy dreams in her mind. But she
was a woman now and knew the truth of the world.
Women married for security, and men married . . . Why
did men marry? For dynastic reasons, she supposed. Absently she helped the two little girls work as she sorted
out her thoughts.

They married for money sometimes, if they were pulled
about. They married to beget an heir. Marriage was an
exchange of benefits, with each side trying to gain an
equivalency in what they were offering. Even in her hopes
of a match with Mr. Foster, she realized they would be
making an exchange. She would offer him an ancient
and unblemished family history and would make him a
good wife and helpmeet in the village. In return, he
would offer her security and a home of her own, and
perhaps children if they were lucky.

But sometimes . . . sometimes when she allowed herself to dream she longed for that rare union of two
hearts—two souls that upon meeting sang a sweet song
of love together. She had yearned for the pulse-quicken-
ing, earth-shattering delirium of true love, the tender
emotion the poets described. She believed in it fervently
and completely. Then she looked at herself in the mirror.
She was no idiot; she had long known men favored a
pretty face, which she did not possess. Women with that
valuable commodity could look higher and expect more
from a match, with or without love.

Her thoughts drifted back to the previous evening in
the carriage with Lord Justin. His gentle, thoughtful action in providing her with a kerchief, as simple as it was,
was the most gallant she had ever experienced. She had

wanted to lean on him as she wept, and had had to physically restrain herself from laying her head on his shoulder. Wouldn't he have been surprised if she had? she thought with a rueful grimace.

"What play shall we do, Miss Simons?"

Lottie's high treble disrupted her thoughts, and Celestine forced herself to pay attention to her charges. It was all fairy dust, her dreams, the lightest spun sugar—pretty to look at but dissolving at the merest touch. Love and marriage had nothing to do with her, and she must not expect it even from Mr. Foster. He was likely just being kind in his attentions to her.

"I don't know yet, dear. Shall we clean up the schoolroom and ourselves and go look for a good one from the bookshelves?"

It was dark in the room, the morning sun having risen high enough to desert the east side of the building and so the schoolroom. The governess was sleeping, Justin thought, peeking around the door. The schoolroom door swung in on well-oiled hinges, and he could see Miss Simons, her head back in the ratty, overstuffed chair that was drawn up to the fireplace. A tiny fire was almost out in the grate, and she sat curled up with a pile of books on the table beside her and one on her lap. The two girls were downstairs with their mother, practicing at drinking tea in company in preparation for the houseful they would have over Christmas. Elizabeth insisted they do that occasionally with her to accustom them to polite society and the expectations of adults.

He closed the door quietly behind him and walked across the room, wincing when a floorboard creaked under the faded carpet. She *was* sleeping, or she would have heard him and opened her eyes. In repose, her plainness was all too evident. Her hair was a mousy brown and pulled back in a severe bun, too big for her fragile neck. A few tendrils had escaped and curled around her face.

Her skin was pale, but her complexion was freckled, an unforgivable blight, and her mouth was too big for fashion, though her lips were rosy and would no doubt be satisfyingly soft to kiss.

He smiled down at her, thinking how surprised she would be if he did just that. Her figure was slight, and the worn gray dress she wore did nothing to enhance it, probably hiding any attributes she did possess. She was a schoolroom mouse, the perfect governess, likely to tempt neither master nor servant to take liberties with her. What a sad life for a woman of so much intelligence and gentle wit as he had found her to possess in the hours he had spent with her.

After Elizabeth's intolerable accusations that morning he had ridden for two hours in a blind rage that contrasted sharply with the tranquillity he had thought he had achieved. His sister-in-law was an interfering harpy, and her demand for absolute control over those in her sphere was disturbing—worse than disturbing! It was demonic! Why should a governess not have a life of her own, the chance to savor the joy and sweetness other women took for granted? Was it evil to offer Celestine Simons a few stolen moments of romance?

He thought not. She might not agree right now, but he felt sure that if she knew her job to be secure, she would sing another tune entirely. Her fear of him originated in her need for this paltry position; release her from the fear and she would welcome his attentions. He knew when a woman responded to him, and had felt the suppressed longing radiate in waves from her. He would help her free that hidden core of passion.

He would see that no ill befell her. There was no good reason why she should not enjoy his considerable skill at lovemaking, but to overcome her scruples without telling her that little secret; now *that* was a challenge worthy of him. She would be grateful, eventually, when he taught her how sweet stolen kisses could taste. It would give her something to dream about in her spinsterhood. And perhaps Elizabeth would learn a salutary lesson from the experience; she would find that one could allow one's dependents the freedom to live a little, and no harm would come of it. Together he and Celestine would strike a blow for all of the meddling marchioness's household.

He knelt beside her and noted again her hands, folded together in her lap. The knuckles and joints were swollen and he wondered if they were painful—if she suffered. Her expression in sleep was smooth, with no hint of suffering, but she was really not old enough for lines of pain to have etched themselves permanently . . . yet.

That would come, no doubt. In ten years, even less, she would be even more faded and would have pinched lines between her brows, under her eyes and around her generous mouth. Soon even her limited attractions would have faded away, leaving a sad little songbird whose feathers had lost their luster. He felt a tiny pang at that moment and wondered if he had eaten something that had disagreed with him, for that small twinge was persistent, and he could only think of indigestion as its cause.

Gently, he lifted one of her hands from the other and caressed it, rubbing lightly the swollen joints. She shifted restlessly, and her lips parted. He watched as she shifted again. Under her ill-fitting gown was a suggestion of small, well-shaped breasts and gently flaring hips. Odd that when one was this close the freckles under her eyes were charming, a dusting of tiny dots just over her nose. Her complexion was so fair that on her eyelids he could see the delicate tracery of blue veins under the milky whiteness. He raised her hand and touched his lips to the swollen knuckles of her right hand.

"Mmmm?" she murmured and flexed her fingers.

He did it again, letting his warm breath caress the back of her hand, then pressed his lips in turn to each painful joint. He watched her face as he did that, and saw a tiny smile hover on her lips and a soft sigh escape, as she murmured again.

"Justin."

His name came out as a sigh, her voice soft and caressing, and a shiver ran down his spine. Her voice held the
seductive warmth of a lover in the velvety darkness of the
night. Ah, sweet success; it was so close he could taste the
ambrosial flavor of his favorite dish! She clearly was already besotted with him; it was merely a matter of making
her admit as much when awake. He waited for the triumph to flood his being. And waited.

He shrugged.

He supposed that it would come when she admitted it
to his face, as other ladies and not-ladies had done in his
long career of seduction. It was a game that was won
when a woman gave him her heart, or at least said she
did, with winsome professions of undying devotion that
he never believed for a second. He had no real illusions
on that score. Few women gave their heart or their hand
without a mercenary motive, and that was fine. The triumph was in capturing their undivided attention and
tempting them into throwing away everything for him. It
was a game he seldom lost.

The conquest would be all the sweeter this time, surely,
because his motives were to some degree altruistic. He
would win his bet with himself, and show Elizabeth, at
the same time, that a governess was also a woman, and
should be allowed a woman's right to romance. All would
emerge winners in this tender game, including Celestine
Simons, who would have a brief, piquant season of love
to remember.

The governess's large gray eyes fluttered open, and she
appeared disoriented. Her gaze fixed on Justin's face, her
eyes widened, and she snatched her hand from his grasp.
"My lord," she gasped. "What . . . what . . . ?"

"I had hoped to be like the prince from the fairy-tale
and awaken Sleeping Beauty with a kiss."

She pressed the back of her right hand to her lips and
her eyes widened. They really were the most remarkable
shade of gray with a thick fringe of dark lashes. Looking
so frightened and bewildered she was almost pretty, Justin

thought. Almost? Perhaps he was being unduly harsh. Many a London debutante, boasting no more attractions than Miss Simons, had been called a beauty. Clothe her more elegantly and dress her hair in the latest fashion and she would not disgrace Almack's.

"No," he answered the unvoiced question in her exquisite eyes. "I did not take that liberty. I merely pressed an ardent salute on your hand, the very hand you have pressed to your lips."

"Oh, my lord, you must not!" She rose in her agitation, a wince of pain flitting across her face as she stood. Her stance was hunched, and she straightened with difficulty. Not meeting his eyes, she picked up a pile of books from the table beside her chair and retreated to a low white shelf suited to the height of young children, where she started to shelve the books that she held. A heavy tome dropped from her hands and he bent to pick it up for her as she rubbed her knuckles.

"It was an innocent expression of my devotion to you, Miss Simons." A smile played over his lips. He retrieved the rest of the books from the table and handed them to her one by one. "My, my. *Gibson's Book of Children's Plays. Plays For The Very Young. Almanac of Plays Intended for a Youthful Audience.* What is this all about?"

She turned back to him and took another book from his outstretched hand. "The children are making puppets. We are planning a play for the family, but I cannot find a suitable one for the season." She frowned and bit her lip. "They are so excited about it, and I don't want it to fall flat because of the wrong material."

Justin tilted his head to one side, considering the matter. "What about *A Midsummer Night's Dream?*"

The governess surprised him with a laugh, a light tinkling sound that would be the envy of many a schoolroom chit trying to learn social skills. "Does not the very title make it ineligible, my lord, as well as a hundred other things? Shakespeare is much too old for Lottie, let us not even mention Gwen."

"However, it seems to me that it has the right feel, if you know what I mean—fairies and enchanted forests—in fact I seem to remember that the play was performed for her majesty Queen Elizabeth at Christmas. Tell you what." He shelved the last two books for her, then took her hand and drew her back to her chair. "Sit, Miss Simons. I have a proposition for you."

She looked alarmed and the vague idea floating around in Justin's brain solidified. The very thing! What he had in mind would bring him into much closer contact with her, and allow him to break down her defenses. She was susceptible to him, he knew. Her murmuring of his name had given it away even though she was not aware of it. But she had reservations that must be overcome, and he required time to do that. In the interests of a true challenge he had forsworn reassuring her that he would intercept her employer's wrath and make sure that she was not turned off without a reference, that most feared of plights. That would make her too easy a pigeon to pluck, and he had long ago learned that the sweetness of success in any venture was commensurate with the uncertainty of the outcome.

And so he would win this game without making it any easier for himself. If he involved himself in this puppet play it would require spending a little time with her and further his aims; Elizabeth would be suspicious no doubt, but would likely not interfere in something to do with her daughters.

Celestine pulled her hand away from him and her pale cheeks turned rosy. From any other woman he would have suspected coquetry, but there was no pretense in her. She folded her hands together and sat demurely looking down at them as he knelt beside her chair. He chuckled to himself, aware of the absurdity of his position. It was a picture of the gallant swain offering heart and hand to a young maiden. But he must focus on the matter at hand.

"There is nothing suitable in the books, you say, and

it must be something very special and suited to the season. Would you allow me to write a short play for my nieces? Just a brief one, with a nod, perhaps, to Will's summer fantasy?"

Her lips parted and she was startled enough to look up into his eyes. "You would do that?"

He gazed at her lips, distracted for a moment in spite of himself. He looked forward to caressing their softness, and becoming her teacher in a lesson of love. "For my nieces? Of course. It may not be fashionable to admit, but I love the little pusses."

"And they love you," she said softly, those full petal lips curving in a smile that took his breath away. "They often speak of you, you know. I knew you before I met you, through Lottie's stories. She was very disappointed when you didn't come last summer. And it isn't just the sweets you bring them. You have a way with them, my lord."

Her voice was low and sweet, not the affected, shrill tone of Miss Chambly or the overly-correct diction of the one before her. A warmth spread through his inner regions and he smiled back up at her, surprised at how gratified he was that she had known of his existence and had spoken of him with his nieces. "Now, that's another thing. If we are to work together, I want no more of this 'my lording'! And that is an order! You must call me Justin." That one murmuring of his name hadn't been enough; he wanted to hear her say it again, with just that soft tone she had used.

She stiffened, and he saw that he had gone too far. "That would not be at all proper, sir." She rose and shook the wrinkles from her dress. "I . . . I must see to the girls . . ."

"Stop!" He took her arm. "You are doing it again, Miss Simons. You are running away."

"No, my lord—I am seeing to my duty. And it is not at all proper to be here with you alone."

"Why? You are not some green girl who needs chaperoning, my dear. You are a grown woman." He pulled her closer, wanting to dissipate the nervousness he felt tremble through her body. He spoke quietly with the reassuring tone that usually calmed the most giddy filly. He did not want her to be frightened of him; he only had the best of intentions. Besides, he could not believe she was truly frightened of him, only of discovery and the price she would pay; he would make sure she did not suffer from his attentions. He couldn't explain that to her now, but . . .

"Come, my dear, you have no reason to be afraid of me. I promise, I will never do you harm." Almost against his own will he pulled her toward him until their bodies were touching at the knee and her bosom grazed his chest.

Her eyes widened. "I-I must go, my lord." She pulled away and ran from the room, her gray skirts billowing out behind her.

Five

Panting, Celestine almost collided with a footman on the landing as she raced inelegantly down the stairs from the third-floor schoolroom. As the footman bowed and continued on his stately way, not betraying by even a lifted eyebrow the surprise he must have felt at her precipitate descent, the governess stopped and put her hand over her heart. Lord St. Claire was right. She did run from him, and with good reason. She was ill-equipped to parry his teasing thrusts.

How disappointed she was in him. The evening before he had been quietly kind, even deferential, and she thought his teasing, mocking flattery was over. But to suggest she call him by his given name—that alone was highly improper. And he had kissed her hand as she slept! She held her right hand to her flaming cheek.

She gazed down at her swollen knuckles, wondering why he had done that and how he had surmounted the distaste he must feel when he looked at her ugly hands. He was so elegant and perfect, and yet he seemed to be pursuing her, a plain governess, merely for sport. He was like a hunter, denied his favorite game, who would take up a gun to shoot a crippled deer or elderly hare just to keep in practice.

Maybe that was it. Maybe when enticing targets presented themselves, he would abandon the chase.

It would be so much easier if she could hate him or

even dislike him. But there was something within him that called out to her, that beckoned like a lover whispering softly from the shadows, and now he haunted her dreams. His company was delightful when he chose to be himself. Walking with him in Ellerbeck had been a revelation. She never would have suspected a member of the aristocracy could be so unaffected and relaxed. They had spent whole afternoons together, romping with the children outside, or cozy by the fireplace as he read adventure stories for Lottie in his low, cultivated voice. The gentleness he revealed in the carriage on the way home from choir practice had finally shattered her self-control.

Surely she could not be so much of a goose as to fall in love with him! No, it wasn't that, she assured herself. He was beyond the realm of her experience and she did not know how to deal with him. He discomposed her, that was all. Celestine took a deep breath and sedately walked down the staircase to the first floor.

Still, he was despicable to be taking advantage of her precarious position in the household, and without even the excuse of attraction. For Celestine was a realist. She knew her attractions were few and not such as to send a young nobleman crazy with love or lust. She had lived in the world long enough to be aware men favored a pretty face over inner beauty. No, he was amusing himself at her expense and she would not put up with it. Her peace—nay, her very *future*—depended on it.

She composed herself and entered the drawing room. The scene there was one of domestic felicity. Young Augustus St. Claire, viscount and future marquess of Ladymead, had arrived home from school and, with all the superiority of adolescence, was studying Gilbert, the baby of the family, who sat on their mother's lap. Lottie and Gwen were seated on either side of Lady St. Claire on the heavy green brocade sofa.

"Miss Simons," the marchioness called out, seeing the governess lingering uncertainly by the door. "Come and help me with the girls. They have prepared something for their brother's arrival, have they not?" Lady St. Claire's beautiful face was alight with maternal pride as she surveyed her brood, and indeed they were a fine-looking family.

Celestine crossed the room and took the two girls to stand in front of young Augustus St. Claire. She knelt on the deep, soft carpet. *"En Français, mes enfants,"* she whispered, holding the little girls' hands in her own.

Lottie's eyes lit up, but Gwen looked very uncertain and stuck two fingers in her mouth.

"Bonjour, mon frère," Lottie said, curtsying. "Et . . . ." She stopped and looked at her governess.

Celestine whispered a word to her.

Lottie nodded. *"Et joyeux Noël."*

Gwen had remained silent. Celestine decided it was best not to prod her, as she clearly had no memory of the brief passage, even though they had practiced it just that morning. Lady St. Claire was adamant though, her thin, arched brows furrowed over her eyes.

"Now, Gwen!" she commanded, her voice stern. "Take your fingers out of your mouth and say what you are supposed to say."

The little girl looked frightened and eyed her big brother, who looked down at her with barely concealed impatience, with trepidation.

"Well, say something, brat," he said, his voice breaking awkwardly. He was very like his father, with a wide, high forehead and commanding presence even at his young age. He stood with his hands behind his back in unconscious imitation of the marquess.

Gwen's lower lip trembled and her blue eyes grew wide. She sniffed once and a fat tear rolled down her cheek.

"Infant," Augustus said, turning away in disgust. "Just as stupid as she was when I went away to Michaelmas term."

Celestine gasped and was speechless. She longed to deliver a set down to the young man, but Lady St. Claire had made very clear to her that the heir of the household was not her responsibility.

"I think you should apologize to your little sister, Gus, old man," a steely voice said from the door.

Celestine whirled to see the boy's uncle, one booted foot resting negligently over the other. He was elegant and assured, as always, his buff breeches immaculate and his bottle-green coat perfectly fitted. He glanced at her and a half smile played over his lips, as though he was remembering the little scene between them just minutes before.

"Uncle Justin!" Gus cried and ran to him.

Justin's expression became stern, though, and he crossed his arms over his chest in an uncompromising attitude of disapproval. "I said you should apologize to your little sister. She is a small child and a female, and a gentleman is always courteous to children and women."

Gus swallowed, clearly wounded by the mild reprimand from his hero. He returned to his sisters, knelt down by Gwen, and said, "I *am* sorry, little one. Forgive me?"

Gwen nodded and ran into his arms, planting a wet kiss on his smooth cheek. He got up looking sheepish and wiping the moisture from his face with his sleeve, then looked hesitantly toward his uncle.

"*Now* I am glad to see you," Lord St. Claire said, and stepped forward with his arms held open, ready to hug his nephew. He took another look at him, though. The boy stood eye to eye with him, and he stuck out his hand instead.

Gus flushed and pumped his hand enthusiastically.

Celestine was impressed by the nobleman's handling of the situation. Gus had been corrected without the bluster of his father or the waspishness of his mother. There was definitely more to the man than met the eye. What a puzzle he was! She would swear one minute there was nothing more going on in his brain than the question of whether to wear the green jacket or the blue, and then he would surprise her with his thoughtfulness or wit. She quietly guided the two girls from the room to turn them over to Elise for their luncheon and started up the stairs behind them.

"Miss Simons."

Lord St. Claire's cool, amused voice followed her up the stairs, making her pause and turn reluctantly.

"Shall I consider our conversation in the schoolroom to have ended affirmatively? Shall I undertake that little commission? I would so like to be of service to you."

Celestine gazed down at his handsome face and sparkling eyes. "I expect you will please yourself, my lord," she said, with a faint smile.

"I always do," he chuckled. "I always do."

Lady Emily Delafont, Marchioness of Sedgely, traveled in her stylish equipage with her companion and maiden aunt-by-marriage, Lady Dodo Delafont. From Yorkshire to the Lake District through the Pennines was quite a trip, but the weather had held so far and it was preferable to being alone for Christmas yet again.

Not that she would have been absolutely alone. Of course there was Dodo. She looked across the carriage, dim in the dull December light, at her attenuated aunt, whose long lankiness was so completely opposite to her own short pudginess.

Dodo was very like her nephew, Emily's estranged husband Baxter Delafont, in looks. Baxter was tall and lean, with dark wings of black hair and an eternally sardonic expression on his handsome face. However, Dodo was completely unlike him in character, hiding a romantic, warm heart under a gruff exterior. Emily sighed. She was grateful to Dodo for her support since her five-year-old separation from her husband of fifteen years, but life was beginning to take on a stultifying sameness that was very much like being trapped in amber. Her life was in suspension to be resumed at some later, unspecified date.

It would be nice to see Elizabeth again. It had been

years since they had seen each other, she realized with a start, though they corresponded regularly. The invitation to share Christmas with the St. Claires had been a complete surprise, but a welcome one in so many ways.

There was the relief from boredom it would offer. Life in Yorkshire in the winter could be deadly dull, though she loved it in all its seasons. It was a harsh area in many ways, and there had been difficulties in recent years with Luddites and loom-breakers and hard years of poverty for many people. But it was beautiful, too, in a wild, untamed way, and she did what she could for the people of her village. They had been good to her in return.

Also in favor of the invitation was the opportunity to renew her friendship with Elizabeth, her bosom bow from their years at Miss Lillian's Fine Academy for Young Ladies. While she was with her husband, she and Elizabeth had seen each other regularly during the social whirl of the London Season.

But Emily had retired from that life when she and her husband had gone their separate ways five years before, and Elizabeth had long been busy with her children. Exchanging letters was not the same as sharing a nice long coze, curled up with a cup of tea in some secluded nook. That was what they had done as girls, and she hoped they would have the chance for a few such conversations over the Christmas season. Her visit was to be at least three weeks long.

But mostly there was the chance to see her niece, Celestine Simons. When she had heard of Celestine's predicament after her father's death, the absolute poverty she had been reduced to since her father's income was entailed to a male cousin, she had offered the girl a home. But Celestine had a stubborn, independent streak and would not hear of inflicting herself on dear Aunt Emily, as she had written back. Instead she had asked for help in finding a governess position with a good family, which Emily had been glad to do.

Luckily, she had still been in correspondence with

Elizabeth and had asked about the possibility of a governess's post, either with them or with someone of their
acquaintance. A letter of regret from Elizabeth, stating
that she had no open position nor did she know of one,
had been swiftly followed by a letter outlining the affair
of the unfortunate Chambly girl at Christmas and Elizabeth's determination to end the governess's employ at
Ladymead. Of course Justin, an acquaintance from many
years ago, had acted the part of a complete cad, but,
according to Lady St. Claire, the young governess was full
of ideas above her station and had set her cap at the
nobleman. Elizabeth, in need of someone immediately,
decided to hire Celestine on Emily's recommendation.

The carriage turned a corner and Emily let down the
window, letting in a blast of cold, crisp air.

"How much farther, Gorse?" she called to her coachman.

"We've made the turn into the estate, milady. Another
mile or two, mayhap, accordin' to the directions."

"Good! On we go, then." Emily glanced around her
curiously. There was a long row of trees on one side of
the drive, bare and dark in the fading half-light of a mid-
December afternoon. It wouldn't be long before sunset,
as they were only a few weeks away from the shortest day
of the year. In the distance, she could see a copse and a
lake, probably frozen or close to it already, and in the
distance, the fells. They had already traveled through the
Pennines, a trip Emily had never made before, and she
was thrilled by the new scenery.

"Are you intending to freeze us to death before we get
there, my dear?" a querulous voice muttered.

"Of course not, dear Dodo," Emily laughed. She put
up the window and sat back, smoothing her wine-colored,
fur-trimmed cape down over her ample figure. She threw
her dark fur muff over to her aunt. "Use this if your
hands are cold. It is deliciously warm—*too* warm for my
plump hands."

Soon after that they pulled up to the house and Emily

eagerly stepped down with the aid of her groom's hand. She gazed up at Ladymead with pleasure.

"What a lovely house!"

It was more modern than her own gloomy home in Yorkshire, but the appellation of "house" was far too modest for it. It had been built in the last century to replace the ancient pile, as Elizabeth called the old house, now a picturesque ruin, and was constructed of a large central section of three stories built of gray stone, with two similar wings, one all windows, clearly a conservatory. The top was castellated, looking for all the world like a crown.

Emily and Dodo moved up the steps and into a huge hall with chandeliers gleaming against the day's gloominess. Welcoming warmth enfolded them, and a tall, good-looking footman took their wraps. Their maidservant followed a few hours behind in another carriage, along with their baggage.

"Emmy!" Elizabeth St. Claire swept into the hall, a vision in dark green silk. She wrapped Emily in a perfumed embrace and then held her away from her, eyeing her up and down. "Put on a few pounds, my dear?" Her tone was arch.

Emily's cheeks, pink from the chill air, burned to a deeper color. "I would say we all put a little weight on over the years, but you, my dear, are impossibly slim, and after four children!"

Elizabeth laughed, delightedly. "Now I remember why I loved you so well at school. Such a well-turned compliment, and after my discourtesy! You are far too kind." She took her friend's arm and led her into the drawing room.

Once there, Emily turned and said, "Do you know my aunt, Lady Dianne Delafont?"

Elizabeth put out her hand and took the older woman's, holding it for a moment. She glanced over at Emily. "Very like Baxter, is she not?"

Emily shook her head. "In some ways, but in many more ways not."

Plainspoken Elizabeth! She had often offended in their girlhood days, and many thought plain, shy, country girl Emily befriended her only because of her elevated rank, for Elizabeth was the daughter of an earl and the betrothed, from the cradle, of the then-future Marquess of Ladymead.

But for some reason she and Elizabeth had gotten along from the beginning. Perhaps it was the very dissimilarity of their characters. Elizabeth was tart and astringent, outspoken and bold, while Emily was quiet and shy, with a sweetness that overlooked many faults. Her shyness had dissipated over the years, and she was less likely to suffer fools gladly, but because of the age of her attachment to Elizabeth she still disregarded the woman's acrimonious character.

"You must be absolutely perishing for refreshment," Elizabeth said. "Andrew, tea," she told the hovering footman. "And please tell Miss Simons I would like to see her here. Elise can look after the children for a while." She turned back to her guests and made sure they were comfortably ensconced in chairs, then seated herself.

"I hope my niece is working out." Emily sighed as she settled into a comfortable chair. It was such a relief after days in a carriage. She looked forward to a warm, comfortable bed that night, too. Inn beds were just not the same, no matter how competent the landlord. "From the letters I have received, I would say she likes her position very much."

"Oh, my darling, she is absolutely perfect. I would not say so to her face, of course, for I would not have her get puffed up, but I bless the day that little chit Chambly threw her cap at Justin. She did me a favor by being so presumptuous."

Emily sighed. "Was not some of the fault your brother-in-law's?"

"Men!" the marchioness said dismissively, waving one

elegant hand. "They have no control where a pretty face is concerned, and a wise woman uses that to her benefit. I do not blame the chit for trying to better her position. Who would want to work as a governess when one could be the wife of a lord, especially one as rich and handsome as Justin? However, not in my house and not with my brother-in-law! Justin will marry, and it will be to a girl who can bring something to the marriage other than a lot of blond hair and a simper."

"Still, Lord St. Claire has quite a reputation in town for raising a lady's expectations, only to dash them at the very last possible minute."

"He is a scamp," Elizabeth admitted, "and I have told him he must mend his ways. I have invited a few eligibles for the Christmas season to see if I can fire him off into holy wedlock. August wishes it, and I have promised to do my best."

"Unless you are willing to court them and give them a ring, I do not see how you can force the issue." Emily was amused, as always, by Elizabeth's forthright manner, and was eager to see her friend's brother-in-law again after a number of years, to see how he looked and behaved. He would be—she counted in her head—all of thirty-two now, and had been breaking hearts for twelve of those years.

"I have done my part in hiring Miss Simons. I knew she was perfect the moment I saw her. I would have hired her anyway, just for your sake, my dear, but she is so plain and shy—and, my dear, those hands! Impossibly ugly! Justin is particular about those kinds of things." She stretched her own elegant, slim ones out in front of her.

Emily stiffened. "Lizbet, you go too far," she said quietly, using her friend's pet name to soften her words.

The marchioness reddened in an unusual display of chagrin. "Oh, my darling, I am sorry. I know she is your kin, but you must see . . . with Justin the way he is . . ."

They were interrupted by a cry of pleasure from the door and Celestine's soft voice. "Aunt Emily!" She raced across the room as her aunt rose, and they embraced. "Oh, Aunt, it is so good to see you!"

Emily hugged her fiercely for a moment, then held her niece away from her and looked her over. Celestine was Emily's older sister's only child. Pansy, a dozen years Emily's senior, had married a scholarly older gentleman, and Celestine had been the light of his life. Since her mother had died when the child was very young, father and daughter had been unusually close, and when the old gentleman finally died after a long, debilitating illness, Celestine had suffered. The pain was compounded by the abrupt realization she had no place to live, as the estate was entailed and she had little money of her own.

Emily was only seven years older than her niece and felt a kinship with her, a solid bond that would have encouraged her to offer her niece anything. She had offered Celestine a home or an independent income, but Celestine begged to be allowed to make her own way. She had no expectations of having children of her own, she said. Failing that, she wished to work with children. Thus, after spending the previous Christmas with Emily and Dodo, she had traveled straight to her new governess position.

Her letters since then had been very cheerful, but looking her over now Emily thought Celestine looked paler than normal, and surely she had lost weight. Was something troubling her? Or was her pallor just the result of the season and too little outdoor exercise? And her hands were swollen again with arthritis, a painful condition that must make her work all the more difficult.

Conversation took a general turn, with Elizabeth doing much of the talking concerning her plans for the holidays and who else would make up the house party. She had invited a widowed friend with a daughter who had made her comeout several Seasons previously. An older couple, acquaintances of the marquess, would also spend much of the season at Ladymead. They had two daughters, both of marriageable age, one just out of the schoolroom and headed to London for her first Season in the spring.

Emily saw Elizabeth's hand in all of that, and was amused, as she ate cream buns and drank tea, with wondering how her machinations would work. Would Justin St. Claire be caught in parson's mousetrap at last, or would he escape once again to wreak havoc the next Season on young girls' hearts and widows' reputations? She rather thought she would wager on Justin.

He strolled in as they enjoyed their tea. He was an old acquaintance of Emily's and came over to kiss her hand gallantly.

"You look positively radiant, my lady. Ravishing! That deep wine color suits your complexion." He threw a side glance at Celestine, whose eyes were determinedly studying the floor, and his eyebrows pulled down in puzzlement.

"Celestine is my niece," Emily said, answering his unasked question. "Elizabeth was kind enough to send for her when I arrived so we could visit."

The nobleman nodded, but his gaze stayed on the governess. Was that the trouble, Emily wondered. Despite Elizabeth's best precautions, was the rascal pestering Celestine? The girl had little experience with how to handle a roué, and if he had determined to set her up as his flirt, or worse, she would not know how to react. But that was ridiculous. Though overly blunt, Elizabeth had been quite right. Celestine was plain and not very socially adept—not at all St. Claire's usual type.

He actually favored *two* types in his annual prowl of London—beautiful young girls in their first or second Season, and mature, sophisticated widows or wives ready for a little flirtation. The first type he seemed to enjoy making fall in love with him. The second type was pure dalliance.

Celestine was neither. She was twenty-eight, long past the first blush of youth. But still, she was an innocent, her youthful years taken up in caring for an invalid father in a small village. If she ever fell in love, Emily suspected it would have all the fervor of a first attachment and the strength of a more mature love and could possibly be devastating to her. She watched as Justin St. Claire charmed Dodo while sitting beside Celestine. The girl's face had turned rosy at the feel of his leg accidentally brushing hers or his solicitousness in handing her her tea.

He murmured things to her sometimes that no one else could hear, causing her blush to deepen, and he watched her constantly. It was deeply troubling to Emily, and she was glad she had come, if only to help her niece out of any bind she found herself in as a result of her inexperience with hardened flirts.

Also aware of the byplay was Elizabeth. Her lovely face was pulled into a frown, the purse-string wrinkles around her mouth evidencing her displeasure. Justin laughed and talked, but there was an undercurrent in everything he said and did. Emily decided it was a good thing she was there. Perhaps she could be of some use to her niece, or perhaps she could find a way to deflect the man's attentions. At the very least, she could figure out what his game was—and stop it, if at all possible.

Six

Despicable, *damnable* man, Celestine thought as she rummaged through the scraps of fabric the draper had given her. Justin St. Claire had thoroughly thrown her out of countenance when all she wanted to do was talk to her Aunt Emily. He said not a word out of turn, but if she would reach for something, he would hand it to her before she got to it, allowing his fingers to brush hers. She could feel his steady gaze on her face as she spoke, and she lost the thread of the conversation. His thigh pressed against hers, and then he would apologize *sotto voce* when he 'noticed' it.

Lady St. Claire had looked like a thunder cloud by the end of tea, and she feared she was for it, but time passed and Celestine escaped upstairs with her aunt. Now she was in the blessed quiet of the schoolroom with the two girls. Soon Elise would come to take them off for their baths and bed, but right now Lottie and Gwen were curled up together in a big chair by the fire examining a fairy-tale book, their blond curly heads nodding as they got drowsy and murmured together, while she went through fabrics trying to get ideas for costumes for the puppets they were making.

It was difficult now because Lord St. Claire was creating the story. She had no inkling what it would be and what characters she would need to clothe—if he meant to follow through on his offer. It was entirely possible he would get bored before finishing, or never meant to do it at all—in which case she had better prepare something, rather than depend on the mercurial nobleman.

He was a puzzle. He lived up to his reputation as a rakish tease most of the time. He was adept at conveying his flirtation without saying a word, so her blushes and consciousness must appear to be all on her own side.

But there were times . . . as in the carriage on the way back from choir practice. She had felt a quiet strength emanating from him as her own composure crumbled from the emotionalism of the music she had been a part of. When she sang with the choir in St. George's, she felt she became one with the church and the organ music. Parting from it was painful.

In the darkness of the carriage, she had felt he understood. She had wanted nothing more than to lay her head against his shoulder and cling to him while she regained her control. What would it be like, for once, to lay down her burdens and let someone take care of her? She had always had to be the strong one, for her father had been sick the whole of her adult life.

She didn't regret the necessity that had forced her to be strong, but, oh, the bliss of letting someone else make her decisions for her or carry the load of responsibility she had always assumed. Was that what it would be like to have a husband? If she married the vicar, would she feel a weight ease from her shoulders? Somehow, she thought not. He would expect her, with a perfect right, to assume her share of the duties in the parish.

And she must not fantasize that life with a man like Lord St. Claire would be any different. His lightheartedness would inevitably have its reverse in additional cares and worries for any woman who married him. She, no doubt, would be expected to assume the bulk of the work of managing the household and possibly his estate.

For a moment in the carriage, she had felt there was a well of strength within him that had perhaps gone unappreciated because it remained untapped. In the light of day and with the resumption of his teasing flirtation, she wondered if she had imagined that side of him. Was it her own need she projected on him, or did she really feel the wave of kindness and caring that had rolled over her and soothed her as she held his handkerchief to her eyes in the darkness, inhaling his scent and letting the comfort of it fill her?

She probably would never figure him out. If she could get to the end of his visit without some kind of incident, she would be happy.

But how lovely it had been for those few minutes to feel his quiet strength beside her and imagine what it would be like to have someone to lean on when the world seemed too much. Celestine had no illusions about herself. She knew her own strength had kept her father alive as long as he lived, but she had sacrificed something of herself.

Her body was weak, and sometimes the future frightened her. What would happen if she became crippled from the rheumatism that wracked her body? She'd had little pleasure in the world except her father's company and knowing herself to be all-important to him, and now she had to make her own way. For all that her post was a good one and she came to love the little girls more every day, it was unremitting labor. How marvelous it would be to lay down her burdens and rest, knowing someone else was there to care for her.

It would be so wonderful to be able to relax and enjoy Justin St. Claire's cheerful, sunny company, for he really had a way about him, a bright, happy manner that lifted her heart just to be near.

She stopped sorting the fabrics, appalled at the turn her mind was taking. What was she thinking? He was dallying with her for God knew what reason—probably out of habit or because he needed a flirt at all times. She was a fool to enjoy him, for the moment more company arrived, he would turn his attentions to a more suitable object.

And he didn't mean any of it. He couldn't! His flattery was outrageous, the compliments wildly unsuitable to someone of her plain visage and lack of attractions. He was just filling time until the pretty girls Elizabeth had included in the guest list arrived. Then she would be left in peace in the schoolroom to finish her seasonal work and get Lottie and Gwen ready for their puppet show.

And, since she was thinking of that, she must prepare something, for he would certainly get bored and forget about writing his nieces a play for their puppet theater. It was just flirtation to him, for whatever mysterious reason. Celestine sighed, not sure whether to be glad or sad that her customary good sense kept her from sweet daydreams of love.

Justin stroked out another word and wiped his nib on a pen wipe. This was damnably hard work, writing a play! He hadn't intended to go through with it. It had just been another flirtation, a way to stay close to Miss Simons. But then he had realized if he didn't, the little girls would end up the losers, and he never would disappoint his goddaughters.

Lottie, so bright and clever, with sparkling blue eyes, was the very picture of her mother—and could be as tart-tongued occasionally. Someday she would lead the men of the *ton* a merry dance. Little Gwen, her blue eyes a little puzzled at times, and rarely saying anything one could understand, had a sweetness of expression and innocence that made hurting or disappointing her out of the question. When she laid her blond head against his arm, he would gladly take on anybody who might wound her. He might be an abominable brother, an unconscionable rake, the scourge of the London Season, but he was a good uncle.

Was that what being a father was like? He stared off into space, chewing on the end of the pen as he imagined little ones around him calling him father, pulling at his jacket, climbing on his knee. If the feelings he held for his nieces and nephews were so very strong, what would fatherhood be like? The responsibility terrified him, and he shrugged off the idea. Time enough for that in some distant, hazy future. Right now he must think of this damned play.

And so he sat, pen in hand, and a volume of Shakespeare in front of him. He had been there all morning while the rest of the family went off to church, and he was still at it after nuncheon. Damn. How had the man, the immortal bard, ever done it? The words seemed all wrong when they flowed from the end of his pen.

For a while in the library there was just the scratching of his pen across paper, interrupted occasionally by a muffled curse and the crunch of paper being balled up. Then there were just the pen sounds. He wrote and wrote, continuing long after his hand had started to ache.

He might have something. A story about a lonely prince and a princess who didn't know she was a princess. A tale of true love. He closed the Shakespeare, pushed it away, and chewed the end of the pen.

A lonely prince who had his pick of the most beautiful girls in all the land, but could not find a single one who made his heart sing. His brother, the king, was getting impatient and wanted him to choose a girl to be his princess. The lonely prince—call him . . . Justin frowned down at the paper with unseeing eyes. Call him Aurelius, the golden one, fortunate in birth, countenance, and riches, but without love. He wrote on in the blessed silence of the library. It was a dark, gloomy day outside, and he wrote in the pool of light shed by a branch of tapers.

There was a princess who didn't know she was a princess—call her Calista, the most beautiful one. She lived in a forest, all alone, where no one saw her radiant beauty. She had no mirror, so she did not know she was so fair. The scratching became more fervent as Justin scrawled his ideas, dipping into the ink, blotting his page occasionally.

The lonely prince, Aurelius, tells his brother, Reginald the Mighty, he will set out on a journey across the land. If he has not found the girl he wishes to wed at the end of one month, he will marry anyone Reginald chooses.

Justin sat back in his chair, oblivious to the spots of dark ink soiling his sleeve, as he chewed on the end of his pen. He needed some comic relief. Reginald would choose a girl for him to come home to, the most ugly, long-toothed, pimply female with a high screechy voice and harrying manner. He would do her voice himself, a copy of . . .

The door opened and Elizabeth peeked around. "Justin! There you are. What on earth are you doing?" She came into the shadowy room, one elegant hand planted on her hip.

He flushed. "I . . . uh, I'm helping Miss Simons by writing a play for her and Lottie and Gwen. They're planning a little puppet theater for the holiday company."

Elizabeth's rosebud lips set in a grim line. "Really, Justin! I am counting on you to help me entertain our guests, you know that. And I have the Stimsons and their two daughters arriving this afternoon, and Lady van Hoffen and her daughter Lady Grishelda! You will have no time to be scribbling on some silly piece of work when I need you to conduct them on walks into the village and ice skating and . . ."

Justin turned back to the desk and made another note. Add a wife for the mighty Reginald—Queen Parlia, one who talked and talked and talked. . . .

"Oh, miss, look at the company arriving. Ever so beautiful the ladies are! And their clothes!"

Celestine came upon Elise, with Lottie and Gwen, peering through the spindles of the railing that overlooked the great hall. She stopped and watched with them.

"Look at the beautiful ladies, Miss Simons," Lottie said, crouched down with her arm around her little sister.

A man and woman with two girls around twenty were gathered in the hall, being welcomed by the marquess and marchioness. The man was portly and red-faced, with a distended stomach that confessed a love for fine food and perhaps more wine than was good for him. The woman, on the other hand, was bird-like and slim, and fluttered around her two daughters, her high, fluting voice making worried comments about the cold and its effect on the girls' health.

The daughters were plump and pretty, with dark hair and rosy cheeks, and, as they were swathed in velvet, fur-lined cloaks and had muffs over their gloved hands, they could hardly be freezing. Lord St. Claire joined them all, and soon his good-natured teasing could be heard, at least by Celestine, above the rest.

"Miss Stimson, and Miss Caroline! Why, I didn't even know you were out of the schoolroom, Miss Caroline, but what a beauty you have become!" He lifted each girl's hand to within an inch of his lips, an absolutely correct greeting. "And Mrs. Stimson! One would hardly know you from your daughters, ma'am, you look so young. It must be confusing for all the bucks and beaus of London, telling which is the mother and which are the daughters."

The tiny woman giggled. "Oh, my lord, how you do go on!"

Elizabeth looked on in approval, and as maids and footmen relieved the party of their cloaks and pelisses, muffs and gloves, the company moved out of sight and into the parlor, where their chattering could still be heard as the doors closed.

"My! How I wish I was one of 'em, Miss Simons." Elise sighed. "Dressed so pretty, with nothin' to do but go from party to rout to ball."

Celestine smiled. "I have heard his lordship, the marquess, has a party at Christmas every year for all the ser-

vants of Ladymead. Is that so?" She took Gwen's hand as
she spoke, and Elise took Lottie's.

"Oh, it is, miss! We have such a time! Punch and cakes,
and music from Dobbs and the scullery boy, what is such
a good hand with the violin. You'll see, miss . . . that is,
if you come."

Celestine smiled over at the maid. She knew the difficulty. A governess was neither fish nor fowl, neither servant nor family. She would not take part in the upstairs
parties, and likely would not fit in at the downstairs party.
Her presence would possibly even be resented. It was a
lonely position in many ways, but she could not bemoan
her luck in having a position in such a good family.

"I shall take care of the children while you enjoy yourself, Elise. Perhaps Andrew will dance with you."

Elise's eyes widened as she contemplated the idol of
her life, the fair-haired footman Andrew. Then her face
fell. "He don't notice me, miss. He's ever so stuck up, is
Andrew—and ever so particular about what company he
keeps. Says a children's maid is beneath 'im."

Celestine reached out her hand and touched the girl's
arm. "Never mind. If he can't see what a pretty, sweet
girl you are, he doesn't deserve you."

Elise smiled shyly over at Celestine as they mounted
the stairs to the schoolroom. "Thank you, miss. You are
such a change from that Miss Chambly."

Curiosity got the better of her and Celestine asked,
"What was she like? I haven't heard many speak about
her."

"That's 'cause none of the staff could stand her, she
was that stuck up! Acted like we was all beneath her, and
what's a governess but a servant of a kind, I ask you?
Beggin' your pardon, miss." Elise looked a little shame-
faced. "You're a different type, miss. We all *knows* you're
a cut above us. You got the manners of the gentry, but
you never looks down your nose at us nor demands special treatment, an' that's what makes you a real lady, Mr.
Dobbs says."

Celestine was touched. As they entered the schoolroom and the little girls ran to get a favorite book, she gave the young maid a quick hug. "You're a dear."

Elise flushed. "That Miss Chambly, she had her eye on his lordship, the marquess's brother. The nerve! An' her just a governess! Like he'd take her as a wife."

"Even if he'd wanted to, I'm sure his brother never would have agreed to it."

"Nor her ladyship. She's ever so high in the instep. She's got plans for him, Mr. Dobbs says, an' she's on the lookout for a proper match this Christmas. Says she'll have him wed afore spring."

So that was the plan, Celestine thought. Not just to distract him, but to get him hooked. Well, good luck to the marchioness. With her brother-in-law's proclivity for flirtation, it was not going to be easy.

Miss Caroline Stimson gazed up at Justin from under incredibly long, dark eyelashes and smiled coyly. "La, my lord, but you are a flatterer, I'm sure."

Justin grinned and suppressed an urge to stick his tongue out at her and tell her to give it up, she didn't know how to flirt yet. She did all the cute little tricks, the fingers lightly resting on his arm, the sighs, the languishing glances, but they were done with such childish ingenuousness that it made him more aware than ever of his age. He was fifteen years her senior!

The elder Miss Stimson, her round cheek resting in her palm, was gazing pensively out the window at a distant hill, yet he had the feeling she was not thinking or pondering or even daydreaming so much as striking a pose. It was utterly fetching and utterly false. He could tell she was aware of every word that passed between him and her younger sister. What would she do when the pose did not draw his attention in the way she calculated?

Justin was used to such machinations. Girls were trained early in the arts to catch a husband, he knew, and for a minute he wondered if he had become a little jaded by all the attention lavished on him over the years. He was definitely piqued that Miss Simons would not return his regard, and that, perhaps, was why he was so determinedly pursuing her. Even irritating Elizabeth was only secondary now.

The strange thing was, he found he enjoyed talking with her more than with any woman of his acquaintance. There had been the occasional married woman with whom he had engaged in real conversation, but usually they wanted to gossip about their mutual friends, or flirt to plague their husbands, or initiate a dalliance with him.

He wasn't complaining. Those affairs were often the most rewarding in a purely physical sense. There was nothing like a woman whose needs were ignored by her husband for a good, energetic tumble. But there had been times when he had wanted something more, and he had not been quite sure what it was. It was a little worrying to realize being with the governess satisfied that need. The times spent walking with her in the village, romping with the children, and just sitting reading by the fire with her and Lottie and Gwen had been the most enjoyable of his stay so far.

"St. Claire, you have hardly said two words to me since we arrived! And you are usually so entertaining."

He leaped to his feet as Lady Emily Delafont stood before him. With some relief, he offered her the seat on the sofa he had just vacated, the seat next to Miss Caroline, and took an armchair near the older lady. "I shall remedy that oversight this very minute, if you will allow it, ma'am."

Miss Caroline Stimson, who had been trying to engage his attention for the past many minutes, sniffed in annoyance.

"Oh, Lord, don't start calling me 'ma'am' or I shall be sure that not only have I put on too much weight, I am looking old." Lady Delafont sat down, chuckling and smiling at the young girl she shared the sofa with. Miss

Caroline, however, had eyes only for the young nobleman.

"Nonsense, my lady. You must know nothing can detract from your charms. You look radiant, if I may say so. Some ladies look better with—well, shall we say added bounty?" He deliberately let his gaze linger on the neckline of her dress, which displayed at least some of her attractions, pale creamy breasts in a delicious cleavage, set against the deep wine color of her silk dress.

"Scoundrel," she said, coloring faintly. "I should have known my shameless trolling for compliments would be amply rewarded by such a practiced flirt as yourself."

"I cannot believe someone of your loveliness would ever have to angle for what is surely only the truth! Perhaps if Delafont were here . . . but you live apart from him now, do you not?" He lowered his voice and stared intently into her eyes. Here might be an opportunity for intelligent flirtation that could reap more than just an innocent kiss under the mistletoe. Separated and widowed ladies were always the best bet for a little slap and tickle under the covers, as they didn't expect any more than just the fun of lovemaking. He believed in variety in his bed and wouldn't mind exploring a woman of more ample charms.

There was a hint of frost in her voice when she answered though, and he knew he had gone too far too fast. "We are separated."

A misstep. "My apologies, my lady. I treat you as an old friend, you see, and perhaps I do not merit that privilege."

The smile came back to her lips. "You're forgiven."

Miss Caroline, bored with talk that excluded her, flounced away to speak to her sister, and the two of them left the room without a word.

"How remarkably rag-mannered," Lady Delafont said. "However, it does give me the opportunity to speak to you more privately, so I must commend their bad manners for once."

Justin looked at her inquiringly. At that moment his sister-in-law popped her head in the door and looked around inquiringly.

"Hello, Emmy. Justin, where are the Misses Stimson? August and I have just finished conducting their parents on a tour of the house, and wondered if you and they wished to join us in a perambulation of the gardens. Where did they go?" She looked accusingly at Justin.

"I have no idea, Elizabeth. They left the room together, that is all I can say."

The marchioness sighed and gave him a blistering look. "You were to keep them entertained, you dunderhead."

"It was my understanding your orders encompassed all of the company, and Lady Delafont is surely part of that?"

Lady St. Claire caught her friend's eye and rolled her own. "All right. But you could have asked them where they were going."

"I didn't feel the right to inquire, nor did they give me a chance."

She sighed and departed. Justin turned back to Lady Delafont, and in a caressing tone, said, "Now, you were just saying you wished to find me alone." He moved to join her on the sofa, putting his arm over the back close to her shoulders.

"You make it sound highly improper, you practiced scoundrel!" She smiled, but looked a little uncertain.

"I meant no such thing! You wound me, my lady!" He took her rounded, dimpled hand in his and caressed the back with his thumb.

She shook her head. "No wonder Lizbet despairs of you." She pulled her hand away. "What I have to say does not concern me."

"Then I am desolate," he replied.

"What I have to say concerns my niece, Celestine Simons."

Seven

Justin went still.

Emily noted how he paled, his face set in a grim expression. Was he so hardened, then, that he would try to ruin her niece and brook no interference? She had never heard he was an unprincipled bounder, just a hardened flirt. And Celestine was not without friends, not the least of whom was herself. She might be separated from her husband, but she still had the full backing of the 'Delafont' name behind her. She could make things very uncomfortable for Justin among the *ton* if she so desired.

Taking a deep breath, she continued. "I love my niece very much."

"That does you credit, ma'am, and her to have inspired that love." His voice was polite, but frigid.

"She is my eldest sister's daughter. I'm afraid her mother lived only a few years after her birth, so her upbringing was left to my brother-in-law, an older man than his wife. But he was a good man—a learned scholar, a quiet, retiring sort, unfortunately possessed of very little in the way of fortune, and that little entailed. My niece lived in a country village her whole life, never traveling to London or even Bath. She nursed her father through his long illness to his death. I'm afraid she has known very little of the world."

Emily watched Justin and saw some softening of his expression.

"She seems . . . a very sweet young woman, if I might be so bold, ma'am."

To her surprise, his words sounded genuine. But then she shouldn't be surprised, knowing Celestine as she did. Her niece had a rare, luminous quality and quiet goodness many people found engaging—not that she would have expected someone like Justin St. Claire to appreciate her niece's subdued charm.

"Not 'ma'am,' Justin. We were friends once, were we not, when you were a young sprig just down from Oxford and I was a society matron? Much has changed, but not that." She tried to see below the exterior, beneath the shell he seemed to have covered himself with in the meantime. When she had first met him, as Elizabeth's new brother-in-law, he had been an open, engaging young man, full of high spirits and energy. Too many years in London had made him brittle and, according to rumor, a hardened *roué*.

He grinned at her. "Please don't remind me of my callow youth, Emily. I cannot believe I was ever that young."

"You were an entertaining sort, even then. You've always had the ability to enjoy the foibles of society and laugh at them."

"Damned funny, half of it is, if you do not mind my language."

"Don't censor yourself for me. I lived with Baxter for too many years not to have heard all the possible curse words, and a few he invented as well." She turned away from the memory of her husband, who was traveling somewhere in Europe, and kept her focus firmly on the task at hand. It hurt too much to think of Baxter. "I was speaking of Celestine."

"You were. To what end, you have not said."

"I have an end in mind, but just hear me out first. My niece is very special. I think she is beautiful, but then, I am biased. I know the world sees her freckles and mousy brown hair and how her hands get when she is suffering a relapse."

Justin frowned and looked down at his own square, broad, strong hands. "What is wrong with her, ma'am— Emily—if I might be so bold to inquire?"

"Rheumatism. She had a fever when she was young, and her joints became inflamed. Since then she occasionally gets these outbreaks. They have worsened as she has gotten older. She suffers in the cold weather so much! Some mornings I know it is pure torture for her to rise from her bed, though she would not thank me for telling anyone that. She is very private. She had an outbreak last winter as well, but I saw some improvement while she stayed with me last Christmas through my insistence on hot bathing every morning and a liniment my house-keeper swears by. But I am afraid that, left alone, Celestine does not take care of herself properly."

"Why not?"

Emily pursed her lips, frowning as she gazed unseeing at the wall. "She is accustomed to helping others, and I believe she feels she shouldn't spare the time for her own needs. Perhaps I am wrong, but I cannot get her to spend the time on herself she needs. And now, as a governess, she will wear herself to a shade taking care of the little girls. No governess gets a hot bath every morning and an adequate fire in her room. She is there to serve, and Celestine will always do her duty."

"Is she fit for the job? Why did she not stay with you, Emily, if you don't mind my presumption? Surely she would be better off not working at all? I am sorry for my plain speaking, but it seems obvious to me."

Emily sighed. "To me also. Do not think you have of-fended me, for it is exactly what I wished. I wanted her to stay with me, and I would have settled money on her if she would have allowed it, but she resisted. I think the lure of working with children makes her so adamant about working as a governess. I have none and never will, or I probably could have convinced her to stay."

"So why not arrange a suitable marriage for her?"

She made an impatient gesture. "Surely you are not such an innocent after all those years on the town. You are four years my junior but have the advantage on me for London Seasons. You know what Society is like. I am sure an eligible connection could be formed if she would allow me to settle money on her, but she will not take it and I will not force her. She has the right to self-determination. I am afraid, for the marriage mart, she has not sufficient personal attractions . . . she is not . . . that is to say, her attributes are all internal."

"A nugget of gold wrapped in plain broadcloth." Justin's voice was quiet and his gaze averted to the window. His expression was pensive.

She stared at him curiously. He was so different sometimes, and she had the feeling there was a strong, good man within him he did his best to ignore. It was such a waste, in her estimation, but by London standards he was only doing what was expected of him.

But was it possible he did see Celestine's attributes and honor them? "You do have a way with words on occasion, Justin. I could not have expressed it better. Her faults are all to her own detriment. She is too self-effacing. She will not consider herself when there is the welfare of others at hand. She is too modest about her accomplishments, which are numerous, and too ready to see her faults, which are few and superficial."

"She is a paragon of virtue, in other words," Justin said, with a hint of disdain in his voice. "Much like my saintly brother."

Emily gave him a sharp glance. Something had changed in his attitude again, and the curtain of cynicism had descended and was firmly in place. She had meant only to point out the innocence of her niece, her inability to fend off advances she would not expect.

"She is not perfect—no human is. But she is loving and kind and sweet, and I love her very much." There was a bit of defiance in her own voice, Emily realized.

She frowned. What an exasperating man Justin St. Claire could be—sometimes quite human, then changing like a shadow in the night into a pattern card of the frivolous London beau. Elizabeth had confessed in a long conversation the previous night that she despaired of his ever settling down, and in the meantime his escapades with widows and wives, actresses and opera dancers, were embarrassing to the marquess, who was a rising star in the House of Lords.

"Familial love—it does you credit, my dear," Justin said. "But I still fail to see where all this is leading."

"I noticed your behavior in the parlor yesterday afternoon," Emily said, with more steel in her voice than she intended. She shifted on the sofa to look him directly in the eye. "You were flirting with her, and I want to know what your intentions are."

Justin's eyes widened in incredulity. "You are asking if I intend to court your niece?"

His sarcasm was painfully obvious. Emily, afraid she had botched the whole job rather badly, hurriedly said, "No, of course not! I just want you to know she is a complete innocent. She has no idea about flirtation and men's ways. She has never been . . ." The growing anger on his face stopped her.

"And I taint her with my evil ways, is that it?" His voice was bitter, his well-formed mouth twisted into a scowl.

"Of course not, you idiot." Emily sighed in exasperation and folded her plump, soft hands together in her lap. She stiffened her back. She must have her say, no matter how irritated he was getting. "But surely you must have seen how flustered she became when you merely brushed her hand with yours, or gazed at her in that way you have. You are engaging in a game with an innocent who does not know the rules. I am asking you to leave her alone!"

Justin rose stiffly, his resentment evident in the way he held himself. "I assure you, Lady Delafont, I have no intention of harming your niece or tampering with her in any way! Her precious innocence will remain intact so she can die a virtuous old maid, as you clearly wish. I would not *dream* of seducing her into my bed and tainting her with my foul body! Now, if you will excuse me, my sister wishes me to entertain the other guests!"

Justin strode out of the room and through the hall, shouting at a footman to inform the grooms he wished his horse saddled. It was the outside of enough to be virtually accused of intending to bed the woman's sallow, plain niece! Emily Delafont's mind had clearly been poisoned by Elizabeth and her poor opinion of him. He needed fresh air. He needed to get out of the constraining presence of Ladymead. Too many more run-ins like this and his riding would be much improved through bruising practice.

He allowed his valet, Dooley, who had appeared at his summons, to aid him with his coat, waving him away with a curt command when he was done.

Of all the idiotic . . . what did Emily think he was planning—to seduce the poor, plain, naive thing? In all his years on the London Season he had *never* taken a young lady's reputation away from her. He may have dallied with her affections—if young ladies of the *ton* had any genuine feeling in the first place, which he doubted—but he had never gone over the line.

Yet now he was cast in the role of an evil seducer of pure young maidens and plain old spinsters.

He strode out into the brisk, frosty air, ignoring the call from his sister and brother to join them with the young Misses Stimson. He would bolt rather than do the pretty to one of those simpering, vapid misses. He almost *ran* back the stables and mounted Alphonse, taking the reins from the groom and trotting away over the frozen ground.

A far hill beckoned and he leaned forward, urging Alphonse, who was fresh and eager, to gallop. It mattered not that he wasn't dressed for riding. All that mattered was working this latest affront out of his system. Fifteen minutes of bruising riding worked out the worst of his fury, and he slowed to a canter as he crested the hill and looked out over the valley where Ellerbeck nestled, snug against the bosom of Eller Rise, as the low hill was called.

He thought of his own neglected estate not far from Ladymead. To his own mind, it was even prettier than his brother's house—smaller and more intimate—but it always seemed cold and lonely when he went there to confer with his bailiff and estate manager, so he was seldom in residence.

Perhaps Elizabeth was right about one thing. Maybe he should start looking around for a wife to start populating Questmere, his home, with little St. Claires. Somehow the thought of children did not frighten him half so much as the notion of a wife. Children he knew how to deal with, but a woman—a *wife*—would require a level of intimacy he had never achieved with anyone, unless he planned to follow the usual *tonnish* pattern and marry a young chit, get an heir upon her, and leave her home while he returned to London.

It was not, for some reason, an appealing thought. Someday he would marry, but he would be damned if he would fall in with Elizabeth's plan to consider the Stimson girls or the van Hoffen chit, who was arriving on the morrow, as a possible spouse.

He would go to the London Season this spring with the intent to look around and choose a wife, a girl with some conversation, some beauty, and no pretension. No simpering airs for him. He wanted a woman who could love him—not just his money and title and estate, but him.

Was that possible? Was there such a woman in the world? In his experience the whole mating ritual of the London Season was as cold-blooded as choosing a brood mare to mate with a stallion. You examined a girl's bloodlines, looked her over for physical flaws, made sure the seller, her family, wasn't hiding any faults of temperament, and then you made your offer. If it wasn't accepted, you moved on to the next.

A few of his friends had succumbed to the entreaties of their families, especially those who were eldest sons and needed to beget an heir. Some seemed relatively happy, but most were carrying on much as they would have when single, only with an avidity and desperation that hinted at a home life not to be tolerated for any length of time.

With no pressing need to breed an heir, he saw no reason why he should tie himself down too early. And he would not be hen-led! He didn't want a doormat for a wife, but he also didn't want a harridan like his sister-in-law.

He trotted down a hill, noting he was heading for the church. He remembered the feelings he had in the dark two evenings before as he listened to Celestine's beautiful voice in the chill dimness. One pure, sweet moment of truth had been visited upon him in the gloomy confines of the chapel. He yearned for that susceptibility, that fragile, heartrending instant of raw emotion he had experienced, even though it had left him feeling exposed and chafed as though by a biting wind. His wife, when he chose one, should sing like that, he thought. If she could do that, she could cut through to his very soul and lift it, as Celestine had done that night.

He dismounted and tied the horse to the gate, then strolled up the walk to the church, an old structure of gray stone covered in leafless ivy. The family had attended service just that morning, but he had not accompanied them. He went to the side door they had entered the night of the choir practice and found himself alone in the church. He shivered.

What had he felt that night? A peculiar sort of melancholy had swept over him. That was why he had wept at the sound of the governess's voice, and it explained the odd connection he felt to her, the openness of heart he had experienced in the carriage. That was the only way he could account for his protectiveness toward her, his desire to pull her to him and soothe her worries.

What had Emily said? That Celestine took on other people's burdens and never minded her own. But then, Lady Delafont was biased. He had to admit, though, in light of Emily's glowing recommendation of the girl, he was more curious about her. He had been intent on flirting with her, amused and maybe challenged because it was so difficult. Now he was genuinely curious.

Not that he would heed Lady Delafont's warning to stay away. What right had she to determine *his* actions? Absolutely none. She was as bad as Elizabeth, maybe worse. She acted like he was evil and would taint the saintly Celestine, or corrupt her with his attentions. Elizabeth was just worried about having to turn away another governess and find a replacement. She despised anyone or anything that challenged her absolute control in her household.

Why did everyone make such a fuss about a little harmless flirtation? He didn't intend to bed her. He liked older women as lovers and preferred beauties, not plain little spinsters. She would probably lie beneath him like a log, and he preferred a wilder ride. If he undressed her and touched her body with knowing hands, hands that had aroused many a woman, she would likely shudder and make him feel like a lecherous fiend.

Or would she gaze at him with passion flaming in those huge, luminous eyes, and open her luscious mouth under his? He shook his head and snorted in amusement. That was the second time he had thought of her in that manner, and it was quite ridiculous. One had only to look at her to see she was not formed for passion, but for goodness and contemplation—piety, good works, *sainthood!* He liked an earthier type to bed, preferably experienced.

Of course, that would never do when he chose a wife. He would not want a passionate little wench for a wife, because he had no intention of sharing her with anyone else. When a woman was his, she was *his,* for however long the affair lasted, and a marriage was intended to last for a lifetime. He wouldn't want a wife if he would always have to wonder with whom she was lying.

A noise alerted him that he was no longer alone.

"Ah, Lord St. Claire, how nice to see you again. We missed you this morning." It was the vicar bustling cheerfully up the aisle, papers in hand.

"Hello. I was enchanted by the beauty of the church when I visited for choir practice, but I am afraid I slept in this morning—missed the service. So I made free to come in now to look around." Justin held out his hand and shook the vicar's. The man had a respectable grip, and was just deferential enough for their difference of rank.

"Marvelous, sir. I must say I believe it a charming building," he said, glancing around with pride. "Though to someone who has seen the Abbey or St. Paul's, it does seem a trifle small." There was just the hint of pretension in the man's voice, and he spoke with the air of one man of the world to another.

"Yes, well, they are hardly meant to be compared, are they? But each has its charms. I am looking forward to your Christmas presentation. Miss Simons has a lovely voice, do you not think so? She is a valuable addition to your choir."

"Most definitely," the vicar said, blinking a little at the rapid change in subject. He continued, though, very quickly. "Miss Simons would be a valuable addition wherever she went, I believe." His tone was proprietary. "I confess, I shudder to think of her ever leaving Ellerbeck. In fact, I have thought of making her residence here a more permanent sort."

Justin caught the side glance from the vicar, and wondered whether the man was warning him off or checking for approval. Warning, he decided. The reverend seemed too sure of his own good fortune if he should speak, and Justin supposed his own attendance at the choir practice was odd enough to set tongues wagging.

"More permanent? You mean hiring her as your house-keeper? Do you think that is really proper? I hear she is from an excessively good family." Mischief lit the noble-man's eyes, but the vicar, without a humorous bone in his body, was appalled.

"Of course I did not mean that, my lord! I would never . . . oh, I believe you jest, sir! I mean to ask the young lady to be my wife. I have been observing her for some time and she conducts herself with just the sort of self-effacement and humility I would wish in a wife. And I have heard her family is good, though I believe she is in reduced circumstances. I have no need of a dowry, as I have an independent income in addition to your brother's generous allotment. I have reason to believe the lady would not be averse to my paying court."

Contempt welled in Justin's heart. On the outside all deference, the vicar was really an upstart, a popinjay of the worst sort. He was evaluating Celestine's worth for his hand! It was ridiculous. She had more than one title in her family background. What did he have?

But the vicar had good reason to be confident, he feared. Celestine was not averse to him, and could prob-ably be persuaded to think she was very lucky if he deigned to marry her. According to Emily, she did not think much of her own worth and would be grateful for the opportunity to marry and have children of her own. She would work herself to the bone trying to be worthy of the honor of being the vicar's wife, and he would ex-pect it of her, never giving a moment's thought to her condition and how she should have some care herself.

The thought disturbed him more than he liked to think. Celestine Simons was a gentle soul—good with chil-dren, responsible, caring. Other people were first in her thoughts always, it seemed. Would the vicar ever appre-ciate her true worth? Did he love her, or was he just think-ing about damned bloodlines and family history?

Justin bid the vicar good-bye and strode back out into the wintry sunshine. Dark clouds loomed on the horizon, foretelling some unsettled weather to come. They were matched by the gloom in his heart. He felt pulled down, depressed.

What was wrong with him? This was rubbish! He needed to sweat it out of his system, that was all. Alphonse still had not got the vigor worked out of him, so once out of the village, Justin gave the frisky gelding his head and they galloped up the hill to the crest and stopped to look over the other side, down at Ladymead.

Perhaps he could accomplish two goals at once by flirting with Miss Celestine Simons. He could frustrate Elizabeth, always a goal with him. He could not abide a managing female, and she was the worst of that sort. August gave her her head, as she did not dare try to manage him, at least not in any way he noticed.

At the same time, he could perhaps elevate Miss Simons's low opinion of herself. In his experience flattery, no matter how outrageous, always touched a deep need in a female to be appreciated. More than one young lady had come away from a flirtation with him with an overblown opinion of her own attractions. He counted it a kindness to flirt with some of the young girls in their first Season. He knew himself to be attractive to them, and it did their self-esteem good to receive attention from him. If it stopped Miss Simons from allowing herself to be a doormat when she eventually married that vicar, what's-his-name, then he would have done her a good turn, indeed.

With a little glow of virtue, he trotted back to the Ladymead stables, and left Alphonse to a groom's care. He had a flirtation to continue. All in a good cause, of course. Or mostly, anyway.

Eight

The next day, the last of the house party arrived, a Lady van Hoffen, who had attained her title through marriage with an aged European nobleman, and her daughter, Grishelda. Grishelda was a plain young lady with an intelligent expression and a cool smile that didn't quite reach her eyes. Her mother was a buxom, beautiful redhead of perhaps forty years, flamboyantly dressed and eager to flirt with Justin, whom she knew from London.

He wondered at his lack of interest. A whispered word from him would have her slipping from her chamber to join him in his bed that very night, a temptation he would not normally have foregone. The lusty widow was eager to wed her daughter to him, but would likely be just as eager to start an affair, and she might not find the two aims mutually exclusive.

But something in him rebelled at her flirtatious glances and sly innuendoes. He caught the daughter watching him with thoughtful, intelligent eyes, and the knowledge that more than one person would know of their liaison made him squirm. He injected a frosty note in his replies to the lady and evaded her after that. She was a little too obvious for him.

Outside the snow started, first coating the fells with a light dusting, then drifting into the valley where Ladymead nestled among copses. After the Sabbath pause, when much of the staff was given a half day off to attend evening services, life at Ladymead was back up to full bustle.

Justin found he was expected to join in with whatever activities Elizabeth had planned, which that day consisted of conducting the young ladies on an extensive tour of the house, the conservatory, the library, and finally the gallery, with all the family paintings needing to be explained. Justin, bored to flinders with the Stimson misses, was grateful that Lady Grishelda was an intelligent young woman who did not seem to believe every encounter with him must be spent in flirtation. How had she managed to escape the influence of her mother?

Maybe there were women in the world who would make intelligent, conversable wives after all, Justin thought. Her demeanor was cool, though, without being haughty, and he was not sure she was the type of woman who could be heated up by passion. He couldn't imagine bedding a woman like that, one who would remain well-bred and chilly even in the bedroom.

They walked together along the hallway.

"I really think that is it, ladies," Justin said, pausing at the end of the hall near the stairs, and turning back to the two Stimson sisters.

"Fustian. What is this door here?" the younger one said, putting her hand on a brass doorknob.

"That is just to the upstairs rooms, the third floor."

"And what are those," the elder Stimson sister asked, "the attics where you keep the ghosts?" She giggled.

Justin smiled. "Nothing nearly so romantic, I am afraid. The servants' quarters, of course, the nursery, and the schoolroom."

"Oh, is that where the little girls would be? Those darling little creatures we have hardly caught a glimpse of so far?" said Miss Caroline, her childish simper firmly in place. She turned the knob and started up the stairs. "I have a great love of children!" she called as she danced up the stairs. "And I wish to visit them."

"She hasn't been long enough out of the schoolroom

that I should think she'd want to go back so soon," Justin
muttered, drawing a smile from his companion, the sensible Lady Grishelda.

Charlotte Stimson was already starting up the stairs behind her irrepressible sister, and Lady Grishelda shrugged.
"I think we had best follow them up, or they are apt to
cause havoc in the governess's domain, and I should hate
to add to her burden."

"Very true," Justin said.

When he got to the door, Charlotte and Caroline were
already in the schoolroom, fluttering around and cooing
over the little girls, causing, as Lady Grishelda had pre-
dicted, havoc.

Lottie was in her element, preening for the admiring
young ladies, her blond head turning this way and that
as she spoke to the two young women, but Gwen was
frightened by their noise and fuss and was clinging to
Celestine's gray skirts. Lady Grishelda's calm, thoughtful
eyes took in the sight and she crouched down to speak
softly to the little girl, drawing her out so Celestine could
attend to the Stimsons' unending questions and repress
Lottie's spiraling spirits, which threatened to send the little girl out of control.

Near a globe, a clustered bunch of holly and a sprig
of mistletoe rested on the long table that served as a desk
for the girls. Celestine had apparently been conducting
a lesson on the origin of Christmas, since that was all
Lottie or Gwen could be interested in at that time of year.
They weren't formal lessons, really, just something to
keep them occupied and out of trouble, she said, her
calm, melodious voice cutting through the babble of children and Stimsons.

Justin listened to her as she explained she had been
speaking of pagan beliefs and the origin of the Yule log,
mistletoe, and the reason for bringing evergreen boughs
in to decorate with, when the company had burst through
the doors. Caroline Stimson picked up the sprig of mis-

tletoe on the table and twirled over to Justin, her muslin skirts belling out around her, holding it over her head.

"Give you any ideas, Lord St. Claire?" She giggled again.

Her older sister frowned and Lady Grishelda glanced up sharply from her murmured conference with Gwen. As a piece of flirtation, it was over the top for a schoolroom miss. Justin was most interested in Celestine's reaction, though, and when he saw her wide gray eyes fixed on his face, he smirked. Some devil in him induced him to mischief, and he had been given the perfect opportunity.

"Why, Miss Caroline," he said, his eyebrows raised and his blue eyes glittering in the dim light from the window, "are you sure you should be tempting a known rake such as myself with your lovely countenance? Do you know what you are asking for?"

The girl laughed, a high, brittle sound, as her cheeks reddened. Her elder sister frowned and snatched the greenery from her hand. "That's enough, Caro," she snapped.

Lady Grishelda stood, her movement fluid and graceful. "I think we have interfered for long enough on Miss Simons's time." Her voice was steady and brooked no dispute.

She would make a formidable mother and wife, Justin thought. If a man wasn't careful, she would likely have him reformed into a boring, steady old married man before he knew what hit him—if she were even interested in marriage. Lady Grishelda emanated an air of stern practicality that seemed to preclude any of the softer feelings of love and desire.

"I believe Lady St. Claire mentioned a game of battledore and shuttlecocks in the large salon," she said, her eyebrows raised. Her comment was directed toward the Stimson girls, who were a few years younger than she.

The two Stimsons swept out of the room, leaving a puzzled Lottie in their wake. They hadn't even bothered to say good-bye to her. Justin drifted from the room, but

Lady Grishelda paused in the doorway. She said good-bye to the children, then looked up at the governess.

"I am sorry, Miss Simons, that we interfered in that way. Your job is no doubt difficult enough at this time of year without the added stir of company in your domain."

Celestine smiled into the woman's kind, pale blue eyes. "It is quite all right, my lady. Lottie, at least, enjoyed the break, and it was kind of you to soothe Gwen. She is not one for fuss and noise, I am afraid. Most people frighten the poor little dear, but you have a way with her."

"May I visit without the accompaniment of the others sometime, perhaps when the children are at luncheon or otherwise engaged? I have some need of information you are particularly suited to give me."

Celestine raised her eyebrows at this. "I, my lady? If I can be of any help, I am at your service, but . . ."

Lady Grishelda smiled. "Believe me, it is nothing onerous. I am forming a school in our village, and I am taking a survey of every professional educator of my acquaintance as to curriculum. Your opinion would be valued."

Celestine flushed with pleasure. It was a rare thing for her to be consulted on anything, and she felt a kinship with the plain young woman with the sensible manners. "I . . . I would be honored to help, my lady. Though I have been a governess for less than a year, I used to help out at our school in the village where I was raised. It was one of the joys of my life and it was a very successful school, so I may have some insights to offer."

"Splendid. I look forward to some rational conversation," Lady Grishelda said, ruefully glancing back down the hall, where they could still hear the Stimsons' raised voices. "Until then," she said, and smiled her farewell.

Justin awaited her outside the schoolroom. "That was well done, my lady," he said quietly, glancing back at Celestine's smiling face and giving her a small wave. Celestine's smile died and she looked away. Damn. That silly bit of horseplay with the mistletoe had offended her. Now he would have to make up lost ground.

Lady Grishelda's calm demeanor cracked slightly as they strolled down the hall. "Those Stimson girls should have shackles! They have no sense that there are people in this world who must earn their living and who may not all appreciate a couple of little idiots bursting in on their day." She cast a side glance at Justin. "My apologies for the slight to your sister-in-law's guests, sir."

"No apology needed, my lady. Our opinions in this matter coincide exactly. May I hope they always stay as closely aligned." He grinned at her.

She narrowed her pale eyes and gazed into his with a puzzled expression. "I must say, sir, you are not at all what I expected when my mother spoke of you. And she did speak of you—at great and detailed length."

They descended the stairs together at a stately pace.

"And what were you expecting?"

"A wolf, sir. An attractive beast, but dangerous, so I am told."

Justin let out a shout of laughter at the young lady's forthright disclosure. "Ah, but perhaps I am just a wolf masquerading in sheep's clothing, my dear—the better to allay your fears."

Lady Grishelda slanted him an incredulous stare. "Lord St. Claire, I am no simpering debutante, nor am I a fashionable impure. There is no need of flirtatious asides with me, you know."

Justin grimaced. "Impaled," he said, his hand over his heart. "You have cut me to the quick, my dear. And I was hoping for a spot of *intelligent* flirtation this Season."

Lady Grishelda smiled. "You shall look to my mama for that, sir. She will indulge you in any type of flirtation you like."

Celestine remained distracted long after her visitors retreated. The little girls were called for tea, and she tidied the schoolroom, then sat down with her sewing basket.

Lady Grishelda embodied everything Celestine had

ever thought a young lady of the *ton* should be. She was gracious and graceful, kind and intelligent and would be an admirable foil for Justin St. Claire's high spirits and rackety ways. This Christmas season would, perhaps, see the start of a friendship between them that, given time, could blossom into something more. She was just the kind of woman to settle him.

Celestine sighed. She rather hoped so. It would do Lord St. Claire good to have someone serious to set his feet on a more mature, intelligent path. She ignored the painful little voice in her own heart that pleaded for notice, arguing she was that same type and perhaps with more appreciation for his lightheartedness, and firmly set her mind on her work. The elegant, attractive, and witty aristocrat was not for such as she, even if things were different and she had been blessed with beauty as well as wit. Her situation precluded an alliance with a man of his exalted position.

And anyway she was not confident she would have the vigor to reform a rake. That would require a woman of unusual strength of character combined with a serious disposition and determination—Lady Grishelda van Hoffen.

She yawned. She was so tired in the afternoons. She struggled to stay awake as she sewed some basic garments for the puppets, the heads of which were now drying on a side table along the north wall of the schoolroom. There were enough for six characters. She hoped that would be enough.

Her eyes drifted shut and she slept, drifting immediately into a vivid dream.

She was walking in a grove of pine trees, their scent heavy on the cold breeze. She glanced down at herself and found she was cloaked in a red velvet cape trimmed in ermine, and she started. Where had she ever gotten such a fine garment? There was snow all around, but she knew, for some reason, she must stay right there and wait.

For what?

She wasn't sure, but she was to wait. Her breath came out in steamy puffs, and she could hear the trees creaking in the cold, weighed down as they were with a blanket of snow. Darkness was closing in. She should return home, or she would be trapped in the dark with a snowstorm coming.

She heard a thundering of hooves through the forest and a great, black horse came into view, its rider clad in a black cape. He swung himself down from his mount and came toward her.

"Justin," she whispered, gazing up into his handsome face. His expression was one of desperate need—desire, even. His blue eyes glittered like sapphires in the dim light.

"Celestine," he said, and clasped her into his arms, holding her close. Then he bent his head and his lips touched hers softly, warm and reassuring in the cold breeze. "Come away with me, my love, and I will give you everything your heart desires. I will treasure you all the days of my life. I don't care what my brother says, or Elizabeth—I love you. Come away with me."

Celestine's lips curved in a smile as she relaxed into a deep sleep, curled up in her chair in the darkening schoolroom.

The evening was gloomy, with a howling wind that rattled the glass and blew down the chimneys. The company was gathered in the drawing room after dinner, the men drinking port and the ladies taking coffee. Small groups had formed and Justin restlessly moved from one to another, listening to the conversation and trying to avoid Lady van Hoffen's winks and grimaces.

He was feeling irritable and out of sorts, and he didn't know why. He approached the hearth and gazed into the crackling blaze, swirling his drink in his stemmed glass. What in God's name was wrong with him? He had everything a man could hope for in life and more: wealth,

title, health, family, and good looks to top it off. Enough
women had extolled his manly virtues that he did not
think it was vanity to believe himself good-looking. When
he looked in his own mirror, he only saw the usual set
of features arranged in the usual way, but women seemed
to find his appearance pleasing enough. He would be a
fool not to notice that *and* take advantage of it.

All of that aside, why was he staring broodingly into
the fire instead of flirting with the voluptuous widow who
wanted to warm his bed, or even with the giddy, pretty
Stimson girls? He glanced around the room. Charlotte
and Caroline Stimson were at the piano. Their glossy dark
heads were bent together as they worked out a duet. Elizabeth sat with Dodo and Emily Delafont, and Mrs. Stimson
listened in as she did some kind of complex needlework.

Mr. Stimson, August, and Lady van Hoffen were by the
coffee tray. The widow was flirting with August—or trying
to. Justin wished her well of it. August was a painfully
righteous gentleman and would likely not recognize it for
what it was, an attempt to draw Justin over, or even for
what it wasn't, an attempt to draw the marquess into her
bed. Lady Grishelda was looking over a book, seemingly
needing no outside companionship.

He envied her. She was so self-contained. She appeared
to need no one, perfectly content to go her own way and
live with her own thoughts. That was the result of unblemished morality, no doubt. Justin tossed back the rest
of the port, grimaced, and set the glass on the mantle.
Was he getting maudlin again? Certainly not—he was
merely bored. What did he want to be doing right now?

Strangely enough, he longed to get back to writing his
little fable for the girls. He wondered if Celestine would
like it. Would she frown and criticize, or just cast her
luminous eyes down and say, "It is fine, my lord," because
he was her employer's brother? Or would her glowing
eyes turn up to meet his as she said, "Oh, well done,
Justin. It is perfect!"

Damn. That was ridiculous. Even if she approved, she

would hardly use his given name. She had made it clear such a privilege was not what she aspired to. But the one instance she had used it, when she was asleep and had murmured it, had given him a hunger to hear her say it again. He didn't think he had ever heard a woman say his name in quite that tone. It had sounded like an endearment on her lips.

He wished he knew what her reaction would be to his play. It was important to him that she approved, though he hardly knew why. Why did it matter? And why had he attempted that tawdry bit of flirtation in front of her in the schoolroom that afternoon? Had he expected to see hurt, anger, jealousy? All he had surprised in her fine gray eyes was puzzlement and disapproval.

What did she do in the evening, he wondered. The girls were in bed, or in Elise's care by now, so there were no more demands on her time. He found himself possessed by a powerful curiosity. He excused himself to Elizabeth and slipped from the room.

She would likely be in her own room, a sanctum he could not invade, but it was just possible she was in the schoolroom preparing for the next day. He took the stairs two at a time, but slowed before he got to the third floor. No need to alert her to his presence too soon by galloping like a racehorse.

It was quiet up there. The maids and footmen would no doubt be sitting down to dinner in the servants' dining hall. Perhaps that was where Celestine was, too. But no, there was a light in the schoolroom. Silently, he crept forward and looked in the partially open door. She was by the fireplace, but there was no fire lit. He frowned.

She was sewing something gray by the light of a dim candle on the table beside her. Every few stitches she would stop, rub her knuckles, then go on, laboriously setting stitch after stitch in a straight line. At one point, she sighed, set the sewing on her lap, and leaned her head back. Her eyes fluttered to a close and she seemed

almost to sleep for a moment. Then she shook herself
and continued with her work.

Justin remembered what Emily had said about Celestine's ailment. Her hands were painful, almost crippled, when she was in the throes of an attack of arthritis,
and she failed to take care of herself as she should. How
did one take care of arthritis? He cast his mind back to
his uncle, who had suffered from the ailment.

Uncle Solomon had sworn by the mineral water baths
at Bath. That connected with something Emily had said
in her little speech to him. Justin headed back the way
he had come, his face a mask of concentration.

Nine

Celestine hummed a joyful tune as she worked on the puppets while Lottie and Gwen were out for a walk with Elise. The evening before, she had indulged in a nice long chat with Aunt Emily. She barely remembered her mother, who had died when Celestine was so young. Emily, though young enough to be an older sister to her, had given her all the mothering she had ever had, and her presence now was soothing. She had expected it to be a solitary and dreary Christmas, her first away from family, but now it didn't seem so bad.

It was unexpectedly lonely being a governess, something she never would have imagined. Until her father died, she had been a respectably situated spinster in a small village, with a circle of friends and acquaintances that, if not wide, was loving. She had been in a position to distribute some largesse from her kitchen and had taken part in her church's campaigns on behalf of the needy.

Her father's death, leaving her with virtually nothing, and then her move to Ladymead, had changed everything. Now she was a servant and yet not a servant. She was employed by the marquess and marchioness, so she was certainly not in a position to socialize with them, and yet the servants thought her to be in a very different class from them. When she entered the servants' hall or the kitchen for something, merry conversation would cease, and she would be greeted in a stilted fashion. They were kind and helpful, and she believed they liked and respected her, but she knew they wouldn't be comfortable again until she left.

And so for almost a year she had been isolated from adult conversation and starved for contact and conversation with her social equals. Emily's visit was a blessed relief—though it didn't come without a price, she had discovered the previous night. Emily was aghast at how far she had let the arthritis go without attempting to treat it in any way. Sitting on Celestine's bed, Emily had rubbed her cook's ointment into her niece's painful hands, chastising her all the while for not taking care of herself.

"You would think you *wanted* to be a cripple," she had fussed, massaging the aching joints with the greasy formula, an ointment that made Celestine's flesh tingle and glow. "You *must* take care of yourself!"

"There is too much to do! Much more interesting things than taking care of myself," she had protested.

"And how will you be able to do those interesting things when you are confined to bed unable to move?" Emily scolded. "Not taking care of yourself is a sin against God. He gave you a brain and a body and expects you to do your best with both."

When morning came, another sample of Emily's determination had been displayed when two maids came into her bedchamber pulling a copper hip bath. They had proceeded to fill it with steaming water. When Celestine argued, they would only say his lordship said it was to be so, and left it for her.

It had been pure luxury to sink into warm water at the time of day when her whole body rebelled against allowing her to get out of bed. As a result, her morning had progressed with less pain than usual. It was bad of Emily to intercede on her behalf with the marquess, or more likely the marchioness, but it was welcome interference and improved her ability to do her job. The ache was somewhat better already and she had more energy than she had felt for months.

She had already spoken to young Augustus that morning, and he had expressed an interest in building a small puppet theater with the estate carpenter, so he was gone to pester for the materials. Now she just had to think of a suitable play to put on and they would be in business.

A light tap at the door made her look up. It was Lord St. Claire, holding a sheaf of papers and looking rather sheepish. She invited him in, smiling unconsciously at his handsome face and grin.

She did like his smile. His face was narrow, with high cheekbones and a mobile, sensuous mouth. His eyes were the startling blue of a summer sky, with silky, dark lashes and heavy brows over them, keeping them from any suggestion of femininity. His hair was a dark tumble, and she wished she could reach out to touch that one stubborn lock that fell over his forehead.

But it was his smile that made him so devastatingly attractive. He glowed from the inside with health and vitality and something else—a sweetness Celestine believed he didn't know he possessed. What had started as a very good day was made better by his presence, and she had forgiven and forgotten his high-spirited piece of foolishness with the Stimson girl and the mistletoe. A man like Justin St. Claire must be forgiven his boyish pranks.

They spoke of commonplace things for a few minutes: the children, the weather, the season, all of the guests. He seemed nervous, and she wondered what the sheaf of paper was for. But she was kept from inquiring when her thoughts wandered off as he spoke. She gazed at him as he paced the schoolroom and remembered the dream she had of meeting him in the forest.

Was it wrong to dream of him like that? She didn't know. There was no harm in it, she supposed, and she couldn't control the dream fantasies that took her places she could not in reality go. It was as close as she would ever get to being kissed by him, her dream kisses, and she defiantly decided she would *not* feel guilty! She saw him gazing at her expectantly and floundered for something to say.

"I . . . I'm sorry. What was that?"

"So may I? Would you mind?"

Celestine scrambled frantically in her brain, wondering what it was he was asking.

"I . . . I suppose . . ."

"Good!" He took the chair across from her and rattled his sheaf of papers. He cleared his throat and began.

"Once upon a time there was a wayward prince named Aurelius. He was a jolly sort, always having fun and traveling, but underneath he was really very lonely. One day the prince's brother, the king, an extremely serious man known as Reginald the Mighty, who believed everyone else should be just as serious as he, said, 'Aurelius, you must choose a bride.' "

Celestine sighed in relief. This must be the story he was writing for the puppet theater. A fairy-tale? From *him*?

He read on. The lonely prince searched the kingdom for his match, but came back empty-handed, only to be faced with his brother's wife, who had chosen him a girl to wed. She was screechy. She was ugly. She was missing teeth, and spoke in a high-pitched . . .

Celestine broke out laughing and Justin glanced up, a grin on his beautiful face.

"Do you like my prince's wife-to-be?"

"She is perfect!" Celestine laughed, setting aside her sewing and clapping her hands together. "I shall have such fun creating a puppet to portray her!"

"But now I'm stuck." Justin glanced down at his papers again. "I don't know how to get the prince to his Princess Calista, who is living out in the forest where she has charmed the birds and the woodland creatures and can speak to them." He was silent for a moment. He cleared his throat and stared at his hands. "Will it be . . . will it be suitable?"

"Suitable?"

"For the play . . . for the girls. Can you do something with it?"

Was he so unsure of himself? She gazed at his face while his eyes scanned the paper. It occurred to her he was actually enjoying himself writing the piece, and she was touched. She did not know what his usual life consisted of, but from things said by Lady Elizabeth and Emily, he was a man about town dashing from club to ballroom to racetrack to mill. That he should enjoy himself writing a play for his nieces was unexpected.

"It's delightful, my lord, but it needs very simple dialogue before we can put it on."

"Of course," St. Claire said, hitting his forehead lightly. "I should have thought of that. But how can I help the prince find his princess?" His voice lowered to a caressing baritone. "He is so lonely, and the right woman is waiting for him, but how does he find her?"

He was doing it again, Celestine thought, glancing with dismay into the aristocrat's expressive eyes. As if he didn't have enough ladies to flirt with! She had seen him with the Stimson girls and the ravishing Lady van Hoffen. Did he need to make a slave of every woman in his sphere of influence?

Carefully, she said, "I think you will find some way, my lord. If you will excuse me, I must find out if the girls are back from their walk yet." She rose to go.

Justin caught her hand. "Don't go yet." He pulled her back, then stood and held her hand, touching her knuckles gently with his thumb. "How are your hands today? Are they any better?"

Celestine flushed with mortification. She wanted to snatch her hand away and hide it behind her, but he had a light but powerful grip on it. His long, strong fingers curled around hers, and it wouldn't do to have a tug of war. His closeness was disconcerting—the warmth that radiated from his body, the scent of some hair pomade or cologne, the way his wide shoulders and sturdy body blocked everything else from her view. "They are a little better, my lord. Now I really must . . ." She tugged on her hand, but he didn't let go.

She watched in horror as he lifted her hand and touched the swollen knuckles, each in turn, with his lips. His warm breath bathed them in heat. She felt hot and cold flushes over her whole body, and a queer sick feeling in the pit of her stomach. His other hand came up and his fingers threaded into her hair. Somehow he worked the pins loose, and her chestnut hair started a slow slide, tumbling down her back and over her shoulders in rich waves. She couldn't breathe or move.

"Don't run, Celestine. Don't be afraid of me. I would never harm you."

His voice was a low murmur and she felt herself falling under his spell—felt her heart throbbing and swelling with desire. What was he doing to her with just a touch, just a word?

He turned her hand over and his lips caressed her palm in a lingering kiss, then her wrist. She felt her pulse leap. His free hand stole around her waist and he pulled her closer, trapping her other hand between them. Her eyes fluttered closed as she felt his body, the heat searing through the thin fabric of her dress and chemise. She swallowed, willing away the dizziness that threatened to turn her world black.

"Celestine."

It was like a whisper from a dream and she glanced up under her lashes and opened her mouth to ask him what he wanted. His lips came down against hers, their warmth and softness taking her breath away and shadowing her mind with confusion.

She had never been kissed by anyone but her father and her aunt in her whole life, and this, of course, was completely different. It was as though Justin were reaching in to some hidden and untouched part of her, stroking it and petting it into purring satisfaction. She felt his lips move over hers, then a tentative, delicate thrust as his tongue lightly touched her lips and dared to lap at her own tongue.

She felt herself relax and soften against him, unable to fight the sweet languor that stole over her. The kiss went on and on, their tongues touching, his thrusting into her mouth with more urgent power. Both of his arms were around her now. Her hands found his broad shoulders and she clung to him, feeling his muscles flex and tighten. One of his broad hands was splayed over the back of her head, holding her lips to his own with a firm and steady hand. The other hand was caressing her back, sliding down her backbone, cradling her rounded bottom and molding her against the hard planes of his body. . . .

She pulled her mouth away from his and gasped. Pushing against his shoulders, she managed to wrench herself from his arms. There was a spark of desire deep within his brilliant blue eyes. He was breathing heavily, panting almost. She was wretchedly aware of how much she longed to be back in his arms—how bereft she felt after tearing herself away—but she straightened and took a deep breath.

"That, my lord, is quite enough of that!" Her voice was trembling.

"Oh, I don't think so," he said, advancing on her and holding out his arms. His voice was low and seductive, rasping the words and giving them dark, dangerous meaning, and his eyes were sea blue now, warm and inviting, offering bliss and fulfillment to her if she acquiesced. "Come back, Celestine, come back. You know you want to. Just for one more kiss."

"No," she said, backing away. She hastily twisted her hair up into an untidy bun and with clumsy fingers stabbed the pins she had retrieved from the floor back into it.

His eyes blazed. Why was she being so difficult? He had felt her melting against him like warm candle wax, molding her soft curves against his body. He had been surprised—no, amazed—at the shapeliness of her body under the hideous, high-necked gray dress she wore. Her curves were womanly, her hair like spun silk, her response to his touch loverlike in its passionate intensity. The kiss had lingered and become a mating, his tongue thrusting into her hot sweetness until he felt as though he would go mad with desire. If he could just get her to admit she felt the same, maybe he wouldn't stop at just a kiss to irk his sister-in-law. He was hungry for more. Beneath her prim exterior she was molten fire, a sensual volcano ready to explode.

"Celestine, don't deny what is between us. I have had plenty of experience, enough to know you would find more joy in my arms than you have ever felt in your entire life. You are a woman who needs to be loved."

Her gray eyes went flinty, and she seemed to petrify in front of him. Her spine stiffened with indignation. "That will never happen, my lord. I ask you to leave my schoolroom. *Please!*"

His hand came up to caress one long strand of silky hair, a stray from the untidy bun, but she batted his fingers away and moved to the other side of her chair, clutching it like a buoy.

Justin knew he would get no further at that moment. But she wanted him, he could feel it in his bones. She wanted his touch, maybe more. Her face was pale, the light dusting of freckles under her eyes making her look ridiculously young, like a schoolgirl. He remembered how her waist-length, unbound hair hung over her shoulder like a silk scarf. Her lips were flushed pink from his kisses and glistened with a touch of moisture. He swallowed, knowing his physical condition was such that she would be able to tell she had aroused him if she knew what to look for. He did not want to risk frightening her just yet with his passionate response to the feel of her in his arms. A strategic retreat was called for.

"I suppose I should go back and work on turning my fairy-tale into a play," he said, picking up his sheaf of papers and holding them in front of his breeches. "Will you read it when it is done and tell me if you wish any changes?" He was aiming for a lightness of tone to reassure her. He didn't think he had quite succeeded, but she appeared to relax a little.

"I . . . certainly, my lord."

A light tap came at the door. Both of them whirled at the sound and Lady Grishelda smiled. "I hope I am not interrupting anything?"

"No, of course not," Celestine said, relieved she had not been a few moments earlier. Or what if she had and had just come back? That thought was horrifying and Celestine swayed dizzily, holding on to the chair for support. But there was no consciousness in the young woman's face. "Please come in."

"I thought we might have that talk, but if you are busy?" She looked inquiringly at the sheaf of papers in Justin's hands.

"No. I was just leaving." Justin bowed stiffly, his cheeks pink. "Excuse me, ladies."

Celestine sighed with relief. How much longer was he to stay at Ladymead, and how would she last? If he had more torture devised for her in the guise of his expert kissing, she would have to think of ways to evade him. Her virtue alone was no protection, it appeared. She turned to her visitor and invited her to sit in the chair just vacated.

"Lord St. Claire was consulting me about a play he is writing for the puppet show the girls will be putting on for Christmas."

Lady Grishelda eyed her steadily, her gaze flitting over Celestine's flushed cheeks, sparkling eyes, and the stray strand of hair that trailed over her shoulder. "No explanation is necessary, Miss Simons. I will not carry tales that Lord St. Claire was visiting the schoolroom."

Celestine shifted in embarrassment to have her light chat seen through so easily. There was such a thing as rather too much perspicacity and candor, she decided, and the young woman in front of her was guilty of both.

"I did not think you would. Nonetheless, that was his reason for being here. Now, of what would you like to speak?"

Lady Grishelda's calm eyes narrowed thoughtfully and she compressed her lips. But when she spoke, it was about her school and her desire to make it truly useful for the children of her village.

Celestine felt the tension leave her as they spoke. It was bewildering, after a year of virtual isolation, to find herself sought out by such a variety of people. Her aunt, so close and dear to her; Lady Grishelda, so intelligent and well spoken; and Lord St. Claire, so . . . so handsome and gentle and merry and . . . try as she might, Celestine could not rid herself of the memory of Justin St. Claire's kiss. Even as she spoke to the young woman in front of her, conversing about books and students, another part of her mind was dealing with the aftereffects of her first kiss.

She wanted to revel in it. She wanted to go somewhere quiet and relive every precious second, from the first touch of his hand until the moment when she had regrettably come to her senses. Regrettably? Yes, she was sorry she had parted from him. And yet if they had stayed like that Lady Grishelda would have had a scandalous tale to tell had she so desired.

For a few minutes she had been a woman—not daughter or niece or governess, not parishioner or friend or neighbor, just a woman, being kissed and caressed by a man with fire in his veins. As inexperienced as she was, she had recognized the look in the nobleman's eyes when he had at last released her. The naked desire there had thrilled her to the core, making her quiver. It was a powerful sensation to arouse a man like Justin St. Claire, who was surely used to beautiful courtesans and lovely society ladies.

But he *was* a man, and according to a married friend of hers from the village where she grew up, men could get that way over any woman. Jessie, married to a successful draper in their small village, had called it being in rut, in a disdainful way. So maybe there was nothing so very wonderful in his feeling that way over her. It was a lowering thought.

She was conscious that her conversation with Lady Grishelda had become more personal. The other young woman was speaking of her intention never to marry.

"Never?" Celestine asked, watching the calm face before her.

"No. I believe women surrender too much in marriage. We give up our self-determination."

"But do we ever have that in the first place, my lady?" Celestine asked. "Aren't we always subject to the whims of men? I escaped that only because nobody wants me in marriage, and I have no close male relatives."

The younger woman got up and paced to the window. "I will be frank, and what I say may shock you." She stood staring out at the landscape, the hills dusted with a light layer of snow. "My mother has lived her life for men. She needs men—needs their support, their approval, their minds, their bodies. She is a leech, sucking strength and self-confidence from them. I disdain her way of life."

"But that does not mean you must do without marriage," Celestine said softly. "You are an intelligent, attractive, caring woman, and marriage . . ."

"Would end all chance to use my abilities in any way I wished!" She was vehement, turning from the window with a blaze of determination in her pale-blue eyes. "I will live my life for myself! I will *not* become some man's plaything to discard when he has found a new toy."

Celestine, taken aback by the twists of Grishelda's conversation, was puzzled. But a ray of light pierced the dark. "You see your mother as being used by men, do you not?"

Grishelda nodded.

"Some might say it is the other way around, that Lady van Hoffen is the one who has the ultimate freedom of choosing, instead of being the chosen. She is, after all, in control of her own life."

Grishelda's expression twisted. "That is not so. My mother is notorious, yes, but her choices are limited. She is avid in the pursuit of admiration, and any man who feigns it will find himself in her bed that night. What kind of choice is that?"

Celestine was silent.

"I have shocked you." She came back to sit down. She arranged her neat, modest dress around her and folded her long-fingered, elegant hands in her lap. When she looked up again, her eyes held a militant gleam. "I am sorry. Perhaps I have seen too much of life as a result of my mother's . . . predilections. But I see it as revelatory. I see how men use and discard women, how women are only sought as long as they are young and attractive or can pretend to those virtues. I abhor such treatment, and so I will forego the pain of such abandonment in favor of a higher course, a course of service to the poor."

"Very laudatory," Celestine murmured. But she could not help thinking that in Lady Grishelda's position, surely she could continue her life of service *and* have a life of her own: a husband, children, *love*. If she had the young woman's advantages of position and wealth, she knew exactly what she would do. She would make every attempt to attach Justin St. Claire and marry him, whatever the future held. That was the truth of the matter. A lifetime of kisses and caresses like the ones he had given her would more than make up for the loss of self-determination she would suffer upon marrying. Perhaps if she were wealthy and independent like Lady Grishelda, she would feel differently. She would never know.

Something inside told her whether he knew it or not, Lord St. Claire was ready to change his life by taking a wife. There was a restlessness, a bored air, that told her he was ready to start living as an adult instead of as an eternal youth flitting from affair to affair.

But she was a poor governess with no beauty, no wealth,

and no position. And she had best not forget that, nor the fact that there would never be anything between her and the aristocrat beyond the sensual fulfillment he sought. The gap between their social positions was vast. More than a gap, it was an abyss. All he could offer her was ruin. She *must* remember that, or she would surely lose herself—or at the very least, her virtue.

Ten

Justin strode from the schoolroom to his bedchamber. It would *not* do to enter his sister's parlor in a state of raging arousal. Unbelievable that he should be so affected by a prim, gray mouse of a governess. He had bedded courtesans, society wives, some of the most beautiful women in England!

He had thought himself in control of the situation—had expected to arouse her desire, then leave her hanging. After all, this whole thing had started as a way to tweak Elizabeth's nose—to get the governess to fall under his spell and have a little fun.

Instead Celestine pushed *him* away, leaving him to deal with his problem. It was just being male, he supposed. She was a warm and willing bundle in his arms and his body had prepared itself accordingly. After too many years of mindless seduction, he was not used to having to exercise control.

Warm. Willing. When he had gazed down into her liquid gray eyes, he would have sworn she was beautiful in that moment, even though he knew better. Her skin was so pale as to be translucent, like the very best bone china, with that enchanting sprinkle of freckles over her small nose. Her mouth, too large for fashion, was well suited to satisfy a man's hunger. He had been right about that. He had plundered the depths of her mouth, erotic images flooding his brain as he imagined her sensual lips employed in delectably arousing ways. As he thrust into her mouth, he had wanted nothing more than to lay her back on the schoolroom table and show her how pleasurable was the sweet mating dance of man and woman. A fine sweat broke out on his brow.

Her hair, so mousy-looking bundled back into a bun, was a glorious silken mane that hung around her shoulders like a curtain. He could see it fanned across a pillow, her pale, perfect skin glowing with vitality from the passionate exercise he was giving her as she writhed beneath him while he thrust into her welcoming body. He could teach her things, arousing things . . . he shook his fogged head, trying to clear it.

He hungered for her. For *her!* He sat down on his bed and ran his fingers through his curls as he considered that fact. He need not go without fulfillment, even here in the hinterlands of the Lake District. He knew at that moment, in his condition, he could have found Lady van Hoffen and she would gladly have given him satisfaction. Her reputation preceded her to Ladymead as a woman eager to lie down for any man with the time and inclination. She was well known in London as a vigorous and athletic lover; her abilities were bandied about in every men's club he frequented.

But he didn't want Lady van Hoffen. He didn't want just a willing receptacle to pour himself into. For all her aristocratic pretensions, Lady van Hoffen was a scheming little whore, not circumspect when it came to choosing sexual partners, nor discreet in her *amours*.

Had he ever passed up a willing woman when he was randy? Not in his memory. His lust had been aroused by more than one female ineligible to bed by virtue of being young and unmarried, and he had always satisfied himself with some willing courtesan. He would not be caught in parson's mousetrap for nibbling forbidden cheese. Any food would satisfy when one was hungry. But not this time.

He sighed and lay back on his bed, staring up at the rich, wine-colored brocade hangings and sturdy oak posts as his ardor finally began to abate. For the first time, he thought of Celestine—really *thought* of her and her life. He would swear his kiss was her first—that she was a virgin in *every* way. But after her initial timidity, she had melted against him with a tender passion that aroused him all over again as he thought of it. She had met his darting tongue and searching kiss with ardor and tremulous yearning.

What was different about her, about her kiss and touch? Was it because he was her first? There was astonishing power in that thought, knowing she was absolutely untouched. He had never had a virgin and had always supposed his first would be his wife, whoever she was. What would it be like? Would it be awful, or awe-inspiring?

He supposed that would depend on the girl he chose and her response to his lovemaking. He was generally accounted to be a considerate lover, careful of his partner's pleasure before his own, a fact which apparently had made the rounds in London. Lady van Hoffen had whispered as much to him earlier, as she squeezed his leg. But a virgin would require special care. It would help, he guessed, if the girl had a passionate nature, like Celestine.

There he was, back to her again. There must have been other men who were interested in her in her first bloom. After all, though she was plain to most eyes, she was not ugly, and she had a softly rounded body, pleasing to a man. Her eyes kindled with a spark, his dark, thick brows drew down, and he absently plucked at the figured bed cover.

Had anyone else seen her eyes as he did? She seemed to become a different person in his arms, alight with an inner flame that burned hot and luscious. And yet he had seen something there long ago, before he had kissed her—a sweet confusion in her glance when she looked at him, a wide-eyed look of wonder.

He knew other ladies thought him handsome and had professed to love him. He had been in London for twelve seasons and had had his share of doe-eyed debutantes casting themselves at his feet, dying of love for him—or so the more indiscreet had said. He had been feted, complimented, sought after for most of his thirty-two years.

But he had never felt such a magnetic pull as he had the night he and Celestine came home together with Elise and Mrs. Jacobs in the carriage. He had longed to take her in his arms and hold her—just hold her, nothing more. He wanted to protect her from the vagaries of her life and soothe her pain, comfort her fears. If the maid and housekeeper hadn't been there, he would have.

He had attributed his tears in the church and his tender reaction to Miss Simons's fragility to the overemotionalism he was occasionally prey to. He was the unfortunate inheritor of his mother's disposition. He remembered as a lad occasionally coming upon her weeping over a sad novel or lovely piece of music and knew it was to her he owed his sensitive nature. He had struggled to submerge that side of him. There was no room in a St. Claire man's life for emotionalism. His father had made sure he knew that and had beaten him once for crying over a hurt puppy. But was that all that lay behind his urge to protect and shelter the governess?

He bounded from the bed with a snort of disgust. What in God's name was coming over him? He was acting like a moonling with a first crush, and over a plain little dab of a governess! He needed rational male company—a bottle of port and a game of billiards. That was the logical cure to this illogical burst of inappropriate lust.

Surely lust was all it was.

Lady Emily Delafont paced the conservatory, ostensibly enjoying the orchids and other fine blossoms. What she was really doing was worrying, wringing her fine, soft hands together. She had been appalled at the way her niece had neglected herself in her time at Ladymead. Only with the most strenuous care could she avoid extreme pain for a number of weeks or even months a year, and yet she didn't give herself a second thought, devoting herself to those over-cared-for children of the St. Claires. But Emily saw a danger to her niece more insidious than the merely physical. In their long talk the night before, Emily had drawn Celestine out, gently encouraging her to talk about anything and everything.

She had been starved of adult company for almost a year, so it was no surprise that she poured her heart out, talking nonstop for almost three hours. And in those hours, Celestine had unwittingly exposed more of her heart than perhaps she had intended to.

The girl was halfway in love with Justin St. Claire. She had spoken of his going to choir practice, his quiet praise of her voice, the connection she felt to him in the carriage on the way home, and his gentle treatment of her when her emotions brimmed up.

She spoke with puzzlement of his teasing and flirtation, but there was no anger or disdain. There *was* longing—tender, winsome, full-hearted longing she no doubt did not realize she was revealing. She touched on his looks, but, surprisingly, that did not seem to figure largely in her infatuation.

Celestine was the most sensible of women, but Emily realized all too often they were the very kind to be taken in by a smooth-tongued rogue. Justin was every inch a rogue, a devil with the ladies. In his years in London, he had cut a wide swath through the ranks of debutantes and even the more experienced ladies of the *ton*.

Sometimes Emily thought he wasn't fully aware of his own powers, as ladies often languished on the sidelines in the throes of absolute infatuation with him, when he had done no more than bow to them or say a kind word. There was something about Justin that called to a deep, yearning place in a woman's soul, the place where tenderness resided. And yet he was a rakehell and a *roué*. Her sweet niece was falling in love with a cad who could not begin to appreciate her fine, deep qualities.

She did not think she was being too partial when she

spoke or thought of her niece as sweet, loving, dutiful, and intelligent. But there was more to Celestine. There was also strength—a deep, abiding strength of character, and an awesome optimism despite the uneven hand she had been dealt. She did not see herself as unfortunate, with the curse of arthritis and poverty heaped on top of loneliness and spinsterhood. Celestine had lost most of what mattered to her in life: her health, her father, her home, and her position in society, and yet she had a determined cheerfulness of character that was motivated solely by her lack of self-centeredness.

That was what Emily had been trying to say to Justin. Instead he had seen her interference as offensive and had sneered at her enumeration of her niece's sterling qualities. And this was the first man Celestine would fall in love with? As likable as Justin was—and it was impossible to hate him even when one saw him for the rogue he was—she could cheerfully consign him to the devil that moment.

So what could she do? Watch and wait, she supposed, and be there to guard Celestine or to pick up the pieces of her shattered heart when Justin revealed himself for the heartless cad he had always been—and hope it would happen soon, so Emily *would* be there. She prayed Justin's visit did not outlast her own. From what she had heard, he intended to take himself back to town for the New Year's festivities. Emily turned toward the door and headed back to the parlor and more empty chat with the empty-headed Stimson sisters.

The air sparkled with a crystalline brightness Celestine had never seen before. Lottie and Gwen raced down the path ahead of her, through the light covering of snow, laughing and screaming at the momentum that they built up. Lady St. Claire would go into strong hysterics if she could see her girls acting like such hoydens, but Celestine believed children must be allowed to be children, with all the attendant noise and occasional scraped knees.

She knew she was beaming—grinning in fact—and the sparkling weather and childish laughter could not be the only reason. After a quiet half-hour's reflection over the morning's events, she had decided there was nothing at all wrong with admitting she had tumbled headlong in love with Justin St. Claire. She felt joyous and free, youthful and energized just saying it out loud. "I have fallen in love with Lord Justin St. Claire!" She laughed at the silliness of it.

Where was the harm? He would never know about it. No one would *ever* know about it. She would keep her full heart concealed from everyone and hug her secret knowledge to herself. Pain was inevitable, but right now she was going to enjoy his company when she had it and not feel ashamed of loving.

But she must not allow such trespasses on her person again. That could lead to trouble, and she felt it unfair to engage in actions that would lead to unrealistic expectations on his side—not that he would expect to court her as he would a lady he was considering marriage with, but he certainly might think she would be amenable to a liaison of a less moral kind.

She acquitted him of any serious intentions. He did not conduct himself like a man who would be considering marriage or wooing. It was just his way, and how could he help that? Many girls must have fallen in love with a man so gifted, handsome, and engaging as he was. She was not the first and would not be the last. She could do nothing about it now the damage was done, so she must just relax and let time settle things.

She strolled down the snowy hill after the girls, feeling better than she had for ages. They were walking along a path that led to the edge of the St. Claire property, though the property line was not even in sight yet and wouldn't be for a while. It was a large estate, and the St. Claires were the principal landowners of the area, employing hundreds of people in addition to the household staff: shepherds, dairymaids, gardeners, farmers, ostlers, a blacksmith, and many more.

But the technical part of running the estate was behind Ladymead. Celestine was walking with the girls in the pleasure park, a landscaped area with copses, rolling lawns and a small stream, frozen now in places, gurgling bright and silver in others.

"Miss Simons!"

A voice carried on the wind reached her as she approached the wooden bridge over the small stream on the Ladymead property.

Celestine turned and saw Mr. Foster, the vicar, following her down the path. He was a stark, black blot on the white and blue horizon. She called to the girls, then stopped to wait.

Panting a little, Mr. Foster said as he reached her, "I am so glad I caught you. I have a matter of some importance to discuss with you."

"I am just taking the girls for a walk. This time of year excites the little ones so. They need to work off their fidgets."

"They should be assigned some quiet work!" the reverend said, frowning a bit. "Contemplation is what they need, and perhaps a talk about the true meaning of Christmas."

Celestine bit back the response that first came to her lips and merely said, "Of course, sir. Perhaps you are right."

Foster unbent a little and hands clasped behind his black-coated back, he fell into step with her. Lottie and Gwen were gathering pine cones under a deep green conifer where the snow had not yet drifted in and stuffing them into the pockets of their cloaks. They wanted to decorate the schoolroom, and Celestine had agreed to help them.

"You wanted to speak to me, sir?" she asked. She

smiled up at him, determined not to let the parson's priggish attitude destroy her joy in the day.

He harrumphed once, blowing out his breath in a cloud of steam, and Celestine glanced over at him in some surprise. "I was dismayed, Miss Simons, at the apparent interest Lord St. Claire has taken in you. It cannot have an honorable intent, and I felt it my duty, as your religious advisor, to prepare you in the event he approaches you with an improper suggestion."

Celestine gaped foolishly in her surprise.

Foster took her tiny gasp of outrage as her reaction to this surprising revelation, and said, "I know, Miss Simons. Quite shocking. Being a gently bred female, you will be unacquainted with male lust, and I would not want you to be exploited by a predatory type such as the marquess's brother. The aristocracy have different codes, my dear, if I might be so bold as to call you that. I would protect you from women's inherent weakness of morality.

"I would like to offer my protection in a more solid form. As my betrothed wife, you would be removed from his sphere of influence. I hope you know I consider you everything that is amiable and feel marriage between us would satisfy us both on many levels."

He paused and glanced sideways at Celestine. Possibly he sensed some anger or hostility from her, because he rushed back into speech. "I know you will think me hasty, but I have been observing you for some time, and my decision was not taken lightly. As a man of the cloth, I must think of the worthiness of my wife to be a beacon among women and must judge her ability to exemplify St. Paul's admonition, in his letter to the Ephesians, that women be subject to their husband as their head and master, as their husbands are subject to our Lord . . ."

The rest was lost on Celestine. Anger had bubbled up into her serene heart, darkening the beauty of the day. How dare he? It was one thing for her to acknowledge her own ineligibility as far as an honorable connection with Justin went, but for the vicar to so boldly state she was only an object of lust for his lordship! And he would protect her from her own weakness of morality?

Inwardly she seethed, but she made a strenuous and not entirely successful attempt to keep her anger quelled.

"Lottie, Gwen! We have to go back now. Tea will be waiting!" Her voice sounded harsh, even to herself. Tears blinded her eyes, and she didn't dare venture a word to the man at her side.

Luckily, he was readily able to come to an explanation for her silence. "I believe you are overwhelmed by my offer, my dear. I will give you time to digest it before informing your employers of our intentions. Indeed, I would not have come forward at this busy time of year, except I feared for you in the same household with that . . . that libertine. I believe the knowledge of your impending marriage will strengthen you in your resistance to that animal's lustful predation, but you must feel free to come to me at any time if you feel yourself weak in the face of his licentious and lascivious manner."

Her continued silence and hurried footsteps did not register with the vicar as disapproval. He continued. "I have heard many things of Lord Justin St. Claire. We both attended Oxford—myself several years ahead of him, I might add—and even in those days he was a known gambler and fornicator. I will not shock your tender sensibilities with the raw facts: the soiled doves under his protection, the games of chance and dens of iniquity he was known to frequent. I may have already been too forthright, I fear, judging by your continued silence.

"But he has ever been addicted to the pleasures of the flesh, I believe. My sermon this week shall be on lust, the deadliest of the seven deadly sins. It will be wasted on his ears, if he even attends service, which I doubt. This is where I must part from you, my dear. I must pay my respects to her ladyship and then return home."

He turned to Celestine, his dark eyes intent. "I would like to celebrate our betrothal, my dear. Please do not take what I am about to do amiss. Never fear that I will view you with a lustful eye, for I am not given to a violence of emotions.'' He stepped closer to her, gripped her shoulders, and laid a cold kiss on her forehead, then turned and walked away.

Celestine was too shocked to do anything but submit to his odious, cold salute.

Justin galloped over a hill on his gelding, which danced to a stop as he pulled back on the reins. In the distance, on her way back up the hill toward the house, was Celestine, with Lottie and Gwen gamboling behind, skipping and running.

But there was someone else with the governess, a dark figure. As he watched, the man in the black greatcoat turned an unresisting Celestine toward him and planted a kiss on her face, whereabouts Justin couldn't quite tell. It was enough to see she did not push him away, nor did she slap him after.

By God, it was that smarmy vicar, Mr. Foster! And their relationship must be farther along than he had ever thought for the reverend to be kissing her in broad daylight in view of the children.

A cold swell of some bitter, unidentifiable feeling swept over Justin. He had been wrong, evidently, about her never having been kissed. Was she playing them both like fish on hooks, seeing if she could land one of them, not caring much which? His lips twisted in anger.

And he had thought her an innocent— an untouched, virginal spinster. Maybe she would come to his bed willingly, then, thinking to catch herself a husband that way. Maybe he did not have to spend his time at Ladymead in vigorous exercise to quell the passion roiling through his veins.

Perhaps it was time to press her a little more closely.

Eleven

Days passed. The house party was lively enough, thanks to the children and the Misses Stimson, and it was informal enough that the children occasionally came down to the parlor and entertained the adults with their prattle. Gus was allowed to play billiards with the men and to eat at the table with the adults, a rare treat for him. He slavishly copied Justin's every move and mannerism and took to tying his cravat in an untidy copy of the intricate style Dooley had created for his uncle.

Lottie and Gwen were included in trips into Ellerbeck for gift shopping and even a sleigh ride into the countryside for greenery to decorate with. Celestine worked alone on the puppets, keeping Justin's characters in mind, but she didn't see anything of him and felt the shine go out of her days.

How silly she had become, she thought as she dressed the Reginald puppet, thankful her hands felt so much better and were not as stiff as they had been. She worked in silence by the big window in the schoolroom and contemplated her short acquaintance with her employer's brother. She had begun to think she was in some way special to him, that he appreciated her and found her desirable enough to want to be around her. He hadn't been feigning that, she had thought. But then, he was an acknowledged favorite of the ladies. He probably had the knack of making each and every one of them feel special.

Or his efforts at staying away from her could have another source. There had been one puzzling moment that was likely the cause of his avoiding her.

It had been very late at night, and Celestine was sleepless. The hot bath every morning and Emily's ointment were starting to make her feel better. The swelling was starting to go down on her hands and she was not so fatigued all the time.

Awake with an unusual bout of insomnia, she decided to try some milk from the kitchen, and had crept down the back stairs from her third-floor room. On the landing of the second floor, she had heard a noise and had shrunk back against the wall, momentarily frightened. A shadow, long and menacing, had crept up the wall, and the scuffle of footsteps echoed.

Then a figure hove into view. It was Justin, and with a whimper of relief she had sagged against the wall, hand to her breast over the thumping of her foolish heart. He saw her then and, a little the worse for a bottle of brandy, he had peered at her in the gloom.

"Celestine," he whispered. "That you?"

"Yes," she whispered back.

He came the rest of the way up the stairs and stared at her, holding his candle high, his eyes raking her body in its soft, worn nightrail. He came closer and closer, until he filled her vision. All she could think of was Mr. Foster's admonition to her and his warning about St. Claire's nature.

It had angered her at the time, but it had humbled her as well, and she had rethought her idea that it didn't hurt to love him in silence. Now, with him in front of her, his cravat askew, his jacket missing, his sleeves rolled up over thick forearms, and his hair even more tousled than usual, she could not think at all. She couldn't concentrate on loving him or hating him or avoiding him, not with him this close.

"I . . . I was just going . . ." She started to skitter past him, to head down the stairs. It was too dangerous even being near him. Though she might resent the vicar's lack of faith in her virtue, there was much sense in his warning to her. Justin St. Claire was a man entirely out of her experience, with seductive wiles she hadn't imagined until she was subjected to them. If she was vulnerable to his caresses in the schoolroom in the middle of the day, what might he tempt her to in the middle of the night, with only her nightrail and housecoat on?

He put out one arm and arrested her movement. She gazed down in fascination at that arm, the cord of muscle across it, the bristling dark hairs and lightly tanned skin. She could see the golden tint to his flesh in the dancing candlelight. What did he do outdoors that left his skin tanned, even after summer was gone? Her ungovernable imagination raised the question of whether he was golden all over—his shoulders, his chest, his . . . she turned her face away in confusion.

He set his guttering candle on a nearby table and fingered her hair with his other hand, grasping a handful of it and burying his face in it. His action so startled her that she lifted her face and watched him in fascination. He rubbed it over his face and against his lips, taking deep breaths of her scent. He wound it around his fingers and kissed the silky strands. He finally released her hair, but some stayed snagged on the bristles of his late-day shadow of beard.

She gazed up at him, her eyes wide. Was he drunk, or just a little to go, as the phrase went? He was standing steadily enough, with no waver or stagger. Being so close to him was suffocating. She moved to duck under his arm, but he grasped her shoulder and pushed her against the wall.

And then he kissed her. His breath was perfumed with brandy and his lips were warm and moist on her mouth. He folded her to his chest in a strong embrace.

For a moment she surrendered, tasting the sweet liquor

on his lips and melting into his warm body, feeling herself start to shiver to radiant life in his arms.

This was the glorious feeling she had been aware of the last time he had kissed her! She felt alive, like something stirred in her dormant body, kindled by the touch of this man. She was aware of a vague, poorly understood desire to cling to his heat, his strength, to mold herself to his muscle and sinew.

But the cold voice of reason intruded and she remembered what the vicar had said. Perhaps he was right after all. She was weak and could easily give in to him. She felt it in herself—felt the sweet languor of love steal her breath away and leave her aching for his touch.

She pushed away from him and he released her, but would not let her out of the circle of his arms. His overpowering presence dominated her, and her hands, resting lightly on his shoulders, kneaded the muscles that knotted and flexed beneath her touch. His breathing was fast and harsh and her own matched his for pace. His gaze was deep blue and unfathomable in the dim light of his flickering candle.

"You like kisses, don't you?"

It was a statement, almost an accusation. It puzzled her, but she had no time to think about it. It was imperative she retreat, for if she were caught dallying in the hall with him in her nightrail, inevitable conclusions would be drawn and her employment would be at an end, as would the good reputation of a blameless lifetime.

"You are drunk, sir." She ducked out of his arms and retreated upstairs to her room to safety. For a few minutes she had been frightened he would follow her and make a scene, but he hadn't, and that had been that. Since then he had not accosted her or visited her in the schoolroom, a fact she should have been grateful for, though it left her feeling restless and dissatisfied.

Of course she had not told anyone about her amorous encounters with Lord St. Claire, but she knew her aunt felt something was wrong. Emily still came to her room every night for a talk and the ointment, and their discussions had been long and thorough, but they did not touch on the nobleman. She also did not tell her about the vicar's proposal, if it could be called that.

Later, after their conversation, she realized Mr. Foster had assumed she would accept him. There was not even the pretense of asking for her hand; he had just said they would not announce their nuptials until after the holidays. That angered her more than anything, even more than his assumption of her lack of morals, for some reason.

After the anger came the sadness that spelled the death of her hopes for an honorable marriage with Reverend Robert Foster. She could not even think of looking at him again, much less marrying him. He thought her immoral by nature—clearly thought all women were impure.

She thought about his cold, chaste kiss on her forehead and how it compared with Justin's hot, dangerous kisses. Would Mr. Foster's kiss have been so lacking if she had never experienced Justin? She didn't know—couldn't imagine. That was the problem with experience; you could never go back from it, never undo it.

And she could never retreat from loving Justin. She thought about him all the time, wondering what it was in him that drew her, but she knew she was right to keep him at arm's length, and she should have been glad he seemed to be avoiding her. She caught the occasional glimpse of him with the Stimson girls or Lady Grishelda, and just that morning she had heard him flirting with Lady van Hoffen.

They were in the conservatory. Celestine had gone there to get a plant for the schoolroom and had become entranced just walking up and down the rows of greenery. When she heard a male voice she assumed it was Grundle, the gardener. She heard a feminine counterpoint and realized too late it was Justin and Lady van Hoffen.

Their conversation had been light and flirtatious, with lots of double entendres and laughter, and then there had been silence. She thought they might have left, slipping quietly from the room without closing the door behind them. But from behind a palm tree she had caught sight of the pair, the ample redhead with her fingers buried in his hair as she gave him an openmouthed kiss. He had given her a little push after that and they had moved away, arm in arm, laughing.

A stab of pain and jealousy shot through her, but it finally put his behavior in context for Celestine. Now she understood him. Just as she had initially thought, he could not be around a female without flirting and making her fall in love with him. She was just one in a long line, and she must bear that in mind next time he flirted with her—if he ever did. And still she could not hate him.

She bent back over her work, deftly sewing a cloak on Reginald, and tried to forget about Justin St. Claire. But some things would live in her memory forever: his eyes following her around the room; his low voice, so seductive, in her ear; his kisses, so warm and passionate that any woman could be excused for falling in love with him; and that one perfect moment in the dark confines of the carriage when he had pressed his kerchief into her hand and she had felt a thread between them stretch taut and thicken, a cord binding their souls intimately. He might be unaware of it, but her heart was bound to his by more than lust or desire.

Was it just in her imagination, that connection? Was it for him some flimsy little cobweb she had woven in her mind into strong hemp? Perhaps, but still it bound her to him, and she would forever feel the tug of it wherever he wandered and whomever he chose to bed. Whether he knew it or not, he would always carry around with him her heart, pulsing with the strong beat of his own.

Elizabeth twitched the curtains back to look out on the gloomy December afternoon. "I think it will be perfectly marvelous," she sang, dancing around the room in a rare display of high spirits. Her husband watched her fondly as she circled the room, touching an ornament here, straightening a cushion there. "It has been years since we have had a big Christmas party."

"You have been a little taken up with child bearing and other necessary nuisances," he chuckled.

He was a big man, stretched at his ease on a dainty brocade sofa at the moment, watching his slim wife with appreciation. Few people saw him smile. Even fewer heard him laugh. Only with Elizabeth did he show those rare sides of himself. Their arranged match had miraculously turned into love, and though they had had their troubles, he was forever glad his parents had betrothed him to her when she was still in the cradle and he was in short pants.

"I think my plans are coming along brilliantly," Elizabeth said. "Every day Justin is behaving himself better. He voluntarily took the Misses Stimson for a ride this afternoon! On the whole, though, I believe Lady Grishelda will suit him better."

"If you can keep him out of the clutches of the mother," August growled. "I know my brother, my dear. With a willing widow in hand, he is unlikely to think of marriage, a subject he avoids even when attending the marriage mart."

Elizabeth stopped. "Do you think they are sleeping together?"

"He and Lady van Hoffen? That trollop? Probably doing damned little sleeping."

"August!" She stopped before her husband and allowed him to pull her down on his lap. "Still, I swear before this holiday season is over, I will have him betrothed!"

"You missed your calling, my dear." He gazed into her sparkling blue eyes. She was adorable when she was scheming. It hardly seemed possible that she had a fourteen-year-old son. She still looked so youthful and slender.

"You should be Cupid, and this should be St. Valentine's, not Christmas," he said, with a teasing lilt in his voice.

"Tonight I will test my mettle at our Christmas party. He will fall for one of my guests, just you wait and see."

August St. Claire nuzzled his wife's neck. "Don't be so sure, my love. You are doomed to disappointment. I don't know who will catch my rapscallion brother, but it will have to be someone swift and witty. And she had best be prepared to have him lead her a merry dance before he is snared."

"He sounds more like a hare than a man, my darling."

"More like a fox, if you ask me."

Justin stared out the window of the library, watching a few snowflakes dance against the pane as the day closed in, the sky darkening with twilight and a threatened storm. Elizabeth's party guests were due to start arriving any time now, if they didn't get caught in a ferocious snowstorm before then.

He was not looking forward to this irritating party his sister-in-law had cooked up. Somehow, the brightness had gone out of his holiday, and he couldn't place a finger on the problem. He had been enjoying himself, even down to writing the damned play for Lottie and Gwen—and Celestine. He grimaced.

The other night he had been cupshot and had pawed her like some lecherous old lout. But it had only seemed her due after kissing him as she did in the schoolroom, then kissing that damned vicar—in broad daylight and in front of the children, no less. He ought to have told his brother. But the vicar had as good as stated his intentions to Justin himself in the sanctity of the church. He supposed he could do nothing.

But if she were as good as betrothed, what business had she had responding to him the way she did? How could she look at him with those great, luminous gray eyes and sigh against his lips with the soft sweetness of ardor? He would have sworn he had given her her first kiss, but now he no longer knew. It made him doubt his instincts, which he had long relied on, and he did not like being in a state of doubt. He had sworn to bed her after witnessing that kiss between her and the vicar, but that resolution died after his unseemly drunken groping of her. *No* woman made him lose control . . . except her, it seemed. He didn't like the sensation of losing mastery over his own body and actions, which was what happened every time he kissed her.

He paced away from the window. What in God's name was wrong with him? Why did every thought begin and end with Celestine? He went back to the desk, determined to finish *The Lonely Prince*. Instead he found himself staring with unseeing eyes at the shelves of books on the other wall.

Christmas was just two weeks away. He had achieved his objective of some kissing and cuddling with the prim governess. She had led him much farther than Miss Chambly had. By God, he had pressed himself against Celestine's pliant body and felt her flicker to life against him!

And their kissing had been far from a little innocent bussing on the lips. It had been the kind of deeply passionate embrace that leads to the bedroom and a night of hot, sweaty play under the covers. Or was it more the kind that led to vows of love eternal and all that rot? His mind scurried away from that concept. He should announce his success, mortifying Elizabeth and showing her she did not exert total control over her vassals, and get on with enjoying the holiday season—maybe even bed the widow and vent his unsated lust on a willing woman.

But for some reason, he didn't want to share what had passed between Celestine and himself, even to horrify Elizabeth. He wasn't exactly sure what it was. He had intended a light flirtation, but this was different somehow. He had realized that in the conservatory when the amorous Lady van Hoffen had kissed him, pressing her lush body against his, grinding her hips, and promising more with her darting tongue and experienced hands.

He'd felt distaste, and compared it to his shared embrace with Celestine. Lady van Hoffen's kiss had been tawdry and lewd, somehow. With the governess, kisses had seemed rich in meaning and shared passion. He had pushed Lady van Hoffen away and laughed it off, though he had known she would expect him in her bed that night. She was doomed to disappointment.

He threw down his pen with an exclamation of disgust and ran his fingers through his hair. Celestine. Somehow she was under his skin. Why? Was he getting a conscience?

He sat up straighter and his eyes narrowed. That might be it! He was feeling guilt—guilt for having lured a virginal governess off the narrow path of virtue. Miss Chambly had gone out of her way to entrap him. He'd had no qualms about accepting her kisses. But Celestine was a virtuous young woman apparently destined to become the wife of the local vicar. He had started to doubt whether she was as innocent as she seemed after seeing the vicar kiss her, but he could not remember a single instance of her encouraging him, even that late night on the stairway landing, so perhaps he should absolve her of any fickleness.

He nodded with some satisfaction. He had hit on the solution, and he would find a way to soothe his conscience. He would talk to her and tell her she need not fear him anymore, that he would keep away from her. He remembered his intentions the morning after escorting her home from choir practice. He should have followed through with what was clearly his better self. Perhaps this would be a lesson to him. He would set her mind at ease and assuage his conscience. *Anything* to stop this fixation on a plain, frumpy governess and get on with his Christmas celebration.

That was what he would do. The play was almost done. Perhaps while everyone else was busy with the party that

night, he would take it to her, confess what he had intended, and tell her he would bother her no more. Then
he could stop thinking about her all the time. He set
back to work on the play, his pen scratching across the
surface of the paper at an even pace.

Twelve

"But, Aunt Emily, this is not at all the thing!" Celestine cried, gazing at herself in her aunt's cheval glass.

Emily gazed at her niece's reflection and sighed happily. Celestine was dressed in a deep rose gown of watered silk, cut low enough on the bust for fashion, high enough for modesty. It was crossed with heavy burgundy ribbon, which served to emphasize her well-shaped bosom, and had an overdress of ivory lace. At the bottom were three *rouleaux* of contrasting silk, the top one dancing in an elegant, swirling pattern around the skirt. It was simple and elegant—perfect for her niece.

"Please, don't spoil my enjoyment of this party!" she said, glancing up into Celestine's fine, gray eyes.

The younger woman set her lips in a determined line. "Aunt, I know your intentions are the best, but Lady St. Claire will perish from rage if she sees me dressed up to rival her other female guests! That you wrested an invitation out of her for me to join the festivities is bad enough, but she will expect me to appear in my dowdy governess grays, not dressed like some debutante."

"Oh, surely not a debutante, my dear," Emily replied, her head tilted to one side. She examined her niece with a thoughtful gleam in her eye, then retreated to her wardrobe and retrieved a velvet case from one shelf. Her maid, Agnes, moved competently in the background, restoring order to the piles of dresses and fabric on the bed. Emily came back to the mirror. In one deft movement, she fastened a lovely string of garnets set in gold around Celestine's slender, arching neck.

Celestine stood, hands down at her sides, and gazed at herself in the semidarkness. Agnes had not pulled the curtains yet, and outside a light snow drifted against the window. "It is dressing mutton to look like lamb, Aunt, and you know it," she said quietly. "And not even choice mutton, but the poor scrag end of the flock."

"I'll not have you speak of yourself that way," Emily said sharply, glaring at her niece's reflection. Her voice softened. "It sounds like bitterness, my dear, and I have never known you to be bitter."

"Oh, Aunt!" Celestine turned to Emily and threw her arms around her, feeling the unaccustomed sensation of the soft, silky chemise under the dress rubbing against her naked skin. "I don't mean to be ungrateful. I just don't think it is fitting, and I am sure Lady St. Claire will not, either."

"Let me handle Lizbet. She seems very ferocious, but she is really a lamb if approached the right way."

"We seem to be heavily into sheep herding tonight, with both mutton and lambs," Celestine said, a wry twist to her smile. Still doubtful, she turned to stare at herself in the oval tilted mirror. Her cheeks burned at the knowledge a seamstress had designed the gown, an old one of her aunt's, to lift and amplify a woman's natural attributes. She was not overendowed, but had always felt her reasonable bounty in that area to be immodest at best, lascivious at worst. A governess must blend in with the background, and in this dress she did not.

The rose material of the gown, altered to fit her slenderness, gave her pale skin a luster she had never noted before, and the garnets gleamed in rich perfection on her throat. Emily's clever maid, Agnes, had been busy on her hair, too, pomading it until it shone and coiling it so it looked like chestnut silk. One long tendril caressed her slender neck.

What would Justin think? Her heart pounded at the thought of spending an evening near him, gazing at him, perhaps even conversing with him—*if* Lady St. Claire didn't take one look at her and demand she march upstairs and divest herself of her borrowed finery.

"Shall we go down?" Emily picked up her fan from a table and handed another, adorned with soft, tawny feathers, to Celestine.

"I . . . I guess," Celestine muttered, staring at the pretty fan in her rose-gloved hands.

Downstairs the party gathered in a parlor, awaiting the signal to go in to dinner. Elizabeth had surpassed herself in the opulence of her preparations, and the house had been in an uproar for two days of cleaning, decorating, and cooking. Silver and crystal glittered and shone, and fresh flowers from the greenhouse perfumed the air. Evergreens to honor the season were heaped on tables with red ribbons threaded through them, and holly garlands wound through the staircase spindles and over the banister. Twelve more were to join the twelve of the house party and family for a total of twenty-four sitting down for dinner.

Celestine and Emily had just reached the second to last stair of the curved staircase when the butler announced dinner had been served. The guests poured out of the parlor, with the marquess leading Lady van Hoffen, the highest ranking of the female guests.

Justin followed with Lady Grishelda on his arm. He glanced up and stopped, his face suffusing with red. Grishelda glanced up as well, and a faint look of disapproval flickered over her plain face. Celestine noticed, but then a moment later was riveted by the look in Justin's eyes. Even if she was sent up to her room that moment by Lady St. Claire, it would be worth it.

One moment suspended in time was all it took for the admiration in his eyes to register with Celestine. Chagrined, she admitted to herself she had hoped he would look at her thus, that his eyes would light up and his gaze travel over her stylish hairdo and pretty dress, her long rose gloves and her white arms bare above them. What a trap vanity was, that even a plain governess who knew her limitations could fall prey to it!

"Miss Simons, you look . . . lovely tonight."

His voice rang out in the suddenly silent hall and Elizabeth, distracted until that moment by Mr. Stimson, glanced up to see what her brother-in-law spoke of. Her blue eyes turned frosty and her stare settled on Emily with an accusatory gleam. But there was no way to deliver a set down or reprimand then and there without causing a fuss, and she was committed to this party's being a triumph. A tiny smile, more like a grimace, settled on her lips.

"As we are all *finally* gathered, let us go in to dinner, shall we?" she said, her voice brittle and echoing in the quiet.

Celestine sat through much of dinner toying with her food. It had been a mistake. She could hear Justin's voice, his rich tones and laughter, down the table. He sat between Lady Grishelda and Miss Charlotte Stimson, and turned from one to the other, talking and laughing with both ladies equally. All she could do was listen, straining to make out his words, then castigating herself for the peagoose she was being.

At her end of the table, Celestine was seated between a young sprig who only had eyes for Caroline Stimson on his right, and an older man with graying hair who consumed his food with a rapidity that was luckily equaled by his tidiness. He ate quickly but neatly, with little time for conversation.

He had been introduced to her by Emily, who sat on his other side, as Gavin Knight. The first impression she got of the hawkish, lean gentleman was not a good one, as he raised his quizzing glass and stared down at the bosom of her dress immediately. Celestine had felt naked, as though he had stripped her bare and was evaluating her for purchase.

After that, Celestine was too uncomfortable to make conversation with him, and was glad he seemed devoted to his meal. Once, halfway through the second remove, she thought she felt a hand on her knee. She gasped, and it had been quickly withdrawn, too quickly for her to be sure it was not an accident.

She glanced up and down the table, finding she was right in her conjecture of why Lady St. Claire had allowed herself to be bullied by Emily into inviting Celestine for the dinner. She had invited a local squire and his four handsome sons to dinner, and had overbalanced the table in favor of the gentlemen. Celestine brought the balance back to the correct number so they could be seated, gentleman and lady in turn, around the long table.

After dinner, the ladies retired to the drawing room to await the gentlemen and a few other neighbors of insufficient consequence to invite for dinner. The talk centered around London fashions, gossip, and whispered confidences about gentlemen. Emily glanced over at her from time to time, but her aunt was trapped on a sofa, listening to an ancient lady's reminiscences, so Celestine was left to her own devices. Celestine had thought Lady Grishelda might be companionable, but she was strangely aloof, avoiding the governess's company.

Conversation livened up when the gentlemen arrived, and some of the young ladies were begged for a sample of their musical talents. Charlotte Stimson was first, and she acquitted herself very nicely, with a couple of love ballads and a spirited cotillion piece.

Celestine listened with half her attention, watching Justin circulate, talking easily with gentlemen and ladies. Lady van Hoffen was watching him, too, with hungry eyes. The widow licked her parted lips occasionally and thrust her ample, almost-bared bosom out when he glanced her way.

Emily gave her niece a tiny smile and joined her on the patterned sofa. They listened to the music in silence for a few minutes, and then Emily glanced over at her.

"My dear, it does not do to show your feelings so readily on your face."

Celestine started and stared at her aunt. "Whatever do you mean?"

The older woman gazed at her sadly. With the piano music as cover, and her fan in front of her mouth, she said, "It's happened, hasn't it? You've fallen in love with Justin St. Claire."

Drawing in a deep breath, Celestine curbed the impulse to close her eyes. Was it that obvious? Had she been *so* unguarded? "I . . . I didn't think . . . how do you know?"

"Oh, my dear, I see the same longing in your eyes I saw in my own in the mirror when I first fell for Baxter. Men are the very devil, love, and they are even worse when they know they have our devotion."

"I . . ." Celestine was speechless. She was alarmed lest Justin—or even worse, Lady St. Claire—should read the same message on her face. What was wrong with her? Normally she was the most guarded of young ladies. She had always striven for the appearance of tranquillity even in the midst of emotional turmoil.

It was a bitter dose to swallow, but she saw from a stranger's vantage point the unsuitability of a spinster governess sighing over a handsome aristocrat—more than unsuitability. She was a caricature of the lovelorn, aging ape leader, pining over the unattainable. A ridiculous figure.

"I think I must go for a moment and collect my thoughts." Celestine rose to her feet with a rustle of rose silk.

Emily started to rise with her, but she put her hand out and said, "No, Aunt. I just need a moment to myself. I shall return directly."

She hastened from the room, out into the coolness of the hall. Glancing around, she decided the library was most conducive to a few moments of contemplation. It was a lovely room, large and dark and quiet, contrasted with the stuffy, noisy drawing room. There were a few tapers lit in case some gentleman decided to retire for a cigar, and Celestine breathed deeply of the scent of leather bindings and old tobacco.

She stood in front of the shelves, glancing over the titles, thinking about what her aunt had said to her. How had she let herself get so carried away that she allowed her feelings to show on her face? That was what came of giving in to love, of thinking it didn't matter if she indulged herself just that once. She should have been more guarded, instead of opening herself up to love.

But had there been any choice? She had been in it before she realized it. It had come to her suddenly, when his lips touched hers, that she had wanted him and needed him for some time. But she must master her urges so she did not give herself away to everyone, especially her employers.

The library was chilly and she wished she had a shawl for her bare arms. She rubbed them with her gloved hands and stared up at the books that reached up to the high ceiling, disappearing in the gloom.

A prickling feeling at the base of her skull warned her she was not alone. She turned to find Mr. Knight closing the door and walking across the thick carpet.

"Mr. Knight." Her voice echoed in the dim room.

His face was shadowed, his beaky nose throwing a dark shade across his cheek, his hooded eyes invisible. He continued to walk silently across the room toward her.

"I . . . I just came for a moment of quiet, but it is chilly in here. I think I will return." She had started hustling past him as she spoke, but he shot out one hand and grasped her arm in a powerful grip.

"I would like you to stay." His voice was sepulchral, haunting in its depth and the echo the empty room provided.

Celestine shivered. She glanced at the door, still fifteen feet or more away, and took a shaky breath. Maintaining an air of bright incomprehension, she said, "Oh, no. I am sure you wouldn't wish to talk to me. I have no conversation, you know. In fact . . ."

He yanked her to him. Before she knew what was happening, she felt the desk behind her, so she couldn't move back, and he had her arms pinned to her sides. She struggled and opened her mouth to scream, but felt the breath sucked from her as his mouth came down over hers.

She was not strong. Never had she been more aware of it than in that moment when her struggles were as ineffectual as a kitten batting at a person's leg. She was bent backward, and she felt her back would break. As he kissed her, he ground his hips against hers, and she felt a ridge digging into her stomach.

She wrenched one arm free and started beating at his shoulder and back with it, while his mouth clamped on hers with brutal ferocity. She could taste him, the sour tang of uncleaned teeth, the tobacco, the port. Her senses leaped to life and her brain worked frantically, trying to think of a way out.

She knew what rape was. She had known a woman who had experienced it and who had unburdened herself at great and graphic length on the one sympathetic person in her small village, herself. Now she was about to experience all the horrors Mary Walmsley had told her about.

No!

She would not be a victim of this beast. Summoning all her courage, she bit down. Her mouth flooded with the metallic bitterness of blood, and he screamed in pain, raising his arm to strike her.

"NO!"

That roared word came not from her, but from the doorway. Suddenly, her attacker was yanked away from her, and Justin was planting his fist in the man's face. Blood spurted from the beaky nose and streamed down to join the river flowing from his mouth. Knight landed on the floor and scuttled toward the door on his hands and knees.

He gave Justin a look of loathing, then, scrambling to his feet, he turned and ran, bumping the door and stumbling as he went. Celestine wiped her mouth, surprised to find blood, likely Knight's, on her lips. Justin came back to her and put his arm around her shoulders. She trembled against the solid, comforting wall of his chest.

For a moment, neither of them said anything. Then Justin gently pushed her away and looked into her eyes.

"Are you all right, my dear? Shall I call your aunt?"

"No!" Celestine blurted. "No, I will be fine."

"He didn't . . . didn't harm you?"

Justin's hair was mussed and his cravat askew. Celestine automatically straightened it for him, and then her fingers went up to smooth his hair, the fine silkiness slipping through her fingers as she looked up into his eyes, dark in the dim light of the library.

"What made you come in here?" she asked.

He looked down, sheepishly. "I . . . I was looking for you. I saw you leave the room, and I wanted to tell you . . . well, I wanted to let you know how fine you look tonight. Garnets suit you. You should always wear them."

Celestine pulled away from him, her emotions a jumble of fear at the attack, embarrassment that Justin should find her, and worry that Knight would retaliate in some way.

"I think I deserve a little something in gratitude, don't you think?" Justin said, his voice husky as he advanced toward her. He gazed down into her eyes as he pulled her close and lowered his face to hers. "Don't you want to thank me, Celestine?"

Before their lips touched, Celestine pulled away. "No, my lord. I . . . I must return, or go up to my room."

He expected favors out of gratitude! Celestine was burning with shame. Had the scene he witnessed left him thinking she had met Knight here and it had gotten out of hand? Or did he think she was soiled goods now, to be pawed at will?

"Don't be a ninny! Let me comfort you, Celestine. I promise you, I shall make you feel much better."

"You are no better than he!" Celestine panted, circling the desk away from Justin. "Is that all men want? To impose themselves and their animal desires on women? I could have handled Mr. Knight, my lord, and I would appreciate it if you do not think you can claim my favors out of some misplaced gratitude!"

It was more than she had intended to say. Indeed, it wasn't even fair, but she felt harassed, hunted, like a deer pursued through the forest by ravening wolves. There was a light in his eyes she didn't like in the slightest, and she must quench it.

It worked. His brightness was extinguished, to be replaced by coldness.

"You would compare me to that . . . that *beast* who attacked you?"

"Why not? So you handle yourself with more suaveness. You still want the same thing, don't you?" There was more vehemence and bitterness in her voice than she had intended, but her anger built, anger at being toyed with by him for his own mysterious ends, and pain at the knowledge there could never be anything more between them but an exchange of her favors for his protection. That was the only avenue available to a poor governess and a rich aristocrat.

Justin drew himself up, a cool hauteur settling over his perfect features. "I had not realized my friendliness was so repugnant to you. You seemed not to mind my caresses so very much. I had reason to believe I was not the only one who sought your favors. And all because I wanted to give you a little romance, a little something to remember in your spinsterhood!"

His face twisted in an ugly grimace. "I thought when you were old, it would be pleasant for you to look back and be able to say once you were kissed by a lord! I felt sorry for you, but I see my pity was wasted. I will bother you no more."

He whirled and exited the room, but at the door he stopped. He was silent for a moment, then sighed. Not meeting her eyes, he said, his voice more gentle, more like his usual tone, "I will give out that I saw you in the hall, and you were headed up to your room with a sick headache. Would you like me to send your aunt to you?"

Celestine's whispered "No," echoed in the still room and she watched him quietly leave, shutting the door behind him to give her some privacy.

Humiliation rushed in on her, filling her eyes and aching in her breast, threatening to burst out and consume her. So that was what his attentions were motivated by! She was an object of pity, to be offered the bones of a few kisses and caresses to remember in her lonely old age. Self-pity washed over her and tears streamed down her face and dripped off her chin.

And he wouldn't bother her after that—oh, no, not after what she had said to him. Had she really compared him to that animal who had attacked her? How could she have?

If only she could go back a half hour, or even fifteen minutes—go back and take back the words she had said. Maybe he wouldn't have told her the truth then. Maybe he would have kissed her again, held her close to her heart, and she could have believed he cared for her a little.

But it was better this way, she tried to tell herself. Better to know the truth. Better to have no illusions. Wasn't it?

But she would give anything just to believe it for a while. She would give anything to feel herself loved by Justin St. Claire, as far out of reach to her as the stars in the sky—out of reach not only by virtue of his position, but by his brilliance, his very being. How many other women felt as she did about him?

Too many to count, perhaps. She sat down behind the desk and laid her head on the blotter, soaking it with her salty tears. And she just one of the many.

Thirteen

The water was starting to cool and Celestine reluctantly climbed from the copper hip bath, drying herself and dressing in the chilly confines of her chamber. The heat from the water had seeped into her bones and made it so much easier to get up and move around.

She examined herself in the cracked mirror above the tall old dresser. She had sustained no bruises from Mr. Knight's attack, but she felt different somehow, more vulnerable. Should she tell someone? Did he do this to other women? Who would believe her, and what could they do about it?

The helplessness of her position frightened her. If she did tell someone, she would almost certainly lose her position. Lady St. Claire would never stand for a woman in her employ to be accusing a wealthy acquaintance of attempting rape. She would become notorious, not he.

That was what had happened to Mary Walmsley, the village woman she knew who had been raped. Mary had been a maid at a bishop's house in London. One of the bishop's acquaintances did the horrible deed to her, not once but repeatedly, and when she became pregnant and could hold her silence no longer, she was dismissed. It was bandied about she had hoped to trap the man into marriage and was taking out her spite on him when it didn't work. She was an immoral slut, gossip said, who had lured the man into her bed.

Mary, a chaste innocent when she left the village, returned a broken woman, only to be shunned by some of the more narrow-minded citizens even in her hometown. She and her child lived in poverty, ineligible for the charity of the church because of her supposed transgression.

Celestine could do nothing but hope no one else ended up alone with Mr. Knight.

Anna and Betty, the two strong maids-of-all-work, came in and started to haul the bath out to the hall, but they fell back when Lady St. Claire entered the room. It was unheard of for her to mount to the third floor unless it was to visit the schoolroom, and Betty gaped in astonishment.

Lady St. Claire was at her most regal, chin up, head held high. She gazed at the bath with a frown on her lovely face.

"What is that doing in here?"

Celestine, rising from a curtsy, looked at her in consternation. "It is my morning bath, my lady. The bath you and the marquess kindly ordered."

"I? Or August?" Her eyebrows were arched in high curves over her startling blue eyes. "I never did such a thing," she stated. "A morning bath for the hired help? We cannot tie up the maids that way, especially with a house full of guests. This is monstrous! How did this come about?"

"B-b-but I was told Lord St. Claire . . ."

"Beggin' yer pardon, my lady," Anna, a stout, red-faced country girl, said, gazing nervously at her employer. "It was Lord St. Claire, the marquess's *brother*, what ordered a bath for Miss Simons ev'ry mornin'. Sed as how it wuz for her artyritis."

Lady St. Claire's face blanched, then turned pink. "Justin?" Her whole frame trembled with indignation. "This is absolutely unheard of and will stop this instant! He has no authority . . . we have a house full of guests, and I cannot . . ." She ran out of words, speechless with rage.

"Go!" she ordered Anna and Betty, and they quickly tugged the bath away, shutting the door behind them.

Lady St. Claire circled Celestine, eyeing her usual gray dress and nodding. Celestine's mind worked furiously. Was she going to be fired? What if she was? Those thoughts superseded others in her brain, but she knew later, when she had time to reflect, she would wonder at Justin's kindness in thinking of the bath for her arthritis.

The marchioness drew to a halt in front of Celestine. "I came up here to ask what you meant last night by prancing around in front of my guests in finery ill-befitting your station, after my *kindness* in allowing you to join the festivities."

Taking a deep breath and letting it out slowly, Celestine considered what to say. She would not blame her aunt. Emily had only thought to give her some pleasure, and she would not repay that kindness with tattling.

She swallowed. "I am sorry, my lady. It was ill-considered of me. I . . . I only thought since you kindly invited me to dine, I should . . ."

"I was humiliated in front of my friends. Lady van Hoffen could not believe I allowed my governess to dress up in silks and jewels and pass herself off as one of the guests! And to finish off your insolence, you disappear, and I must find out from Justin you retired to your room with the headache!"

Celestine gazed down at the bare wood floor. This was it. She was going to be let go, and likely without a reference. Aunt Emily would take her in, but she could not impose on her for long without finding another job. She had hoped to keep this one until Lottie and Gwen were ready to make their London debut.

She glanced up at the marchioness. Lady St. Claire had seemed quite happy with her work until now. Maybe she could be appealed to. It went against the grain to grovel, but she really wanted to stay. She had come to love the girls, and she was enchanted with the Lake District, the magnificent fells and varied scenery. Never would she be so lucky as to find such an elevated situation again.

And never would she see Justin again! A jagged rush of pain took her breath away for a moment. Never see him again—never gaze into the blue of his brilliant eyes, never hear his husky, masculine voice, the voice that sent chills rushing down her spine . . .

She must not think of Justin. Her feelings for him were tumultuous and confused. Right now her job was at stake.

"M-my lady, please accept my apologies for last night. I . . . I realized the folly of my actions even as I went in to dinner, but I saw no graceful way out. That is why I retired to my room so early." It was close enough to the truth. She *had* felt it to be a mistake.

Lady St. Claire's face softened. Her tightly clenched mouth relaxed and she gazed into Celestine's eyes. "All right. I accept your apology. You have been so good with the children, and I have been very pleased with your work so far. I would not want to lose you. Let us forget about this and go on as before, Miss Simons. But the morning bathing must stop. It is much too inconvenient for the maids to be hauling water and the bath all the way up here."

Celestine dropped a curtsy. "Thank you, my lady. You will not regret it, I promise you."

"See that I don't."

Justin stroked the cue and slammed a ball into the corner pocket. How could she treat him as if he were in the same class as that bounder, Knight? What would a prissy little gray mouse of a governess know about men and what that depraved animal's intentions were? Did she know she was within moments of his lifting her skirts and forcefully invading her soft body with his? He had heard whispers about Knight before, about his willingness to abuse women he considered of a lower class.

Justin had gone directly from the library to challenge

the bastard to a fight, but the coward had already fled the house, leaving his would-be batterer with an excess of angry energy. He knocked several more balls into pockets, paying no attention to how he got them there, or in what order, as he remembered his frustration and sleepless night. Celestine's words had haunted him as he tossed and turned beneath the covers, and even an early morning ride had not rid him of the echo of her voice.

The rest of the men lounged in big leather chairs by the hearth in the billiards room, smoking cigars and drinking coffee, but he didn't feel like joining in with conversations about horses or land problems or the taxation laws. He was brooding and he knew it. It was totally unlike him, and it made him even angrier that Celestine Simons, spinster governess, somehow had the power to leave him feeling humiliated and uncomfortable with himself. He liked to feel good about himself and usually did, so what was wrong this morning?

He had saved her from God knows what fate, damn it! Knight was a brutish type. He had known men who enjoyed sexual conquest more if the woman was unwilling, and it sickened him to the core. And she had the ingratitude . . . Justin stopped and laid down his cue stick. He passed one long-fingered hand through his hair and paced away from the table to stare up at a painting of some ancient St. Claire ancestor that hung on the wall.

Ingratitude?

He stalked away from the painting and stared, unseeing, through the window.

She had just been attacked—had been in fear for her virtue and maybe for her life, for all she knew. And he had waltzed in, driven the animal off, then demanded a reward for his good deed—while she was frightened. While she was still dealing with the aftermath of what must be a most terrifying experience for a woman.

He remembered her wide, panicked eyes and heaving breast, the fear etched in every feature of her face from those wide eyes to the added pallor of her skin, and the blood on her lip from valiantly biting the detestable Knight. She had been in shock and he had taken brute advantage of that.

And then on top of that he had been unforgivably brutal in what he had said to her. He had been unfeeling, and he was ashamed. How could he ever make that up to her?

But still, he was nothing like that animal, Knight. He did not go around forcing his attentions on women. In fact, they usually initiated the lovemaking. He had never lacked for female companionship in his life. At that moment there were two women in the house hoping for his attention and another panting to get into his bed. Maybe he would take Lady van Hoffen up on her blatant attempts at seduction. Maybe that was what he needed, instead of fixating on a prim, plain governess with no attractions except for a sweet voice and big gray eyes.

The image of Celestine as she appeared the previous evening rose up in his mind. It wasn't quite true she had no attractions. He remembered glancing up at the staircase and seeing her, radiant in rose silk, her hair gleaming in the light from the chandelier. She had gazed down at him, an unreadable look on her oval face.

In that moment he had forgotten anything but that he had kissed those full lips and they were delicious. He had felt that soft, feminine body and found it arousing. He had touched her soul one night in a dark church and found it unbearably beautiful.

There was a simple beauty in her lack of pretension and her honest gaze. She didn't simper or smirk or flirt or giggle like other women did in his presence. Was that why he couldn't stop thinking about her? Or was he just piqued because she hadn't responded to his lovemaking as other women did? And what was he going to do about it?

Celestine kept to herself the next few days, avoiding the house party as much as possible. She concentrated all her attention on keeping her job, voluntarily taking on extra work like caring for Bertie while his nursemaid was pressed into service fetching and carrying for the guests.

She was sitting in the schoolroom with Bertie on her lap when Lady Grishelda tapped lightly on the door and asked to join her.

"Please do," Celestine cried. Except for her aunt, she had spoken to no one for days, and she realized she had become spoiled by the company of Justin, Lady Grishelda, and Emily. It would be lonely when they all left again.

"Where are the little girls?" Lady Grishelda said, sitting in a chair opposite Celestine and tucking her lavender skirts around her legs.

"The Misses Stimson longed to go skating, and they wished to take Lottie and Gwen with them. Elise accompanied them to look after their needs. I have Bertie to take care of right now, so I couldn't join them."

The other woman gazed critically at the little boy, who was snuggled on Celestine's lap, his head on her chest, fast asleep. "Ugly little brutes, aren't they? Boy children, I mean."

Celestine gazed at her in shocked silence.

"Oh, I know women are supposed to dote on the little monsters, but I am not much of one for children, beyond feeling they should be clothed and fed and educated properly, of course. You appear to like them, though. Am I right?"

"Yes. Sometimes I feel Lottie and Gwen are my own, and then I realize I will likely never have the opportunity to have children. It saddens me sometimes."

"But surely what you are doing is better? You are your own woman, independent, making your own way, beholden to no one."

Celestine gazed over at the plainly dressed young woman in front of her, and then laughed softly. "Ah, yes. The women's freedom movement." She looked down tenderly at Bertie's fuzzy head resting on her bosom and

held his hand in hers, rubbing the tender skin with her
thumb. His hand flexed and curled around her finger,
and he sighed sleepily, adjusting himself on her lap.

He was a warm little bundle, fragrant from his bath,
with that particular "baby" smell. Celestine rubbed her
lips over his satiny-soft hair. She caught Lady Grishelda's
curious gaze on her again, and said, "I would give up in
a moment whatever independence I have for a man I
love, a home, and children."

"But right now you are controlled by no man. You
make your own way and your own decisions!" The young
woman's gaze was incredulous, her pale-blue eyes wide in
disbelief.

"You believe that?" Celestine said, thinking about Mr.
Knight's attack, Justin's rescue, and her precarious position at Ladymead. "I don't really, you know. I was lucky
to get this position. The marquess is a good man, the
marchioness a fair woman, and the working conditions
better than many governesses could hope for. But still,
my employment could be terminated at any time for anything, even their whims. And if they dismissed me without
a reference, I would find it difficult to get another job.
I'll never starve; I am luckier than most, for I have an
aunt who would take me in. But I *do* want to earn my
keep, and I want to work with children. So much for making my own decisions. That is their extent."

Lady Grishelda was speechless for a moment. Then she
colored faintly. "I . . . I'm afraid you must have had a bit
of a hard time after the dinner party the other evening."

Celestine glanced at her curiously. "How did you
know?"

"My mother spent a good half hour pouring a lovely
helping of vitriol in the marchioness's ear about your im-
pudence in dressing in silk when you should have known
your station."

Celestine remembered Lady van Hoffen's whispered
conference with Lady St. Claire and the venomous
glances darted her way. The marchioness had said as

much when she berated Celestine for her presumption. And she remembered something else, too.

"I think perhaps," she said, slowly, "you did not approve, either, my lady. I saw how you gazed at me when I came down the stairs. Pardon me if I am too bold, but I was curious to know what you were thinking."

Lady Grishelda plucked at the worn fabric of the chair arm and gazed into the hearth, now containing only embers of the fire that was there. "I must admit, I was shocked. I thought we had a kinship, you and I." She looked into Celestine's eyes with honesty and forthrightness.

"I thought you more sensible than to want silks and satins and jewels. I thought we had in common our belief that marriage, as an institution, is designed for men by men, and that you would not lower yourself to dress frivolously for the purpose of attracting notice." She lifted her square chin at that. "I am sorry if I am too blunt."

"No, I invited your honesty."

A tiny smile lifted the corners of the woman's thin lips. "Many people claim to respect honesty, but few do, in reality."

"That is true." Celestine stared pensively into the fireplace, at the flickering coals that still radiated waves of warmth. She cuddled Bertie to her. "And I think it is a fair question, why I dressed myself in silks and jewels this once. I am plain. I have always been plain, and I have arthritis as an affliction. Also, my life until a year ago was devoted to my father."

"I have heard about your loss. I'm sorry," Lady Grishelda murmured. "How difficult caring for your father must have been for you, not having your freedom or any ability to plan for your future."

"I loved him, and I would do it all over again exactly the same way." Her lips curved up in a smile and her gray eyes were glazed as she stared back into the past. She laid her cheek against the little boy's downy head. "My father was the sweetest, dearest man who ever lived.

He wanted so much for me to have a Season and a chance at marriage, but I refused. We could have afforded it, barely. Aunt Emily would have sponsored me. But Papa would not have been able to go with me and I could not leave him alone with only servants to look after him."

Lady Grishelda said nothing, but eyed her curiously. Celestine caught the glance and continued. "You're wondering what that had to do with my dressing inappropriately two evenings ago. You see, it was a first for me, and I could not resist. You have made the choice to eschew beautiful silks and jewels. For me the choice was made by life. When Aunt Emily coaxed me to wear that dress, one of her own cut down to my size, I could have said no. Perhaps I should have said no; it nearly cost me my job. But I wanted to know, just once, what it felt like to walk down the stairs in a lovely gown and join the company at dinner under the glittering chandeliers at a beautifully set dining table."

Looking down at her hands, Lady Grishelda murmured, "And it was spoiled for you by my mother's ill-natured gossip and my reproving glare. I am so sorry, Miss Simons. I had no right . . ."

"Please." Celestine hushed her. "That one moment was worth it. I didn't lose my job, and everything is still the way it was."

"I think perhaps freedom is a much more complicated issue than I perceived," Lady Grishelda said.

Nodding, Celestine said, "In a perfect world, women and men would be free to use their talents and abilities without the strictures of their place in society or their sex to bind them, but we live in an imperfect world. I, for one, can only do the best with what I have been given."

Silence fell between the two women, each one lost in her own thoughts. The schoolroom clock tapped out the seconds, and the embers in the grate crackled and moved as coal disintegrated into ash.

"Will you call me Celestine, instead of Miss Simons? I feel we are friends, if that is not too presumptuous."

Lady Grishelda looked up with shining eyes. "I would be honored, Celestine. But only if you call me May."

"May?"

"My middle name. I *hate* my name," she said, frowning. "It was a family name that I am forced to use. May is the name my mother chose, and what she calls me when she remembers to talk to me at all."

Celestine heard the anguish behind the words, but felt the area too painful to probe.

The young woman brightened a moment later, though, and said, "I hear you sing. I wish you had stayed long enough the other night so we could have heard you. I adore good singing, though my own voice is more like that of a frog than a bird, I am afraid."

"I will be singing a solo in the Christmas pageant on Friday night at the church. I hope you will come."

"Aren't you nervous to perform in front of everyone like that?"

Celestine considered the question, her head to one side as she absently smoothed Bertie's hair. "Not really. Oh, if I think about it, yes, I am nervous. But I know when I start to sing all of that will leave me. I'll be fine."

"I look forward to it, Celestine. I really do."

The two young women smiled across at each other, a bond forged, a friendship made, a bargain sealed.

Fourteen

His very presence must be repugnant to her, Justin thought bitterly, but he could not help that. He had promised something and a gentleman always kept his word. He tapped on the door of the schoolroom and entered, finding her with her head bent over as she worked on something at the table. She glanced up and paused, seeing him.

"Lord St. Claire! I . . . what can I do for you?"

"I finished the play, Miss Simons," he said, his voice stiff and formal. "I felt you might need it to make any changes you see fit, and to make and design your puppets accordingly."

"Oh, I am done the puppets, my lord," she said, her cheeks pinkening as she moved away from the table so he could see past her.

He glanced, then looked again and chuckled despite his awkwardness near her. *Papier-mâché* puppet heads clearly recognizable as Aurelius, Reginald, Parlia, Calista, and the ugly girl, Hepzibah, were lined up on the table. Aurelius had crisp brown hair and blue eyes, while Calista was a stunning blond with violet eyes. The ugly girl who was being betrothed to Prince Aurelius was hook-nosed and snaggletoothed and had a wart on her nose. The clothes for Aurelius and his queen, laid out in front of each puppet head, were very regal, fit for forest royalty in shades of green and brown. Scraps of lace adorned the queen's dress.

"Very good, Miss Simons. I only hope the play is up to the standards of the players." He handed her the sheaf of papers and turned to go. He turned back before he got to the door but did not meet her gaze. "The, uh, Calista puppet, though—she should have gray eyes. And, uh, brown hair. Very *long* brown hair, silky and beautiful. And freckles." His voice was husky, and he cleared his throat. "I find I have a certain fondness for large gray eyes and freckles."

"I wish you would let me help you, my dear," Emily said to her niece, as the governess got ready in her aunt's chamber.

"Hmm? Help me?" Celestine turned around in front of the cheval glass, examining her lavender dress, making sure it was absolutely tidy.

"Yes, *help* you. Financially. So you won't have to stay a governess forever. You could even have a long-delayed London Season, if you wished," Emily answered in frustration.

Her niece was the most infuriating person on earth. Thanks to a brilliant marriage many years ago and a separation settlement with an ample allowance from her husband, Baxter Delafont, Marquess of Sedgeley, Emily had more money than she knew what to do with. And shut away in self-imposed exile in Yorkshire, she had very little to spend it on. Her gowns were several years out of date and she had not bought anything for herself for quite a while.

She would have loved to spend some of her bounty on her niece. But Celestine had never been willing to accept more than the smallest trumpery gifts. Emily wanted to make her independent—settle some money on her, give her a dowry—but the girl refused. She watched her fuss over her plain lavender gown and simple heart locket, her only adornment, getting ready for the Christmas pageant concert at the church that evening.

Celestine was a serious woman, even as she had been a serious, steady girl. She needed some *fun* in her life. Instead, from the time she was sixteen she had nursed her seriously ill father. After his death, she had immediately taken on the job of governess to the St. Claire children.

And yet, under that serious, calm, intelligent *façade,* Emily had always sensed a wild, passionate side that came out only when Celestine sang. Then one could hear the longing, the untamed turbulence of her soul, keening in high, lovely tones sad enough to make an angel weep. Celestine was an example of what happened when a strong character set all its effort on taming and subduing the ferocious desire and tremulous longing of a wild heart.

Was she imagining things? Was Celestine's outward serenity a reflection of inner tranquillity? She thought not, but her niece was reticent and Emily was loath to pry. Sometimes all a woman had was her inner life.

Beyond her one momentous admission that she had fallen in love with Justin St. Claire, Celestine had said nothing. She had retired that night without another word to anyone, and Emily had left her in peace to recover from her fractured heart as best she could. No one else could help you. Emily knew that from bitter personal experience over the last five years of separation from a husband she had loved always.

She watched in concern the stiffness of Celestine's movements. "Are the hot baths no longer helping, my dear?"

"I . . . I am no longer taking the baths."

"What? Why not?" Emily, angry, rose from her chair to stand in front of her niece. "Do you *want* to be crippled? Those baths are the only thing that will get you through the rest of the winter in comfort. My dear, you were *improving!* Why would you stop taking them?"

Celestine colored and fiddled with the locket. "I did not cancel them. Lady St. Claire did."

"Why? Was she not the one who instigated them in the first place?"

Celestine turned away, but Emily took her shoulder and turned her around, searching her expression for clues.

"I . . . no, apparently neither Lord nor Lady St. Claire ordered the hot bath every morning."

"Then who?" Emily's elegant brows arched in puzzlement.

"It was Lord *Justin* St. Claire."

Emily was stunned. She knew Justin, knew him well. He was a nice enough fellow, witty and handsome, but a care-for-nothing sort, the epitome of a *tonnish* rake. He was elegant and lazy and charming. He was also without scruples or morals as far as women were concerned, only kept from seduction of innocents by his lack of desire for marriage and horror of being shunned in society, or at least so she had always deemed him.

Yet he had ordered a plain spinster governess in his brother's employ was to have a hot bath every morning to ease her arthritic joints. It seemed unlikely, and she questioned Celestine closely, but the maid had informed her of the fact in the presence of the marchioness. The brothers were both occasionally referred to as Lord St. Claire, and so Celestine had assumed the older brother was meant—natural enough, since it was his house and his authority to order the servants around.

Emily sat back down in her chair by the fireplace as Celestine prepared to go to the church before everyone else. This required some thought. Anytime someone did something completely out of character, it required thought. Justin St. Claire, bothering about the comfort of a governess? It definitely needed contemplation.

"Not that way, Dooley!" Justin ripped another cravat from his neck and flung it on the floor. He grabbed one and tried it himself but failed, and finally resigned himself to his valet's competent ministrations.

"I suppose that will have to do," he said finally, fastening a ruby stickpin in the folds and surveying his reflection in his mirror. He caught the grimace on his man's face. "I know I've been a bear, Dooley. My apologies, old man."

"Not necessary, my lord." He picked up Justin's hat, gloves, and stick and handed them to him, then retired to pick up the half dozen spoiled cravats on the floor.

"Yes, it is necessary. You know, there is a saying no man is a hero to his valet. I suppose that is true, for at the end of the day we are all just men, and we have our moods and our fits and our weaknesses. A valet sees them all, perhaps more than even a wife. I am sorry if I have been impossible lately, Dooley."

He turned to glance at the thin, colorless man behind him as he pulled on his gloves. Dooley straightened.

"May I say, my lord, it has always been a pleasure to serve you. You are normally the most equable of men, but each man is fallible." A ghost of a smile flitted across his bony visage. "My Bessy has to put up with my frightful moods, and is marvelous sweet about it, sir."

For the first time Justin gazed at Dooley and saw a man—a tired, thin, aging man who provided for his small family by being valet to a spoiled aristocrat. Dooley was a husband and a father, and yet year after year Justin pulled him away from London and his wife and children at Christmas so he could be dressed and pampered in his accustomed luxury.

It would not do.

"Dooley," he said, casually, "I think you should start training a younger man for your job. A likely young 'un who is looking to step up."

Dooley looked startled and then alarmed. "S-sir? Have I said something to offend? If so, I b-b . . ."

"Don't be a dolt, Dooley. I am merely thinking next year it would be nice if you could stay in London with

your family at Christmas instead of traipsing across the
countryside with me. You could stay and look after the
London house so Sanderson can go home to Hampshire
for a week or two. The house doesn't need a butler when
there's no one to butle, and Sanderson rarely gets the
opportunity to visit his family!"

Dooley looked stunned, and silently bowed over his
armload of cravats. Justin, whistling a tune and cheerier
than he had been in days, exited the room.

All the villagers and country folk for miles around came
to the concert, as well as the gentry. It was a festival of
seasonal music, with a pageant consisting of the retelling
of the story of the birth of Jesus. It was a scene doubtlessly
replayed an endless number of times around the country
and greeted with the same enthusiasm by the congrega-
tion, family, and friends of the participants.

The Ellerbeck choir was neither very good nor very
bad, and they wended their way through a program of
music made bearable by a decent organist and a concert-
master with a good ear and a realistic appreciation of
what his choir was capable of. The concert wound down,
and the angels, shepherd, and wisemen filed out of the
church, followed by Joseph and Mary carrying the holy
babe. A final piece was on the schedule for the choir,
and Justin steeled himself. It was the piece that had emotionally shattered him when he had heard them rehearse
it, the piece with Celestine's solo.

The choir started. He was in the family box along with
his brother, sister, and their houseguests. Lady van Hoffen
had managed to maneuver it so she was beside him, and
she chose that moment to place her hand on his thigh.

He jumped and threw her a look. She chose to see it
as encouragement and her gloved hand began to trail up
his thigh until she brushed against his groin, letting her
fingers delicately flick over him. He cast another beseech-

ing look her way, but she merely responded by squeezing him and licking her lips provocatively.

He moved, pushing her hand away. If she thought she was being titillating, she had spectacularly poor taste. They were in a church with his family. Surely she could see the inappropriateness of her conduct!

Then Celestine's solo started, and he had no attention for anything else. He found himself on the edge of his seat, not even daring to breathe. He *hadn't* just imagined it the first time, this power she wielded over his senses. Even with a restless crowd around him, the smell of hundreds of people, the presence of his family, her voice lifted him up. The crowd hushed in deference to the first truly beautiful thing they had heard all evening, and he closed his eyes.

He was at the height of the vaulted ceiling again, chills running down his back like light fingers. The sweet, agonizingly lovely tones throbbed through his body and he was conscious of nothing but Celestine. He thought back on their awkward friendship, if that was what it could be called.

From the first moment he had determined to seduce her, if not in body, then in mind. It had been a goal to while away a boring tenure in Cumbria, something to do until he could go back to London. Justify it to himself as he might, that he intended to strike a blow for freedom against Elizabeth's tyranny, still it had been a game. Instead, he had become aware of how fine she was, how achingly beautiful her soul. She gave of herself; she sublimated her passions and needs, sacrificing them to the wants and needs of others, taking joy from giving.

But there was a fierce intelligence and spirit behind those calm gray eyes. It was as though her calm exterior was a crucible, containing the molten elements of the earth. He had touched it only when he kissed her and felt her melt to liquid fire against him. What other man would recognize that heat and passion within her and care enough to bring it out?

He knew many men felt any exhibition of passion from a lady was nigh unto admitting she was tainted, a whore in spirit if not in reality. Women were supposed to be void of those feelings, with spirits that lifted them above earthly passion. But those poor, misguided sots mistook passion for the lewd groping of a woman like Lady van Hoffen.

That wasn't passion, that was lust, a single element of the higher feeling. Passion, he had come to believe over the past weeks, had a spiritual element, a refined, sweet aspect involving longing and sacrifice, giving and . . . love. Love?

Justin swallowed hard, his hands gripping the edge of the wood bench as he listened to the song Celestine sang, and then the choir's voices joined her and she was lost in the chorus. The music swelled, filling the small church with a joyful noise that must surely shatter the gorgeous stained glass windows.

And then it was over, and August and Elizabeth were leading the way out of the church into the chilly night air. Justin, numb and bewildered, went through the motions expected of him, joining his family in speaking to the vicar and the choirmaster, a little popinjay named Jenks.

But he paid little attention to what was going on around him. He was on the precipice of something important and wanted to get away for a while and think. But this was a most inopportune time for introspection. Charlotte Stimson was clutching his arm on one side. Her sister took his other arm, and he was hauled down the church steps without even a chance to look for Celestine, to see if she was close by.

There was to be a reception at Ladymead for all the choir and their families. It was the most plebeian event of the year, along with the summer festival held at Ladymead, reflecting the more informal manners of the country. A veritable caravan of carriages, carts, and horses wound its way in the sparkling moonlight up to the big house, as Ladymead was known in the village.

The ballroom was open for the party and Justin circulated amongst the crowd, still lost in thought after what he had been contemplating in church. What did it mean? What had happened to him that he was suddenly lost in high-flown contemplation of love?

He had been wont to describe love as a trap for men and a sop for women. It trapped men into conceiving and caring for families and it made up to women for all the power they lacked in the world. But it had not escaped his attention over the years that his brother's marriage was a love match, and he had never seemed trapped.

Justin could not understand the feelings August appeared to have for Elizabeth. She was beautiful, it was true, but she was bossy, managing, and sharp-tongued. Yet August doted on her. It must be love that made his sensible, intelligent brother overlook the failings of the woman and think she was perfect in spite of myriad faults.

But love just wasn't right for him, even if it did exist. He was not made to cleave to one woman, and his inherent sense of fairness would not allow him to take a wife and then cheat on her. He had thought to take a wife when all the wenching was out of his system, if that day ever came. He never expected to fall in love, though women seemed to fall in love with him every time he bowed to one, or asked one to dance.

Was love, if it existed, a female trait? Were men formed only for sexual conquest? His lovers and mistresses had all been willing to lie with him, some professing to love him, their love soon enough turning cold when the baubles stopped coming. The debutantes he had flirted with recovered from their disastrous love for him as quickly as they realized he had no intention of vying for their hand, and each had gone on to other men and marriage.

But Celestine—she had burned in his arms like an ember. His moments with her had been different from anything he had ever experienced. For a time he had been sure his feelings were entirely sexual. He was convinced that to bed her would be like loving fire, the heat consuming him before his hunger was sated. He would not survive it unscorched. Now he didn't know what to think. There were moments when he had no desire to have sexual intercourse with her, times when what he wanted was to talk to her and watch her or even just be with her.

She was across the room with an elderly woman from the village, bringing her a glass of punch and bending over to speak to her. Was Celestine plain? He remembered thinking so, disparaging her freckles, her pale complexion, her nondescript hair color. Now all he could see was her grace and litheness. He knew what her hair looked like unbound, how it caught light and became a river of shining silk. He had felt how she molded to him until their two bodies became one, even through cloth, so close he could feel her heartbeat.

But more than that, he had felt their souls reach out and touch in the church while she sang. It was as if something inside of her broke free and soared, taking him with her, swirling and diving, unbound and glorious. Would the good, dull reverend ever understand Celestine, ever appreciate her rare magic?

As he thought about the vicar and his avowed intention of marrying Celestine, he saw Mr. Foster wend his way through the crowd and take her aside. She nodded at something he said, a serious expression on her face, and disappeared with him out the doors into the hall.

What were they doing? Where were they going? It was obvious to Justin. He had as good as stated his intention to ask her to marry him. What better place to make the announcement than at the party celebrating Christmas?

Without thinking, he followed. He saw the tail of the reverend's sober black coat disappear behind the drawing-room door, and the door closed quietly. Justin paced uncertainly in the hall. Should he break it up? But that would only put off the inevitable; there was no point to that. And why should he want to, anyway? Should he not want what was best for Celestine? Surely a good marriage was better than life as a governess. He tossed back the glass of brandy he held and set it down on a table.

As he paced up and down in the chilly hall, the door opened and he stopped, frozen in indecision. Foster came out and quietly closed the door behind him. He didn't notice St. Claire standing by a large potted palm, and strolled by with a thoughtful expression on his face.

Justin waited for Celestine to emerge as well. She didn't. What was she waiting for?

Impatiently, Justin finally paced over and opened the door. Her back was to him and she ran her fingers over the keys of the piano. She sat down at the bench, still oblivious to Justin's presence, and touched the keys again, then rubbed her fingers, the swollen knuckles paining her, perhaps.

But then she softly touched the keys again and started singing. Justin stopped, mesmerized. Her head was thrown back and she sang a ballad, in Italian, of lost love and heartbreak, surely an odd choice for a woman just betrothed.

Stealthily he crept in and stopped in the middle of the thick carpet, not wanting to announce his presence just yet. He closed his eyes, too, and felt it once again—the queer tug, almost pain, under his ribs when he thought of her.

He let her voice surround him, caressing him into hazy unawareness of the dim, chilly room and the impropriety of being alone there with the governess. A warmth suffused his body and his fingers itched to touch her, to smooth her silky hair, to hold her trembling body close to his. He wanted . . . he wanted . . .

He wanted to give her his strength, to shore up her own. He wanted to protect her and release her from the pain of her arthritis. He wanted to shelter her from a life that had no place for her except as a plain little governess, ignoring her extraordinary gift of song, and taking only her care for the children as worth barter. He sighed. He wanted the unattainable.

"My lord!"

She had heard him, and whirled on the piano bench.

"Celestine," he said, approaching her.

She stood and started around him, avoiding his eyes. He grasped her arm and pulled her to a stop. She gazed up at him in the gloom, the only light the illumination from a branch of tapers brought in by Foster. Her eyes were huge and dark in the dimness.

She would marry the reverend and her delicate body would probably bear him a dozen children—if she didn't die in childbirth—and she would work herself into an early grave in gratitude for his condescension. She would be dead by the time she was forty. It must not be, he thought, feeling a wave of fierce longing pierce his soul. She was a brilliant bird, with wings to touch the face of God, and all Foster, or any other stupid male for that matter, could see was her drab little mud-hen exterior.

Justin pulled her close, his blue eyes glittering in the candlelight. Even the marquess would not have recognized his laconic, lazy brother at that moment. To Celestine, in that moment, he looked like an avenging archangel, with sparkling blue eyes and tousled gleaming hair, perfect of form and visage.

"Celestine," he whispered. "Your name means heavenly."

She trembled in his hands, shivers running through her whole body. He gripped her tighter, and she gazed up at him. "S-s-singularly inappropriate, is it not, my lord?"

"No, entirely appropriate, my dear. You have the voice of an angel, and the spirit and soul to lift up a mortal man until he can almost see heaven."

"My lord?"

Justin gazed down into her smoky eyes, then down at her trembling, blush pink lips. Her whole body was shuddering under his fingers and she smelled deliciously of lavender water and woman, an intoxicating combination.

He pulled her against him and took her lips in a kiss. She ignited, her cool lips turning to hot coals against his, her chaste, softly rounded body molding sensually against him. He tentatively flicked her lips with his tongue and felt her body jolt with awareness. Her succulent lips opened like rose petals to rain.

He dipped into her mouth, relishing the heat of her, the taste of her, drunk with the wine of Celestine in his blood. He wanted her and she wanted him, and flames licked his loins as he thought of lowering her to the thick pad of the carpet and ravishing her right there and then.

He tried to steer her toward a sofa along the wall, only to find her strangely resistant. He came up for air to find she was struggling in his arms, her poor strength not enough to free her from his powerful grasp.

When he released her lips, she whimpered, almost sobbing, "Please, my lord, let me go!"

At that moment he heard genuine fear in her voice, and he gazed into her eyes, startled. There was terror there—fear of *him!* In surprise, he let go of her arms.

"Celestine, I . . ."

She whirled and stumbled away, not looking back before throwing herself out the door and racing away up the stairs, judging by the sound of her slippers slapping against the marble.

Oh, God, what had he done? He thrust his fingers into his thick, tousled hair. He had taken a girl who had been attacked by a monster just days before and held her against her will while he forced himself on her! And his intentions had been completely dishonorable. What must she think? What was she feeling?

His first instinct was to go after her, but he restrained himself. He was the *last* person she wanted to see—the last one who could comfort her.

He faced the loathsome truth. He was destined for more of this as he got older. He would become one of those elderly *roués,* their faces haggard from dissipation and too many days in the unhealthy air of London. He would leer at women and grapple with younger and younger girls, watching them turn from him in horror at what he had become.

He made himself sick.

Fifteen

"What do you mean, you're leaving? It's a week until Christmas! What's going on, Justin?" August paced back and forth in front of the huge picture window of the billiards room. He stopped and glared down at his brother from his towering height. "What have you done?"

Justin sighed and rubbed his eyes. He hadn't slept at all the night before and had come to this decision after much soul searching. He could not stay and see what he had done to Celestine. She was afraid of him, for God's sake, and he was afraid of himself. Afraid of feelings stirred so deeply it seemed life would never be the same for him again.

"I . . . I have unfinished business, and I should get back to London and take care of it. I have to go to Questmere first, settle up with my bailiff before I go."

"Unfinished business?" August gazed at him in open astonishment, which changed to cynical smugness. "You mean some doxy left unseduced, don't you? What about Lady van Hoffen? Or are you bored by quarry that succumbs too easily?"

Anger flared in the pit of Justin's stomach. He took a swig of his coffee and choked back the angry words that threatened to spill out. He would not quarrel. "Not at all. I have not had that particular honor, Brother. In light of the shameless way your wife has been throwing those three girls at my head the last week, when would I have had time?"

August paused in his perambulation. "Is that what it is? You know, I can call Elizabeth off. I think she is doing this because she thinks it will please me." A fond gleam entered his eyes and a rare smile danced over his thin lips. "I happened to say that I looked forward to the day when you chose a wife and got serious about life, and I think she took that as a command to find you a suitable *parti.*" He chuckled.

Justin gazed at him. When he was young, his brother had seemed like some perfect god to him. August was six years his senior, and their father was forever holding him up as an example of what Justin should be like. "Justin, why are you not more like August—as smart, responsible, bookish, well-spoken . . . everything." And so Justin had turned from his brother's example and become almost the opposite.

Surprisingly, he and August had never really fought. In fact, his older brother had always turned a fairly indulgent eye on his little brother's escapades. Did it confirm his own superiority? Justin abandoned that thought. August had no need of any boosting for his self-worth. He truly was superior in every way, and maybe that was why Justin had always tried so hard to make himself different. He was *good* at being wicked, the one thing he could surpass August at, and so he seduced and drank and gambled his way through Season after London Season.

But there came a time when sin became boring, an endless idle searching after new depravities. What was left after bedding innumerable wenches, drinking his way through enough wine for a vineyard, and gambling every night for a month, except the more degenerate pleasures?

Friends whispered of brothels where you could get any kind of fantasy fulfilled. Virgins could be bought, twisted hungers sated, every form of human degradation offered. He had never participated, because his tastes had never run that way. He had never gambled more than he could afford to lose, never drunk so much he didn't remember what he did the night before. At least he did not have those evils to regret.

Was it time for him to take the opposite track? He gazed up at his brother, who stared thoughtfully out the window. August was a big man, handsome and bluff, and well, happy. He was happy. Justin was cheerful most of the time, but August was deep-down happy. Was that what marriage did for a man?

He took a deep breath and said, "Gus, what does it feel like?"

"Mmm? What does what feel like?"

"Being in love. Does your stomach feel like it's on fire all the time and your thoughts always center on that one woman? And when she's around, you want just to watch her and listen to her, even if she's not paying any attention to you?"

August stopped in front of his younger brother and looked down at him. Justin was lounging back in a large green wing chair, one booted foot negligently propped on the other knee, and he stared up at his brother uneasily. Had he said too much? What *was* he talking about anyway?

His blue eyes narrowed, August examined his brother's face and said, "So that's it, is it? Who is it? Someone here, or someone back in London? Are you running from or running *to* her?"

"You haven't answered my question." Justin sat up in the chair and examined his hands, clenched together now between his knees.

His elder brother opened his mouth to speak, then gazed down at Justin again. He sat down in the twin to his brother's chair and said, "You know, I was going to toss off a witty remark about love being hell or something like that, but you asked a question, and I'll try to answer.

"Do you know what love is? Love is being bored with the friends you used to think were so entertaining, because you would rather be at home with your wife, just sitting together in front of the fire. Love is wishing you could take away every little trouble or pain or sorrow from her, because you can't bear to see her unhappy.

"Love is longing to get home again when you've been forced to be away, because you know she is waiting for you and nothing is the same without her. Love is hating yourself when your wife is screaming in the agony of childbirth, knowing you caused her that pain, and yet loving beyond anything the miracle you created together."

August lumbered to his feet and clapped his brother on the shoulder. "The burning stomach and desperate yearning? That is when you are not sure your love is returned. It's fear, little brother. If you have to go, I will understand and speak with Elizabeth about it. But if you are running away from love, don't do it. It'll follow you. It did me." He strode from the room.

Justin threw himself back in the chair and stared at the figured ceiling. August didn't know the half of it. It was terrifying to think he might be in love with a woman who *loathed* the sight of him. And, worse than that, *feared* him! He wasn't sure about all of what August had said about love, but he could think only of Celestine, and she couldn't even bear the sight of him—avoided him as though he had some horrible disfigurement. No, that wasn't fair. If he were merely disfigured, she would not turn from him in disgust. He was tainted with his past, condemned to suffer because of his reputation as a womanizer.

And then, in a fit of complete honesty, he admitted he was the author of his own misfortune. At every turn he had put forth efforts to seduce her, rather than just treating her with civility and kindness. She turned from him in revulsion and fear because of his treatment of her, and for no other reason. Wouldn't August laugh if he knew!

Wearily he rose and decided to tell Dooley to start packing. They would go to Questmere first, then on to London.

***

Celestine sat close to the fire in the morning parlor listening to the ladies talk.

"Oh, yes, shako hats are completely exploded," Caroline said, her voice languid and bored.

A desultory conversation concerning fashion drifted among the Stimson girls and Lady van Hoffen, occasionally joined by Lady St. Claire. In another small grouping Grishelda van Hoffen, Emily, and her aging companion and aunt-by-marriage, Dodo Delafont, sat quietly talking about village schools and the necessity, with all the changes in society, of educating the illiterate and, more importantly, the children of the illiterate.

"It breaks my heart," Emily said, her low, silken voice full of emotion, "to see the children whose parents will not allow them to come to the school I have set up. I understand they are needed at home, but I set up the curriculum so some could attend only half days and still receive the benefit."

Dodo nodded sharply. "Shortsighted," she said. Her voice was sharp and vinegary. "Parents should be encouraging their little ones to learn their letters. It's the only way for a child of poverty to move up."

Grishelda, her eyes bright with interest, added, "That way the boys could get better paying jobs as secretaries and bailiffs, or even stewards. And the girls could marry better, or work as governesses or housekeepers."

Celestine listened for a while as she stitched a straight hem on a length of dark green cloth. It was intended to be the curtain for the puppet theater Gus and the blacksmith had constructed. The boy showed a talent, for he had designed it, and was now painting it with bright colors. He had shown it to her that morning, out in one of the succession houses.

And she had offered curtains for it, using old ones from the attic and cutting them down to fit. She had lost much of her enthusiasm for the puppet play, but the children,

Lottie and Gus especially, could talk of nothing else, and she could not disappoint them.

She had read the play Justin had written, and she had been touched and impressed by his ability. It was worlds away from the simple fairy tale he had started with. It contained the essence of poetry, she thought, sharply flavored with broad humor, the perfect touch of tart among the sweet.

But out of it all came a simple love story between a lonely prince and the princess who didn't know she was a princess. Where did he learn to write such beautiful words filled with longing and love? Of course, she thought, she should have realized such an accomplished lady's man would have all the right words.

That was what had scared her the previous evening. She had been terrified by the depth and profundity of her emotion toward him, frightened out of her wits by the desires that raced through her heated blood like silvery, darting minnows in a fast flowing stream. She was cool. She was sensible. But Justin St. Claire, *roué* and seducer, could melt her into a puddle of womanly desires and needs with the touch of his hand and the sound of his sensual voice whispering her name. She knew he would do nothing against her will. She did not fear him as she had Mr. Knight. Her fear was of herself and the seductive whispers in her heart that would have her abandon virtue for the sake of one perfect moment of love.

The marquess came into the parlor and whispered something to his wife. She looked startled, then left with him. Lady St. Claire had maintained a haughty distance from her lately, and Celestine worried that her position was still in jeopardy. But maybe it would be best for her if she went elsewhere.

Somewhere she could be sure of not seeing Justin all the time.

She caught a glance from Emily and bent her head over her work again, trying to ignore the pain shooting through her knuckles. They were getting worse again, but she had so much to do! Aunt Emily had offered to help, but she just could not hand over the precious labor of making the dolls for Gwen and Lottie to someone else. They were a gift from her heart to her young charges, and she would finish them before Christmas Eve, somehow. She glanced up at the clock on the mantle. It was time to go up and retrieve the girls from their nap.

"It's all done, my lord," Dooley said, meeting Justin in the hall.

"Good. Excellent. I shall ride Alphonse, as before, and you and Lester can follow me," he said, speaking of his groom. "We shall bide at Questmere for two days and then head to London. With any luck, I shall have you back with your family by Christmas morn, Dooley."

The valet bowed, and headed back up the stairs. Justin sighed deeply, and headed into the parlor to make his good-byes. He paused outside the door.

He was being a coward. He could not leave things as they were. He turned and headed back into the hall, then up the wide, winding staircase. It was afternoon, and he knew she would be alone. He had seen Elise take the children out a half hour before to play in the snow with Gus and the stable dogs.

He opened the door to the stairs to the third floor and walked up to the hallway. The schoolroom door was ajar and he glanced in, hoping he would not disturb her too badly. He needed to make amends and tell her she would never be burdened by his attentions again. He had to set her mind at ease.

She was by the fireplace in the lumpy chair, with her sewing basket beside her. The woman never stopped, he thought with a smile.

But her head was bowed and her shoulders shook. In the silence of the schoolroom he heard a soft sob, and saw her hands twisted in her lap, one rubbing the other.

A doll lay on her knee, with lips and a nose and the beginning of one eye, the needle sticking out of the cloth.

Had she stabbed herself? Another choking sob split the silence. Without another thought he pushed open the door, made his way to her side, and knelt by her.

"My dear, what have you done?" he asked, taking her gnarled hand in his own. "Did you stab yourself?"

With a soft gasp she looked up, into his eyes. She tried to pull her hand from his, but he held it firmly. He glanced down at the doll. It was a soft cloth doll, with lips embroidered in rose silk threads. Its nose was delicately traced in charcoal thread, and one eye was started, but something had gone wrong.

The stitching was clumsy, even to his untutored eye, not at all like the fine work done on the rosebud lips. There, the stitches were flat and smooth, lying so close together they formed a surface like satin. But the eye was coarsely done, with uneven stitches stabbed haphazardly into the creamy cloth.

"What is wrong?" he asked, rubbing her swollen knuckles. How cold and stiff her fingers were, despite the tiny fire in the schoolroom grate.

"N-nothing, my lord," she muttered, pulling at her hand again.

"It is not nothing, Celestine. You are weeping." With his free hand he traced her tears down one cheek to where they dripped from her firm, small chin, touching her gently with the pad of his thumb.

She turned her face away into his palm, and he felt her lips move. Was it a kiss, or was she speaking? He longed to know.

"What is it? Please tell me."

Her shoulders shook and she wept harder, sniffling and sobbing, ineffectually wiping at her eyes with one hand. Justin pulled a large handkerchief out of his pocket and she was about to take it from him, but he held on to it and dried her tears himself, gently wiping the delicate skin under her eyes and the pink, swollen skin of her eyelids.

She had gone still and closed her eyes under his ministrations. He took the doll and laid it on the table beside the chair. "Now, tell me what is wrong. Maybe I can help."

A watery chuckle escaped her. Her voice was thick, clogged with more tears, and she sniffed. "Unless you are adept at fine embroidery, my lord, you cannot help."

"This?" he asked, pointing to the doll. "*This* is what is upsetting you?"

She turned tragic eyes toward him. "Partly. The . . . the doll is for Gwen. It is a Christmas present, and Christmas is only a week away, and m-my hands . . ."

She broke down again, and Justin gazed down at her crabbed, gnarled hands. She had clasped them in her lap, twisting them together. He took them between his own hands and rubbed them, the knotty joints and tender swelling. She would not meet his eyes, and he felt a pang deep in his heart, like it wanted to split in two. If only he could trade places with her, give her his strong, capable hands, his vigorous health!

He eased himself up beside her on the wide old chair, hearing it creak in protest at its double burden. Then he encircled her in his arms and pulled her close. At his gentle touch she wept, sobbing into his cravat, and he murmured soothing words, nonsense words. Her sobs subsided into shuddering sighs and she grew quiet. Her breathing was more even, and deeper. She had cried herself to sleep in his arms.

He felt a tender wonder steal across his heart, and a hard lump deep within him melted with gratitude. This was what he had wanted to do in the carriage the night of the choir practice.

He cradled her against his heart, pulling her to him until she was settled across his lap like a child. He caressed her tear stained cheek and soft brown hair and gazed at the embers of the fire in the grate.

This was what love was.

This was it, what August had spoken of—the pain when she hurt, the desire to protect her; the urgent wish to shelter her and give her his strength. He sighed. The irony did not escape him that of all the beautiful women who had thrown themselves at him over the years he had finally lost his heart and soul to one plain spinster governess.

Plain in everyone else's eyes. Plain no more to him. She was beautiful; more beautiful than the painted courtesans of London or the wide-eyed debutantes of Bath. More beautiful than Botticelli's angels. This angel had the loveliness of spirit no painting could ever capture, and a voice to pierce the heart of God.

He knew now what was missing from his life and what he needed to make him whole. Other people had a sense of their own worth and took it for granted, not realizing what a precious commodity it was. August knew the valuable role he played in the world, and Elizabeth took her identity from that.

He had never felt a part of anything, needed by anyone, wanted. But here and now, in this bare schoolroom, with a sputtering fire and a woman sleeping in his arms, he found his purpose.

Celestine needed him. She might not love him as he loved her, but she *needed* him. Would it be enough? He inhaled her lavender fragrance and shifted her slightly to be more comfortable. There was something so unutterably right about holding her. Surely she would feel it, too, and know she could trust him.

This had nothing to do with passion. Oh, he felt that for her, too, but more importantly he found he could not imagine going back to his daily routine in life: the friends, the wasteland that was London, the clubs, the women. He wanted to make a life with Celestine.

He rubbed his cheek against her hair and felt her stir. She put one hand up on his chest and he bent his head to kiss the swollen knuckles. A smile drifted over her face and settled on her lips. They curved up, and he watched in fascination as a tiny dimple he had never noticed before appeared at the corner of her mouth. He longed to kiss it, but he would not disturb her.

He cradled her in his arms and closed his eyes. All that was left to do was convince her to marry him. In the past, he would have assumed she would jump at the chance. Now he was not so sure.

Sixteen

She came awake slowly, not wanting to leave the delicious dream she had been having. Was still having. Justin held her on his lap and was whispering he would take care of her always—would make everything better for her.

And then he kissed her brow, tenderly and without the abandon he had displayed at other times. He kissed her as though he loved her, not just lusted after her. She smiled and decided to indulge the hazy remnants of this dream, so much more tactile than other dreams, snuggling against the raspy chin above her, Justin's strong, square chin. He smelled of tobacco and hair pomade, a spicy mixture all his own.

And when she rubbed her cheek against him, she could feel the strong pulse of life in his neck. She brushed her lips across the spot and felt the rumble in his chest as he murmured her name. How real this dream was! Not at all like the one of meeting him in the glade with a red velvet cloak.

Her eyes sprang open. She was in the schoolroom. In the chair. On Justin's lap!

She scrambled with little dignity to her feet, wiping the sleep from her eyes with swollen knuckles. "My lord! You must excuse me. If I had known . . ."

He grinned up at her with that delightful, lazy, wicked twinkle. "I was rather enjoying that. Why don't you come back and wiggle around on my lap some more?"

He patted his lap and she fully realized what she had been doing. She felt a fiery blush rise in her breast, neck, and cheeks. Her whole body was probably pink!

"Please accept my apologies for my inappropriate behavior, my lord," she said in her most prim, spinsterish voice.

"I liked it better when you were asleep and called me Justin." He had a vaguely dissatisfied expression on his handsome countenance.

Celestine backed away from him, gripping her hands behind her back. His expression changed and he stood, straightening his riding breeches and rubbing his legs as though massaging the feeling back into them.

"Please, sit down, Celestine. I have something to say to you. I won't tease again, or make you uncomfortable, I promise." His voice was gentle and his expression thoughtful.

She sidled around him and took her seat, sitting on the edge with her hands clasped together, staring down at them. "How . . . how long were we . . . like that?"

"How long did you sleep in my arms? Perhaps an hour. Maybe a little less."

Her eyes opened wide and her startled glance flew to meet him. "Th-that long? Why did you allow it, my lord?"

His blue eyes were unusually serious as he knelt by her side. "I had my reasons. Do you want to know what they were?"

She remembered now that this was how he had been at first, when he found her crying. He had knelt by her side and begged her to tell him what was wrong. The pain had become excruciating, she had told him, and she would not be able to get the dollies done for Lottie and Gwen in time for Christmas. Her hands were not only too painful, but too clumsy. Straight stitching she could still barely handle, but the fine embroidery of the features was beyond her.

It seemed a silly reason to weep, and perhaps there was more to it than that, but she would never admit as much to herself. She had felt hopeless in that moment, and the reality of her life had flooded in on her in a rare moment of self-pity. She was a poor, plain spinster who would go from governess position to governess position until she was too crippled to work anymore. Then she would become some rich woman's companion, perhaps, if she were very lucky. She was ashamed now of the self-indulgence and weakness she had displayed, but the pain had wracked her and made her vulnerable.

And then he had spoken so softly and sympathetically, his low voice a balm to her, and the strangest feeling had swept over her. His voice was like a warm robe, encircling her, enfolding her in delicious warmth and comfort. She thought if only she could have him near her, speaking to her and with her always, she wouldn't mind the pain anymore.

She did not remember what she had been thinking when he had joined her on the chair and pulled her onto his lap. Perhaps she was no longer thinking of anything. Safe and warm, leaning against his broad chest and feeling the steady thump of his heart, the fresh bout of tears had been for all that could never be. Suddenly she was a watering pot with an endless supply of water.

She didn't understand herself. She never gave in to tears—never! When her father died she had wept, for she had loved him deeply, but then she had called an end to tears and had gone about the business of making all the arrangements. A woman from the village had whispered it wasn't natural to have so much self-control, but she had needed it over years of caring for her sickly father. That was her strength, the ability to rise above pain and sorrow and go on.

But today she had released the flood gates, and look what had happened. She had made a fool of herself in front of the only man she would ever love.

She realized he had not said another word, and looked up to find him waiting patiently, watching her, still kneeling at her side. His eyes were shadowed in the growing dimness of the schoolroom, and they shone with the blue of the twilight sky.

"What . . . what did you ask?"

"I asked if you knew *why* I held you in my arms?"

"No," she said hesitantly. "I don't know why. You are very kind to me."

"Fustian," he said. He took one of her hands and stroked it.

It tingled, and she realized her pain was less than it had been before he held her, as though his strength was seeping into her. "Why, then?"

"Celestine, I love you. You are my good angel, and I want you to marry me."

She froze. His voice was so serious. His eyes were beseeching. His attitude was one of supplication. As if such as he would have to beg for anything! He was mocking her, and she had not thought him so unkind. She pulled her hand away and, with great dignity, stood up. "How could you do this to me?" she asked in tones of dark bitterness, her voice trembling and low. "How could you?"

She turned and fled from the room.

Now he reaped the bitter harvest of all his womanizing ways. First Celestine had refused to believe he was serious, or at least that was how he'd interpreted her unaccountable words to him, and now this. He stalked around the library, his long fingers thrust through his hair until it stood on end.

"But it is true. I want to marry Celestine Simons! I *intend* to marry her!" He turned and hammered on the desk, making an ink well and wax pastille jump. "Why can neither of you believe that!"

"Because it is utterly outrageous and in wildly bad taste!" Elizabeth confronted him, doing the talking for herself and her stunned husband, who sat behind the desk staring into space. "This jest would be bad enough, but coming when we have a house full of guests, at *Christmas!* You have gone too far, Justin St. Claire."

Justin's blue eyes flashed. Many a man in London had backed down when faced with the anger in those eyes, but Elizabeth was too enraged to be cautious, and she knew she had the support of her husband in this.

"I have not gone nearly far enough! I intend to ask Lady Delafont, as Celestine's nearest relation, for permission to court her properly."

"Court her!" Elizabeth threw her hands up in the air. "Court the governess!" The sharp peal of her bitter laughter echoed in the room. "If this is some Christmas farce you have cooked up for us, Justin, I must congratulate you. It is bizarre enough to be talked of for many a season." She had paced away from the desk, but now she whirled and strode up to face him. "This is your revenge, isn't it, you bounder, you . . . you . . . ooh! You are just avenging yourself on me for telling you to stay away from her. And so you will ruin my whole house party and even our Christmas for your cruel jest?"

Justin gazed at her with an incredulous expression. "Spoil your party? You think I mean to spoil your party by courting Celestine?" He turned and headed toward the door, but stopped and turned back to glare at her. "I know I have brought on this reaction by my previous philandering ways, but hear me, both of you!" He stabbed an accusing finger at her, including his grimly silent brother.

"I will marry her, if she will have me. I intend to ask her again and again and again until she says yes, and then take her away from here. We will go to Questmere, where we will be married, and I swear never to enter your home until you can show proper courtesy to my wife."

He whirled from the room without another word, and Elizabeth and August were left staring after him.

"I think he is serious," the marquess finally said. His deep voice echoed in the chilly room. "I think my little brother really means it."

* * *

"I will toss her out on her scheming little ear, I promise you, Emily! If I find out your niece had anything to do with this scandalous charade, I will send her to purgatory!"

Emily's face had grown cold with anger. "Elizabeth," she said, in a dangerously quiet voice. "I would stop speaking of my niece as if she were a scheming harlot, if I were you."

Elizabeth raised her neat chin and said, defiantly, "This is my house. I will speak of whomever I want however I want."

"Fine." Emily whirled in her tracks and started out of her friend's dressing room.

"Emily! Where are you going?"

"I am taking my niece and we are heading back to Yorkshire. I will not have her subjected to your tirades, nor to your brother-in-law's predations."

Elizabeth flew past her friend and put her back to the door, not allowing Emily to leave. "I'm sorry! I am, Em, dearest, but I am just so upset!" She put one trembling hand up to her forehead. "I am as much worried about dear Miss Simons as I am about that scamp of a brother of mine. Please, you must be realistic. You *know* he is not serious about her. He breaks the heart of beautiful, wealthy, accomplished ladies every season. Do you truly think he is serious about marrying her?"

She put her small, fine hands on Emily's plump shoulders. "He could hurt her badly, and ruin her in the process. He has never done so before, but I feel he is so furious with me he might not think of the consequences."

Emily felt her heart sink as the truth of Elizabeth's concerns struck home. Celestine loved Justin St. Claire, deeply and truly. But Justin was a gallant who enjoyed making the ladies love him, only to turn fickle after they had given their hearts. He had never gone so far as this before, it was true, but what other explanation was there?

Even she, who knew and loved her niece for who and what she was, could not imagine a conceited coxcomb like Justin St. Claire plighting his troth to Celestine in seriousness.

Of course, Elizabeth was seeing the whole disaster in a highly personal light, but that was her way. She naturally first thought of the effect on her—her comfort, her family, her peace of mind.

That didn't change the essential facts. Emily crossed to Elizabeth's bed, sat down, and patted the space beside her. "Come tell me everything, Lizbet, and we will try to think of a solution *together.* I don't want you going off and muddling things worse."

Celestine walked to the long wall of the frozen garden. Snow blanketed everything, but she put her arms up on the rough stone and listened to the children behind her playing with the stable dog and their brother Gus. They were trying to play fox and hound, but Clydemore, the hound, would not cooperate.

She stared off at the purple fells, mantled now with a coating of white. She had come to Ladymead grateful for the position and looking forward to making a life for herself there, and she had done just that. The children loved her and she had made friends in the village, or at least friendly acquaintances. She had joined in the life of the church and community.

It was a calm, orderly, quiet existence, and unutterably lonely. She had grown up among people she had known all her life and was now cut off from them except for the occasional letter, consigned to the barren world of governess—neither family nor servant, barred from the joys and tribulations of both.

And then came Justin, striding into her life like a beam of dancing sunlight, a herald of joy and vigor. How could she not have fallen in love with him? Which was why, when Mr. Foster had finally proposed, she had said no.

She remembered the shock on his face. He had been sure of her, complacent in what he could offer. She had said nothing except that she did not think they would suit. And all because she could not wed one man while loving another. It wouldn't be fair to him, nor to her.

She became aware she was being watched. She turned and saw Justin approaching her.

He was stunningly handsome in his dark greatcoat, dark wings of hair curling away from his face. She never tired of looking at him, tracing the lines of his square chin, high cheekbones, and sensuous mouth time after time without familiarity dulling the pleasure. And the piercing joy she felt each time had nothing to do with his looks, and everything to do with him, with the inner sweetness she felt was part of him. That was why his mocking proposal had come as such a shock, and why she had reacted with uncharacteristic anger.

She had come to know his many expressions—the teasing laughter, the sensuous gleam, the dark anger. But at this moment there was an unfamiliar expression there, crinkling his eyes in the corners and twisting his mouth. With a little frisson of shock, she realized it was uncertainty. Justin St. Claire was never uncertain!

He joined her at the stone wall, glancing over his shoulder at the children, who still laughed and ran up and down the paths, chased by the barking dog past stone urns and long planters, small fruit trees with snow clinging to their bare branches, and low hedges of herbs. Then he gazed out at the fells. His gloved hand brushed the snow from the top of the wall.

"I daresay you're angry at me," he said, squinting into the winter sunshine.

"Angry? No, I'm not angry, my lord. Not now." It was the truth.

"You . . . you do not think me serious, though."

"No. I do not think you are serious."

"And perhaps there is another reason you reject me. You have already accepted another man's proposal."

Celestine's eyes widened. So *that* was what this was all about! She had been casting around in her mind for a reasonable explanation for his sudden avowal of love and his marriage proposal besides the mockery, which was so unlike him. Was it possible he was trying to steal her heart from Mr. Foster?

She had heard he liked to make girls fall in love with him, only to let them down and dance away from commitment like quicksilver. His competitive instincts had been piqued by the thought that she had a serious suitor for her hand. He intended to win her heart away from Mr. Foster! Well, she would not let him know he had succeeded.

"That, my lord, is my business," she said, glancing at his profile. He winced at her reply. Oh, he was a consummate actor! He had missed his calling in life, she thought, for he should have been on stage.

"True, Miss Simons. I beg you to reconsider your betrothal with him, though." He turned toward her and searched her face with an earnest expression. One gloved hand reached out and touched her gray-wool-clad arm. "Please consider, my dear, the relative merits of our status. Mr. Foster, though no doubt a worthy man, is not rich. Your day-to-day life would be one of some toil, and you are not strong."

Celestine sighed. Would he stop at nothing to gain his point? He would even remind her of her infirmity. She had not thought him so low, and it hurt to know the depths to which he would sink. But she still loved him. She could be disappointed in him, even angry with him, but still love him.

"I could keep you in luxury," he continued, "and you would never want for anything. I am not as wealthy as August, but I am not poor. I could take you to London—we could travel. In winter I could take you to Italy. It is warm in southern Italy throughout the year."

Celestine shivered and her eyes prickled, the ominous harbinger of tears. She blinked them back. When had she become so weak of spirit? But his words conjured up pictures of them in the hot Italian sun, laughing and talking as they explored some ancient ruin or beautiful temple, his arm under hers, supporting her as he gazed at her with those beautiful blue eyes made brighter by reflected sunlight off the dancing waters of the Adriatic. She could see it, could *feel* it, even. What luxury to surrender to loving him and . . . but it would never be. He was just waiting for her surrender, and then he would have won the game.

Could she believe him so cruel? She must, for even Emily, as fair-minded a person as she had ever known, had condemned him as a heartless flirt. He had broken the hearts of countless beautiful heiresses. Was she to believe he had fallen in love with one lonely, plain, arthritic spinster governess when any woman in the country would have gladly accepted him as a mate?

No. Life did not work that way, and she would not believe some miracle had occurred. In this one instance she would not trust her heart, which whispered that not only did he love her, but she deserved his love and could make him a happy man. A woman's heart was a tender organ, full of romantic dreams and hopes. But wishing and hoping do not create reality, she thought.

"Justin, you must not say such"

"Ah, Miss Simons, I had hoped to catch up with you."

Celestine turned to greet Lady Grishelda, stylishly if simply clad in a royal blue pelisse with gold frogging. "Lady Grishelda, we . . . we were discussing Italy," she improvised.

The young woman's calm, intelligent gaze went from Celestine's flushed countenance to Justin's grim, unwelcoming expression.

"If I have interrupted a private conversation, please forgive me."

"No. There is nothing we could possibly be speaking of that would be private," Celestine said. "As a matter of fact, I was just about to take the children in. It is time

for their tea. Perhaps you and his lordship would like to
take a walk, but I must go. Please excuse me."

She turned and walked away, gathering Lottie and poor
little Gwen, who was tired and cold. They went in, leaving
Lord St. Claire and Lady Grishelda at the stone wall.

The children were exhausted from playing outside and
so, after sharing tea with Celestine in the schoolroom,
she consigned them to Elise's care for a nap. Celestine
went in search of her aunt, from whom she wanted some
advice, but as she descended the curved staircase to the
first floor a footman approached her, bowing.

"If you please, Miss, the mistress would like to see you
in the library."

"Thank you. I will go there directly."

Outside the library door she paused, smoothed down
her dress, and took a deep breath. It was probably nothing, she reassured herself. It was most likely something
to do with the children. She pushed the door open and
entered, closing it behind her.

Lady St. Claire stood by the window in the masculine
room that was normally her husband's sole domain. She
looked fragile and feminine by the sturdy oak table covered in map folios, but Celestine was not deceived. The
marchioness was a woman of strong will and acid tongue.
She was capable of malice, but usually restrained it in
favor of acidity.

She turned and gazed at Celestine, her expression unreadable. "Have a seat, Miss Simons."

Celestine's stomach started to tremble. This did not
bode well. She gladly sat down in one of the chairs near
the big oak desk that was the centerpiece of the room.
Lady St. Claire crossed and seated herself behind it, looking dainty and diminutive in her husband's large green
leather armchair. She laid her neat hands palm down on
the surface of the desk.

"I have a few things I wish to say first. My husband and

I have been very happy with your work here. Aside from Gwen's lack of progress in certain areas, we feel you are doing an adequate job."

Celestine grimaced internally. This sounded like a polite way to say she was being let go. The marchioness had never been happy with her youngest daughter's progress, refusing to recognize that Gwen had special needs, and patience was one of them. She was slower than Lottie and probably always would be, but she more than made up for it with her sunny, sweet personality, whereas Lottie could sometimes be the very picture of her mother, a miniature termagant. Celestine could hardly tell the marchioness that, though.

"I am glad you are satisfied with my work, my lady. I have enjoyed the past year." Celestine sat up straight and folded her hands together, concealing her gnarled, knotted knuckles in the folds of her skirt.

Lady St. Claire toyed with her rings. "I hope you can continue to work for us."

"I . . . I hope so, too, my lady."

"But there is a problem. My brother-in-law. He has some absurd notion to marry you. He says he has even asked you." Her bright blue eyes flashed up at Celestine. "Is that so?"

He had told them? He had told them he asked her to marry him? Her head whirled and she sat back, wondering what it meant.

"I said, is that so?" The woman's voice was harder, like flint now.

"Y-yes, my lady."

The marchioness rose and paced behind the desk. Then she stopped and leaned over it, her small hands planted flat on the surface. "You must know it can never be! You, marry the brother of the Marquess of Ladymead? It's absurd!"

Celestine was silent, numb in her amazement, too numb to take exception to the contempt in her employer's voice.

"I want to know what you did to lead him to this end. Did you tell him you are breeding? Have you lain with him?"

The numbness quickly subsided to be replaced by a cold pit of fury. Celestine rose. "You have insulted me beyond any measure, my lady." Her voice was trembling. "I shall leave now."

"Wait!"

Celestine paused, but did not turn back.

"My . . . my apologies." Lady St. Claire's voice was frigid with the effort of making an apology, something she rarely saw the need to do. "Occasionally my temper is too hasty. I would not have you carry tales of ill treatment back to my brother-in-law. I will assume you have not lain with him. I believe you to be of good character, and Emily vouches for you."

Still Celestine did not turn back. Her anger burned cold and dark, and she was grateful for it, as it gave her strength. She stared at the door and waited. Lady St. Claire was clearly not finished.

"I . . . we do not wish to lose you, Miss Simons. The children are sincerely attached to you, and you have done wonders with them. Also, I am very fond of your aunt, and would not wish to hurt her in any way. My solution to our little problem is this. You must go away. Just until Justin is gone, and he *will* return to London. He may fancy himself in love with you at this moment, but he has never stayed that way for long.

"I have spoken with Emily already, and she is prepared to take you back to Yorkshire with her and keep you there until we send for you again. I am not *asking* you to do this." Her voice was steely, like a knife pressed to Celestine's back. "It is the only way you can retain your position with us," she continued. "Also, you must tell Justin neither that you are going nor where."

And so that was that. She could keep her position if she allowed herself to be sent away like a recalcitrant schoolgirl. Her voice surprisingly even, she glanced back at Lady St. Claire and said, "I shall consider what you have told me and my options. I shall tell you in the morning. We are having the puppet play tomorrow. I would hope your ladyship will at least allow me to stay to handle that. The girls have been looking forward to it for some time."

"Of course," Lady St. Claire said.

Celestine turned back and walked quietly to the door. She stopped and looked back at the marchioness. With her chin lifted slightly, she said, "I never gave him reason to feel compelled to ask me to marry him. I would have you know that." She walked out and closed the door behind her.

Seventeen

Emily was outside the library when Celestine emerged. She saw her niece's white, shocked face, and her heart sank. Ever since she had known her, Elizabeth had had a hasty temper and tactless way of dealing with people. Down deep there was a good heart, but it was buried in so much awareness of her elevated rank, conceit for her own pretty looks, familial pride in her historic name, and an acerbic tongue and acid personality that sometimes Emily wondered how they had become friends and stayed that way over the years.

And now she had likely put things all wrong to Celestine. It was a simple matter of protecting Celestine's good name and peace of mind, but who could tell how Elizabeth had broached the subject?

"My dear," Emily said, touching her niece's arm. "May we talk? I feel I should perhaps explain what Lizbet was trying to say."

Celestine turned tragic, gray eyes to her, and murmured, "She accused me of lying with Justin to entrap him into marriage."

Emily clenched her fists to her sides and cursed her childhood friend. Of all the stupid, idiotic, hurtful things to say, and to someone like Celestine—chaste, sweet, and utterly without deviousness or malice! She wanted to march into the library and demand an apology to Celestine from her supposed friend.

Instead, knowing it would not do one iota of good, she put her arm around the younger woman's shoulders as the Misses Stimson entered the hallway from a walk in the winter air. The girls greeted them and chattered about the fine day, and whether it would snow again before Christmas while footmen circled and abigails flew down the stairs to retrieve bonnets and muffs and heavy cloaks.

Emily sighed and guided Celestine over to the stairs. "We need to talk, and we cannot do it in the drawing room or parlor. Those chatterboxes will never leave us alone."

After arranging with one of the hovering footmen for tea to be brought up to them, she led Celestine to her room and settled her in a cozy armchair near the window. She took the matching chair and waited while a maid, who entered not long after, set a tray on the table between them.

She had a comfortable room with a view down the valley. She was almost as fond of Cumbria as she was of Yorkshire. She loved the wildness of the scenery, but realized it was starting to wear on her after two years with little change. Baxter, her estranged husband, was gallivanting over the continent, or so Dodo told her from family news in letters. Dodo was his aunt, and so corresponded with some of the family—at least the ones to whom she was still speaking.

Maybe they should go to London for the coming Season—open Delafont House and see the sights. She would love most of all to take Celestine with her to the routs and balls, the theater and the opera . . . but there was time enough to think about that. Right now she must deal with the situation her beloved niece found herself in.

She poured tea and handed a cup to Celestine, watching carefully as the shock eased from her narrow, pale face. That paleness and the fineness of her other features made her niece's eyes seem huge, she thought. She was like porcelain, except for the spray of freckles across her delicate nose that had not faded as she reached maturity.

What could she say to make things better for a niece she loved like a little sister?

"Sometimes I wonder how I managed to stay friends with Elizabeth those years at school and then in London when we were both married."

"She has a nasty streak," Celestine said, warming her hands around the delicate china cup.

Emily sighed. "She was *not* supposed to insult you like that."

Celestine looked up sharply over the rim of her cup. "You knew she was talking to me? And about what?"

"I knew she was talking to you. I know what she was supposed to say to you. I wanted to speak to you myself, but she insisted it must come from her. I have the feeling she did not adhere to the strict instructions I gave her."

"Did you tell her to threaten my job?" Celestine said, dryly.

"Threaten your job?"

"I am to go back to Yorkshire with you if I want to retain my position at Ladymead."

"Oh, Lord, I never suggested that! That is Lizbet; a hammer blow where a light tap would suffice." Emily reached across the table and laid her plump hand over her niece's. "No, my dear. There is no question of you losing your job. We all know there is no fault to be found in you. We just felt, and I agreed to this, that it might be more comfortable for you to be out of Justin's way while he is here. I suggested you come back to Yorkshire for a while to visit me and Dodo, and then return in a month. He is to think you have decided to take a new position somewhere else. We will say you did not tell anyone where."

Celestine grew quiet.

"I have not pried, dear, because your life is your own. You are of age, and as sensible a woman as I have ever met. But even the most sensible of women fall for cads."

"Are you speaking from personal experience, Aunt?"

"No. Or not exactly. But let me ask you this: I have heard Justin has asked you to marry him. Is that true?"

"He did. I assume it is another step in his campaign to seduce me or to win me over from an attachment he believes I have formed." Celestine put her cup down on the tray with a clatter. "I . . . I cannot believe he told his brother and sister-in-law about it! What does that mean?"

Emily considered that point. He had never come so far with any lady; she knew that of a certainty. Was he finally telling the truth, or was it as Celestine suspected, a ruse to lull her into believing in him to further his seduction? But surely, to tell his brother . . .

"Has he made . . . improper suggestions or advances on you, my dear?" she asked finally.

Celestine flushed and stared down at the floor, tracing a pink rosette in the cream and misty green pattern with the toe of her shoe. "Improper?"

"Yes. Don't go missish on me, Celestine. Did he suggest a liaison? Or did he touch you improperly?" Emily gazed at her, watching the flickering play of emotions over her niece's delicate face.

"Aunt! Now you are as bad as Lady St. Claire! She accused me of lying with him to entrap him."

"Oh, Lord, I don't believe she really thinks that! No! Never say that." She paused and sipped her tea. This was a delicate subject, made more so by Lizbet's ham-handed interference. She must not offend her niece, or suggest she had done anything improper. She would start fresh, from the beginning.

"What is your opinion of why he asked you to marry him and followed up by telling his brother about it? In most men, I would say that indicates sincerity and determination—perhaps even love."

Celestine still gazed down at the floor. She shook her head and said softly, "Oh, no. I do not claim he is in love with me. It cannot be." She looked up, and her gray eyes were sad, though her agitation was calmed. "What could a man like Justin St. Claire see in a poor, plain governess?"

"Careful my dear. That sounds like bitterness or self-pity."

"I am bitter! And self-pitying! It is the outside of enough that a man I have fallen in love with has told me he loves me and asked me to marry him, and I cannot believe him or say yes! Does that not seem ludicrous? Bizarre? And yet I cannot believe him sincere. Everyone around me says it is impossible, and you all know him so much better than I." Celestine sighed, put her teacup down, and covered her face with her gnarled hands. "It is too much," she said, her voice muffled.

Emily was worried for her niece. Celestine had been through tragedy in her life, but she had always met it with equanimity. This affair had been harder on her, it seemed, than even the death of her father. Emily supposed that was because, no matter how sad, the death of her father had been long expected. But Celestine had probably never expected to fall in love, and for it to happen with a man so much above her social position!

Celestine uncovered her face, and a rueful smile lifted her lips. "I am not *really* bitter. I am confused. He has kissed me. He has held me. He found me crying over my pain and he comforted me. He ordered a hot bath for me every morning, knowing it would cure some of my aches." Her expression softened. "I would like to think he was in love with me"—her tone was wistful, full of longing—"but I cannot believe it possible. I don't know what this all means. But I have been mulling it over, and I can only believe the marriage proposal was spurred on by a sense of competition."

"Competition?" Emily was startled. It seemed an unlikely spur to a marriage proposal from a renowned rake.

"I . . ." Celestine looked away. "I may have led him to believe I had agreed to an offer from Mr. Foster—the offer of marriage I told you about, and that I rejected. I believed it would end his pursuit of me."

"Instead it just made him want you the more, as you were someone else's." Emily mused for a minute. It didn't seem quite right. Justin would not enter into a competition with a vicar. Betrothal to another beau usually ended his attentions to a particular girl. But what other explanation was there? Sometimes men were unaccountable— her own husband, Baxter, was a perfect example of that.

"What say you to going with me to Yorkshire?"

"Do I have any choice?"

Emily cursed Elizabeth's clumsiness. Celestine felt backed into a corner, and nothing Emily could say would make her believe there was no threat of her losing her job if she did not comply.

"There is always a choice. I know you still believe your job to be in danger. And I understand if you feel stubborn, loath to let Elizabeth treat you this way. But do not make the mistake of staying here to spite her. If you come with me, do it for the right reasons. You will not be running away, just avoiding a potentially embarrassing situation."

"And how does that differ from running away?"

Emily shrugged.

"Are you giving me the advice you wish you had given yourself before marrying Uncle Baxter? Should you have run away from him?"

Emily gazed over at her niece. Celestine knew she was separated, and knew some of the reasons, but not all. "The circumstances are considerably different, as you must know."

"But you were an impecunious maiden, and there was some family opposition to your marriage, is that not so?"

"Yes, but we were in love." Emily gazed off into the distance. "So in love. I fell in love the moment I saw him. He kissed me just moments after we met, you know." Her cheeks grew rosy.

"You never told me *that*, Aunt." Celestine gazed at her in wonder. "How did that happen?"

"He took me for a dairymaid or a farmer's daughter." She chuckled, a throaty sound. "I was wading across a stream with my skirts pulled up and my feet bare, leading a great, ugly, stubborn beast of a horse. Baxter rode up on a handsome stallion and helped me up the other side, subduing my obstinate animal. Then he demanded a kiss as payment." She stared at the wall, remembering the moment her future husband's lips had first touched hers, the shock of awareness that that was it for her; it was love. She shook herself out of her memory to find Celestine watching her, a smile on her rose-pink lips.

"Tell me." Emily leaned forward in her chair and gazed into Celestine's eyes, the thick gray color of them like slate. "How did it feel when Justin kissed you?"

Celestine's expression became misty and abstracted. "It was . . . I felt like a fire had been started in my heart. I felt like it was spring all of a sudden, and there must be a thousand flowers around me. I wanted to dance and cry and sing. I felt . . . I wanted it to never stop."

Emily watched her shrewdly. "And how did he act?"

"The first time? Like a practiced rogue. But then . . ." Celestine told her aunt about his holding her as she wept and cradling her while she slept in his arms and about her impression he had been murmuring he would take care of her always.

"Is that so?" Emily pursed her lips and her fine, arched brows drew down. She made a decision in that moment she hoped she would not live to regret. She was going to irk a few people, perhaps alienate a lifelong friend. "Is that so? Celestine, we must go. I think it is for the best if we leave the day after tomorrow, very early in the morning. Surely you see the wisdom of this?"

Celestine nodded, her pale, freckled face downcast. "I think you may be right, Aunt. I think I need to get away from him or I will be tempted to actions I may regret later."

She was just nervous, Celestine thought, as she listened to the excited chatter of Gus and Lottie behind the makeshift puppet stage the next afternoon. Somehow it had been arranged that all the company would be in the drawing room to see the play, and more from the village. Miss Hay, the village schoolmistress, had been asked to bring her class.

It was to be a rare treat for the children, with cakes and sweets in the dining room after. Very generous of Lady St. Claire, Celestine had thought with some surprise, but the additional people had made a fun Christmas project into a much bigger event. A week before, Gus had been dragooned into playing the part of Prince Aurelius, while Lottie was to play Princess Calista. Gwen was going to make appropriate animal noises—dogs, cats, and sheep—and Celestine was left to play all the other parts.

Until Justin insisted on playing the part of the ugly girl, Hepzibah.

She refused to think that was why she was more nervous, but it didn't help. She peeked out from behind the stage at the rows of seats. The children were filing in at that moment, their faces bright with anticipation, some of them hopping on one foot, one little boy pulling a girl's braids. They chattered and giggled, eyes big and round as they examined the puppet theater, which, thanks to Gus's startling artistic ability, was quite beautiful.

Miss Hay lined them up to sit on the floor in front of the stage, and the adults drifted in, in groups and singly. Lady Grishelda was watching Miss Hay and the children, but the Stimsons were giggling together as they sat with a young man who had come to visit for the day from the next village. He was the squire's eldest son, and had been smitten by both girls equally when he had come for the Christmas party. He was nice-looking in a florid, beefy way. Both girls competed for his attention, laughing and touching his arm.

Justin darted behind the stage. His blue eyes shone with glee and he rubbed his hands together. He was impossibly handsome in buff breeches and a dark blue, perfectly fitted jacket with gold buttons. "I cannot believe how

much I am looking forward to this!" He grabbed the
Hepzibah puppet and fitted it over his large hand, then
gestured with it and squawked, "And me, too! I'm going
to catch me that handsome Prince Aurelius if I have to
hunt him down with my little bow and arrow!"

Lottie giggled and was shushed by her infinitely superior brother, Gus. Celestine swallowed hard and tried to
ignore Justin's closeness. She felt a little faint, even more
so because it was her responsibility to go out and announce the play. It had not seemed such a big chore
when it was just going to be Lord and Lady St. Claire
and maybe a few others. Now she was terrified.

The chatter from the other side of the stage reached
a crescendo and then calmed. Celestine heard the footmen close the door. Everyone must be there. It was time.

She stepped out from behind the stage, hands clasped
behind her back, and faced the crowd.

"Ladies and gentlemen—and children, too, of course."
She smiled down at the rows of shining clean faces turned
up to her. One little boy was scratching at a scab on his
hand and one girl looked frightened, not quite sure what
to make of the stage and what was about to happen.

Concentrate on the children, she thought. That might help.
"Today, we are going on a journey to a forest—an enchanted forest in a land of magic." She scanned the faces
of the children, their pink cheeks and round eyes signal-
ing their excitement. "Do you all believe in magic?" She
watched the children nod and she lowered her voice almost to a whisper. "You will meet a prince there—a very
handsome prince who longs for love! And you will meet
his family. There is a princess in the story, too, and this
is where the magic comes in, for the princess is very special. You see, all the animals speak to her in a language
only she understands. I hope you enjoy our little play,
and remember. Root for the prince and princess!"

She curtseyed and ducked behind the curtain.

"Bravo, bellissima," Justin said in an intimate tone, smiling into her gray eyes with his bright blue ones. He

glanced around and, seeing that Gus was helping Lottie get up on the stool behind the puppet stage so she could hold up her Princess Calista puppet, continued, "That is what they say in Italy, you know. We could attend the theater there if you marry me. You would adore it. You could translate for me; my Italian is abysmal."

She flushed and turned away, angry that he would continue his nonsense knowing how nervous she must be. What did he think he was doing? She was confused beyond rational thought by his continued pursuit of her in the face of her rejection and his brother's disapproval. Her Aunt Emily was right. She must get away until he left for London. Still, the notion of leaving him caused an ache in her breast, a searing pain she had never experienced before.

She slipped the gaudily dressed Queen Parlia puppet on her hand and motioned for the others to come close, then signaled the footmen stationed on either side of the puppet theater to pull the curtains.

The play started. Justin's words, a little garbled sometimes when Lottie forgot where she was, tumbled forth, with Gwen's bleating and mewing coming at ill-timed intervals. The children laughed at Hepzibah's machinations to steal Aurelius away, and Celestine heard Caroline Stimson sigh over the prince's speech about true love and waiting forever until you found it.

Once they were caught up in it, Celestine found it a little easier to forget Justin was so close, close enough occasionally for his breath to touch the back of her neck, and his muscular thigh to brush hers. He mugged outrageously, improvising new and even sillier lines for Hepzibah—lines that had the audience, even the adults, roaring with laughter. It was a success, and all because of him!

It was a poignant reminder of the bright fire of Justin's star. Even if he was serious about marrying her, which she did not admit for a moment, he deserved a wife who could move comfortably among the other members of his social class. He was witty and brilliant and social. She was intelligent enough to match him any day, but she was quiet and introspective, awkward in elevated company.

They were winding down to the end. Aurelius and Calista had found each other and plighted their troth. Except for the occasional "It's your turn, stupid," from Gus when Lottie missed her cue, the end was touching and sweet, with Justin adding loud, rude kissing noises to their final embrace, sending the audience back into gales of laughter among the sweet sentiments. The puppets bowed and Celestine nodded for the footmen to draw the curtains.

Applause burst out, spontaneous and hearty.

"We are a success, my love," Justin whispered, grabbing her hand and pulling her out to the front of the stage, while he called to Gus, Lottie, and Gwen to follow.

They circled to the front, all except Gwen, Celestine blushingly aware of his strong hand holding hers. Lady St. Claire saw it, too, and frowned, digging her elbow into her husband's ribs. Emily watched her niece and her importunate suitor thoughtfully from her seat, and applauded with the rest.

The children jumped to their feet, led by Gus and his sisters, and headed for the dining room in a tumultuous tumble. Celestine pulled her hand out of Justin's and fled, to retreat to the quiet sanctuary of her room and the packing she had still to do. It was the last time she would see him, and she paused at the door, glancing back. He was watching her go with sadness in his beautiful eyes. Her own eyes filled with tears, and she hurried away before he could see the pain she was feeling, the utter loneliness of knowing they would be apart forever.

Eighteen

In the cold early dawn, Emily, Dodo, and Celestine trundled off in the carriage with the Delafont crest, down the sloping road, over icy ruts, and through the village. Faint light glowed in the windows and smoke curled from chimneys in homes where the man of the house was already out doing his duty to his family and where the woman was tending her household chores. Emily thought if her life had gone in a different direction, she would have been one of those women, married to a respectable but poor farmer or solicitor or shopkeeper. Instead she had met and married a distant, titled relation with whom she had fallen deeply in love and was now separated from for complex and varied reasons.

There was silence in the cozy, dim confines of the elegant traveling vehicle, made warmer by heated bricks buried in straw at their feet. Maybe, Emily thought, the other two were lost in their own contemplation, as she was. Or maybe they were just recovering from the scramble of leaving after a quick breakfast in the half-light of early morning.

The eldest lady of the three, Lady Dodo Delafont, yawned behind a gloved hand and eyed the uncurtained window with distaste. She preferred never to see the cruder side of nature, especially not early in the morning, but in deference to her niece-by-marriage, who enjoyed the scenery, she left the curtains drawn back. She was nominally Emily's companion, though she chose to live with her out of affection and not any need to have a place to stay. She was wealthy in her own right.

But when her nephew had separated from his wife, and her sister-in-law, the widow of the previous Marquess of Sedgeley, had demanded Emily leave the country estate of the marquess, Dodo had offered to go with her. Over two years ago they had removed to the Yorkshire estate Baxter Delafont had deeded to his wife free and clear in the separation settlement. It was the house where Baxter and Emily had first met and was precious to Emily for that reason.

"Why ever must all journeys begin so early in the morning?" Dodo asked, stifling another yawn.

It was an unanswerable question, and so the three continued gazing out their respective windows at the wintry landscape, the first glimmers of silvery morning light casting long shadows from the snow-coated fells into the valley, the shadows shortening as the day advanced. Emily glanced over at her niece from time to time, wondering if she was doing the right thing. She was interfering insufferably in what was essentially a private affair between Celestine and Lord St. Claire.

But it didn't seem to her there had been any real end to things between them. She had seen the tension on Celestine's face after the puppet show the previous day and how her niece had fled with one heartbreaking glance back at her love. Justin had watched her leave the room with unaccountably bleak eyes, and she just could not leave it that they should creep away.

Whatever would become of the two?

For her part, as the carriage trundled along the miles, Celestine was replaying every word, every look, every caress that had occurred between herself and the man she had come to adore. How had it happened? How had she fallen in love with a man so far above her touch as Justin St. Claire? It had taken place, she supposed, in imperceptible degrees, stealing over her like age, one moment at a time.

But it would not do. He could not possibly love her— not really. She had dismissed the competitive angle as unlikely, in light of Emily's doubt of that as a motive for offering for her. Perhaps his offer of marriage had been genuine, but surely what he felt for her was lust at worst, pity at best. Lust she could not understand, since he had at his disposal the luscious and voluptuous Lady van Hoffen, who cast him amorous glances whenever he entered a room. Surely any man with eyes in his head would prefer the beautiful and experienced widow to a plain, arthritic spinster.

So it must be pity. He was capable of great affection, she believed, having observed him with the children, whom he genuinely loved, and he had been gentle and caring toward her. He was, she suspected, a man with a large, untapped well of softer feelings: sympathy, compassion, pity.

He had spoken of taking care of her for the rest of her life, and so perhaps his offer of marriage was real, inspired by concern for her deteriorating health. Certainly that hypothesis was borne out by his solicitousness in ordering her a hot bath every morning.

Could a marriage based on pity thrive?

She gazed out the window at the harsh landscape and contemplated. At first, he would be all compassion for her affliction. It would be such a delicious feeling to be cared for by a man like Justin, especially since her love was real, based on his good qualities and sweetness of character.

But he was like a bright star on the horizon, dimming every other person when he was in the room. Women and men alike were drawn to him, to his energy and wit and fire. And all of that would be hers? Impossible. She could never match his boundless energy or blazing fire, and her wit seemed feeble compared to his. It would be like trying to hold quicksilver, making a marriage with a man like that.

After a while his compassion would remain, but he would tire of her limitations and long for love. He would still be kind to her, but always she would be the one who loved while he grew restless and regretted his benevolent impulse. Or maybe—ghastly thought!—he would find his true love, and yet be stuck with her for the rest of his natural life. Would he take mistresses? Probably. It would kill her if he did.

She would always know, always feel she had robbed him of something precious, the opportunity for real love. She loved him far too much for that. She wanted for him the rich, complex emotion she experienced whenever she thought of him, which was often.

She was physically affected by his nearness. He made her heart thud faster, her pulse race, and her blood heat. His lips on hers made her melt into a warm pool of desire. But more than that, she felt a tenderness toward him inspired by his sparkling personality and sweetness of temperament. She ached to give him love, unstinting and powerful, but feared she could serve him best by leaving him to find his true love, the woman who could capture his heart and his soul. It was better this way.

"What do you mean, Miss Simons is gone?" Justin stared at Gwen and Lottie's maid.

The girl wrung her hands together and said, with a plaintive whine, "It were ever so sudden, milord. It were decided yesterday, but I weren't told till this mornin', when Miss Simons came to bid the wee ones good-bye."

Justin swore fiercely and thrust his fingers through his hair. This was Elizabeth's doing, he would swear.

"Where has she gone?" His words were harsh with anger and the girl flinched. He softened his voice. "Please tell me."

Elise was gazing at him with awe and fear. She gaped

like a fish and, impatient, he exclaimed, "If you do not know, girl, then perhaps Lady Delafont does."

He turned to go, but Elise called out, "She's gone, too, milord. This mornin' right early. Taking Miss Simons with her."

She had gone to Yorkshire; that must be it! He tore down the stairs, taking them two at a time, and flung himself into the breakfast room, where Elizabeth was seated with the Misses Stimson. He strode up to his sister-in-law and stood over her.

"You think you have ended it, Lizzie, but you haven't!" His voice rasped with anger, and she gazed up at him with a mixture of irritation and concern on her pretty, scheming face.

"Whatever do you mean, Justin? Please have a seat. Looking up that way gives me the headache."

"I don't have time to sit. I have a carriage to find! Which way did they go? Are they going straight to Yorkshire or are they heading south?"

"I won't pretend to misunderstand you, Justin," Elizabeth said, her voice cold and haughty. "I would wish you would offer more courtesy to my guests, but obviously you have taken leave of your senses."

The Stimson girls were watching and listening avidly, Caroline stifling a well-bred giggle behind her hand. Justin bowed to them impatiently, and then turned back to Elizabeth.

"Miss Simons has received the offer of another post," Elizabeth said. "She is off to take it this day. Emily is merely conveying her thence, so you need not badger me, Justin. I don't even know where it is. I merely agreed to release her from our employ."

"Threw her out on her ear is more like it," Justin ranted, pacing back and forth by the mahogany dining table. "You two just couldn't accept my choice, could you?" he said. He stopped and looked down at Elizabeth, who calmly tore a buttered muffin into pieces and ate it.

There was silence for a moment. The Stimson sisters'

large, brown eyes gazed at him over the evergreen centerpiece as they waited for the final act of the drama. He mastered the overwhelming urge to throttle his sister-in-law, though he could almost feel the satisfaction of her soft flesh giving way under his strong grip as he choked the life out of her smug, self-satisfied meddling little body.

He was calmer when he finally spoke, having subdued his violent urges. "I meant what I said, you know. I will marry her. Somehow, after a life spent seducing and bedding bored wives and widows"—there were shocked gasps from the girls as he said that, and he was glad—"and breaking the hearts of silly little debutantes, I have found a woman of depth and . . . and sweetness. She is an angel, and far too good for me. In my whole conceited life I have never said anything like that, but it is true. Celestine Simons is an angel, and I mean to marry her."

Elizabeth's expression was frigid. Her next words dropped one by one from her pursed mouth like frozen shards of ice. "You are out of your mind!"

He slammed his fist on the table and the silver danced. The teapot lid jumped and settled back out of kilter, causing the Stimson girls to gasp and clutch each other, their eyes round and big as saucers. He leaned over and glared.

Elizabeth drew back at his ferocious expression. His hair was tousled and his cravat was askew.

"I am finally *in* my right mind. I love Celestine Simons, and I will find her and convince her to marry me if it is the last thing I do on this earth. She will have to take me without my family, though, for I have nothing more to say to you or to August."

He whirled on his boot heel and stormed from the room, shouting to Dobbs to find his valet and order him to start packing yet again. The portly butler glanced around with a strangely covert look, though, and whispered, "My lord, I have a letter for you!"

A thrill shot through Justin as he took the missive, addressed in a slanting, feminine hand. "From Miss Simons?" he said.

"No, my lord. From another lady." Dobbs bowed. "I will see to your valet."

Justin split the wax seal and scanned the letter. A sublime smile spread over his handsome features and he followed the butler up the stairs, passing him as he took the stairs two at a time. He was whistling a tune as he went. Dobbs smiled and nodded. Some gentlemen knew as to who was real gentility and who wasn't among the ladies in this household, Dobbs thought. And St. Claire was one of the smarter ones to have picked out Miss Simons, though he had never thought so before in his long years of service to the present marquess's family.

A day that had started out promising was now, in the early afternoon, closing in suddenly, as sometimes happened in the Pennines. The sky was a leaden gray and flakes of snow, first sparse and then thick, began to fall.

Emily gazed out at the sky with some trepidation. She had not counted on this, though she was about to ask the coachman to stop at an inn anyway, on the excuse she was tired and hungry. She then planned on coming down with some slight malady that would delay their departure until morning. But from the looks of the weather, they wouldn't be leaving anytime soon, regardless of her ruse.

Dodo gloomily stared out at the snow. "It never snows like this in London," she said in a sepulchral tone.

"Of course it does," Emily said. "You just can't tell because it turns mud-brown from soot before it makes it to the ground. Everyone thinks it is just an unusually heavy covering of ash."

"It's very beautiful," Celestine said. "But I daresay not too good for the poor coachman."

Emily nodded sharply. She let down the window and leaned out, shouting up to her driver. "Gorse, are we near an inn?"

The coachman answered in the affirmative, which Emily already knew from previous arrangement with him.

"Let us break our journey, then." She put the window back up and shivered.

Not more than half an hour later, they pulled into the courtyard of an inn in a small village.

"I had hoped to make Penrith before we broke for the night," Emily sighed. Dodo glanced at her sharply.

"Surely if the weather clears we can continue on? It is no later than two in the afternoon," Celestine said. "It's a ways to Yorkshire, and I know you must be impatient to be home," she added.

Emily shook her head and gazed out at the thick shower of snowflakes that fluttered against the window. "I don't think we'll be going anywhere today."

The coachman, Gorse, opened the door and placed a step by it for the ladies to step down onto. One by one, they descended and hurried through the curtain of white into the inn, where welcome heat billowed at them from the noisy public dining room, which was open off the main entrance.

The landlord's wife, instantly assessing the costly garments Emily and Dodo wore, curtseyed and offered to show them into a private dining room where they could shed their cloaks. They followed her beyond the public room into a clean, large chamber where a huge fire blazed in the hearth. It was a low-beamed space, and so the heat stayed at body height. Celestine shed her snow-damp pelisse and moved over to the fire, where some chairs were set in a semicircle.

Emily paced over to a window and pulled back the curtain. "I don't think we will be able to go on tonight," she said. "We don't know how far back Agnes and Peter are following with the luggage." Agnes, the abigail, was traveling with Peter, Gorse's son, who drove the luggage carriage. "I don't want to get so far that the poor girl cannot catch up with us. Better to stay here and have attire to wear tonight and tomorrow morning than to lose my poor girl in the storm."

"Whatever you wish, Aunt," Celestine said over her shoulder.

Dodo had taken a spot by the fire and sighed as she eased off her damp boots. "That suits me just fine, my dears, for I hate long travel at the best of times, and this is not the best of times. At my time of life, a good fire and hot tea are much to be preferred over quick arrival at our destination."

Emily cast a sympathetic look over her shoulder. If everything went as planned, there would be no need to continue the longish journey to Yorkshire. But the storm had cast her plans into doubt, and she would just have to see how things went. She hoped she had done the right thing.

They settled around the fire and the landlady, a Mrs. Shruggs, brought a tray with tea, dark and steaming, and a plate of scones, light as a feather and hot from the oven. Emily broke one open, buttered it, and bit into it with a sigh of pleasure.

"Mmmm," she murmured and swallowed. "Wonderful. At least Mrs. Shruggs is a good cook, so we will not starve." She glanced down at her plump figure ruefully. "Though there is little danger of that for me. I have gained at least three stone in the last five years. No wonder Elizabeth hardly recognized me."

Celestine smiled over at her aunt and sipped the strong, bitter tea. "You are lovely, and you know it," she said.

Emily's smile softened as she gazed at her niece. The fire cast a glow over Celestine's pale oval face. She believed, in the light of what she had observed and what Celestine had told her about Justin's words and actions lately, that Justin *was* in love with her. He had never, to her knowledge, taken so much care over a woman, nor offered to marry her.

She was gambling that it was in Celestine's best interests to marry St. Claire. But was it?

Years ago she would have answered yes unequivocally.

But that was before her own marriage had started to crumble under the pressures of family and her inability to produce an heir for her husband, the Marquess of Sedgely. She was still bitter over the way his mother had interfered in her marriage until there was no peace between her and Baxter, and in that time she had lost her belief that love conquers all.

But it was Celestine she must think of, not herself and her own failure to make her marriage work. Her niece picked at a scone, her gnarled hands reducing it to a pile of crumbs as she stared into the fire, stirred back to crackling life by the attentive landlord just minutes before.

"Celestine, if you could have anything you wanted in life, what would it be?" Emily's voice was quiet in the warm, cozy room.

Dodo opened one eye and glanced over at Emily. Then she sighed, closed her eye again, and leaned her head back in her chair.

Celestine pursed her full lips and her delicate brow furrowed. "Anything?"

"Anything. Or anyone. Just what you believe would make your life perfect."

Celestine's gray eyes lit with a glow and her lips curved up in a smile which became sad after a moment. She turned her head away and said, "I . . . I think you probably know the answer to that already, Aunt."

"I suppose. Maybe that is not an appropriate subject to bring up right now." Emily glanced up at the clock. Would her plan work? What would she do if it didn't? "What can we talk about on this gloomy day to brighten us up?"

"Aunt Emily, do you think a marriage where there is unequal love on both sides can last? Can it be good?"

"I don't know if I am the right one to be asking about good marriages. I am a failure in that respect, my dear."

"Takes two to fail," Dodo said, without opening her eyes. "Or sometimes more. Seems to me you and Baxter had a lot of help from my interfering, long-nosed, busy-body sister-in-law."

"Maybe. But I am sure there are a hundred things I could have done differently that would have changed how things ended. Maybe Baxter and I would still be together if . . ." Her voice broke. She cleared her throat and glanced over at Celestine. "But that is not what you asked, is it?"

Emily had seen compassion on Celestine's face before when she spoke of Baxter, but now there was an added hint of understanding. Unsuccessful love made women compatriots in pain.

She shifted in the hard chair and gazed down at the ruby ring that Baxter had given her when he asked her to marry him. Almost to herself she said, "Marriages with unequal love? Perhaps they can be successful, but it is up to the one who loves more, I think. For you must be prepared to make allowances, to take less than you need or want, to be satisfied with the small things, the perfect moments."

Celestine nodded. She had been pondering all day and had come to the conclusion that perhaps she should have taken Justin at his word and agreed to marry him. Even if he married her out of pity or compassion, he could come to love her in time if she was a good wife to him. Surely a few scraps of his affection, as sweet and beautiful as they were, were better than the bleak nothingness that seemed to stretch out in front of her now.

In her dreams as a young girl, she could have imagined no man more perfect than Justin, not just in form and grace, but in deeper attributes. He might hide it from the world, but she had learned his soul and knew the depth of tenderness and core of sweetness no one else suspected. She had dreamed of marrying someone like him one day, and it had been within her grasp.

But in her heart she knew if she had it to do all over again she would do exactly the same thing. What she did, she did for Justin. Someday, if they had married and he had fallen in love with another woman, his life would be destroyed. She could not do that to him. She wanted love for him, not just the affection and esteem he might hold her in. Even if she never had *him,* at least she had her love for him to remember and hold sacred.

But it would be cold comfort through the long winter nights of her life.

Nineteen

"C'mon, Alphonse, just a little further." The snow was coming down so thick that Justin could see barely a few feet ahead of him. Alphonse hung his head and plodded on unhappily, his dark, glossy coat white from the gathering snow. His hooves slipped occasionally on the wet coating on the road to Yorkshire. Justin shared the horse's misery. His feet were frozen in his Hessians, and snow was drifting into the collar of his coat and melting, to trickle in a cold stream down his back. His gloved hands felt frozen to the reins.

But the only thing to do was press onward. Justin kicked in his heels, desperately trying to get a little speed out of his beast, normally the most high-spirited and quick to respond of any mount he had ever ridden.

He reread the note over in his mind, huddling down into his greatcoat for warmth. It had informed him Emily was taking Celestine back to Yorkshire with her, to take her out of his clutches. But the writer believed in young love and wanted him and Celestine to be happy. So she, the letter writer, would create a diversion and somehow get the carriage to stop at the Fellswater Inn on the road to Penrith.

Lady Dodo Delafont. It had to be that old biddy. Who else would consider him, at thirty-two, to be indulging in young love?

"C'mon, Alphonse," he urged. The carriage had

maybe a two-hour start, but he was slightly faster on horseback, or had been before the weather closed in. He dug in his heels yet again and urged his horse on, leaning forward over the stallion's thick neck and whispering, "Warm mash if you get there quickly, my boy. I have to hurry. I have to find Celestine and make her believe me."

"I am going to retire, my dears," Dodo said, stiffly easing herself out of the chair by the fire. Emily said she would join her after a while in the suite of rooms they had reserved for themselves, and the elderly lady mounted the stairs with a smoking tallow candle to light her way.

They had finished an early repast of rabbit pie, mutton, and apple tart as the day turned to twilight. The coachman had reported there was no possibility of traveling on that day. Indeed, it was now too late, even if they had been of a mind to go on. The luggage carriage had arrived an hour or more earlier, and Emily's abigail was even now making their rooms habitable.

Celestine had retrieved a book from her luggage and was hunched near the fire reading it—or, more accurately, staring at the same page as she had an hour before. Emily, standing near the window, gazed over at her and wondered again if she had done the right thing.

Would he follow her? Did he love Celestine as she suspected? She had known Justin for a long time, and his actions, as described by her niece, sounded wholly unlike him. He had never had any patience with imperfection of any kind. Celestine's crippling arthritis normally would have been abhorrent to him, and so she had thought to test his supposed love.

She glanced out the window at the snow being driven against it with furious force. She had not meant to test it this much! If he made it through this gale, then his love would have to be judged strong indeed. The Justin

she knew, or thought she knew, would not venture out
in such weather even for the promise of an evening of
gambling and beautiful courtesans.

Had he changed over the years she had been away from
London? He was older, certainly, but from what she had
gathered from Elizabeth, his life had not changed a bit.
Every Season saw him back in London, gambling, wenching, drinking, and carousing, with young ladies of the *ton*
falling desperately in love with him, only to be spurned
by the fickle aristocrat. So what had prompted him to
propose marriage to Celestine but genuine love? It was
a puzzle she would not be able to understand until she
saw him again.

The wind howled and darkness closed in around him.
Snow was blowing horizontally across the road, and finally
Justin slipped from Alphonse's back. It was much too per-
ilous to continue riding. If his horse fell, he could break
a leg or land on top of Justin. God, it was cold! His ears
and hands and feet felt ready to fall off, for they had
gone dangerously numb, and he was so wretchedly tired.
He longed to lie down in a gully and sleep . . . sleep . . .
but he must not! To stop was to die.

Leaning into the wind, he led his poor beast through
the gale, desperately trying to keep them on the road,
concentrating on sensing any change in surface or eleva-
tion that would signal they had left the thoroughfare. It
could be fatal if that happened.

He searched for a light through the curtain of white
that surrounded him. Surely there must be an inn somewhere? It had been hours since he had passed the last
one, though there had been several houses he could have
sheltered at if he was not so afraid of missing Celestine.
But now his very survival was in question.

Celestine. Would he see her again? Would he find her?
He leaned into the wicked wind and closed his eyes
against the freezing, wet snow. He must go on.

* * *

Emily pushed away from the window, where she had been gazing out at the harsh night, seeing little but the reflection of the fire against the glass, and returned to the hearth, taking the seat Dodo had vacated. Holding her hands out to the fire, she examined her niece.

Celestine's swollen fingers held the book up before her eyes, but she still wasn't seeing it. Her eyes were misty and unfocused as she appeared to ponder something. Her brow was furrowed and her lips set, her pale complexion set aglow by the blaze.

"Celestine," Emily said gently, leaning over and taking the book.

"Hmm?" she said. "What is it, Aunt? Do you wish to retire as well? I confess, I am tired."

"Tell me what you are thinking, my dear. We have not spoken much about . . . about Justin, and I would not have you avoid the subject."

Celestine shrugged with a sad smile and she sat up, stretching out her spine and laying her head against the back of the chair. "I have been thinking of little else, I must confess. I am foolish, I know, but it seems so strange!"

"What, my dear?"

"That he should say what he said . . . *do* what he did! Why would he risk his family's wrath by saying he wanted to marry me? I just don't understand."

"I have known Justin for many years, my love, and I know that he never does anything just to please someone else. Nor does he do anything just to *spite* someone else. And he has *never* asked anyone to marry him before. How did all this come about?"

Celestine smiled, her gray eyes alight, the sorrow in them turning to a soft, dreamy pleasure. "I . . . I think it *began* as a way to annoy his sister-in-law."

Emily's eyes widened. "Maybe I should take back a part

of that previous statement, for that certainly sounds like spite! What do you mean?"

Celestine explained about the previous governess, which Emily, of course, already knew. She told her aunt about the words she had overheard from Lady St. Claire, about engaging Celestine partly because she was so plain. Then she went on and spoke of Justin's determined pursuit of her. "I think he just wanted to annoy Lady St. Claire by flirting with me in front of her. Either that, or he just cannot help himself. But I expected him to stop when the other ladies arrived, and he didn't."

"Knowing him to be a heartless flirt, how did you come to give your own heart to him?" Emily watched the flickering play of light across the pale oval of her niece's face. Her freckles were stark against the alabaster of her skin and her gray eyes wide and thoughtful. She stared into the fire. When she spoke, her voice had the caressing tone of a lover.

"He . . . he is not always what people see of him. Everyone sees the devil-may-care nobleman, the flirtatious lover of ladies."

Emily waited. There was more coming, and in the quiet of the low-beamed parlor, empty except for them, the only sound was the crackling of the fire and the tock-tock of a clock on the mantle. It was growing late, and the chance was Justin had not followed, after all.

"Sometimes when I sing," Celestine said after a long pause. "I feel my heart is going to burst out of my breast and shatter into a million pieces." Her gnarled hands covered her breast, over her heart. "I feel like a crystal vase after a rehearsal or a performance; one wrong word and I will crumble. Justin understands. I don't know how or why, but he does." Celestine's voice became urgent and she looked up, gazing into her aunt's eyes. "I feel, with him, no words are necessary. Something in his heart reaches out and touches something in mine. Does that not bespeak a good soul—a tender heart?"

Emily was deeply moved, for she understood. It was

how she had felt about Baxter. Oh, not right away, as in Celestine's case, but after they were married. She could look across a room and know what he was thinking . . . feeling. They would exchange glances that held volumes. Baxter could sense when she was in pain or tired without a word said between them.

She reached out and touched Celestine's hands where they now lay knotted together on her lap. "And so you fell in love?"

"Yes. I fell in love. And I had meant to be so sensible! I was ready to accept an offer from Mr. Foster, if he made one. I thought all I wanted out of life was a home of my own, a family, perhaps, and the chance to be a wife and mother with someone I respected. But it wouldn't have been right to marry Mr. Foster with love in my heart for someone else."

Emily nodded, reluctantly. "Though many would call you a fool for letting go of a chance for independence with a respectable man like the vicar, I happen to agree with you. If you were heart-whole, there would be a chance for your marriage, but to carry love for another man . . . it just wouldn't do."

"Justin is not what other people think him, Aunt. He is not shallow or vain. He can be so tender . . ." Her voice choked off, but then she cleared her throat. "It will be a lucky woman who does capture his heart and marry him."

Emily shook her head. She had made her gamble and had apparently lost. It was getting late, and Justin had not come. Perhaps his love wasn't strong enough to make him defy his older brother's authority or the snowstorm wailing outside.

Yawning, Celestine stood. "I think I will go up now. Are you coming?"

"In a few minutes," Emily said. "I'll be up soon." She found and spoke with the landlord who, with his wife, was sitting in comfort, his boots off, before the fire in the dark, smoky kitchen. They would desire breakfast at eight and their carriage ready by nine-thirty, she told them, weather permitting.

She had passed back through the drafty passage toward the dining room when the door swept open and a blast of wind carried in a flurry of snowflakes and a greatcoated stranger. He was covered in white, and until he swept off his hat and coat she did not even recognize him as Justin.

He wiped the snow from his eyes and looked about him, then saw Emily.

"Where is she? Where is Celestine?" he cried, his voice hoarse. He tossed his wet curls out of his eyes.

"Justin!" Emily tried to keep the joy out of her voice. It had seemed impossible just moments before that he would arrive, but now he was here, panting and wet, tossing aside his cumbersome frozen coat to the landlord's wife. Mrs. Shruggs bowed and muttered she would set the gentleman's garments by the fire to dry.

Emily did not want to carry on the conversation that must follow in the cold passageway, and so she strode into their private dining room, knowing Justin would follow. He did not disappoint her.

Justin was frozen-looking and shivering, his wet curls plastered over his forehead, but Emily carefully kept her concern from showing on her face. There would be time enough for that when they had sorted out a few things.

"What do you want with my niece? Have you not cut up her peace enough already?" Emily needed to know his intentions before she allowed him back in her niece's life. Though he had asked Celestine to marry him, Emily wanted to be sure what he felt for her niece was love, not pity or pique or frustration at her elusiveness. She wanted to judge the depth of his feeling for herself.

"It is not I who made her unhappy, but you and my interfering sister-in-law. Between the two of you, you have fair ruined our lives!" He stood before her, dripping and shivering, but he ignored his discomfort. "Where is she? I need to talk to her. I need to find out if she is really engaged to that prissy vicar, or if she has been forced into anything by you meddling shrews—you and Elizabeth."

Emily's heart pounded. She saw raw anger in Justin's face, and she had rarely seen any emotion there stronger than amusement before. He was never stirred beyond languid flirtation when it came to women, though he could attract them with just a simmering look from his brilliant blue eyes.

"I am all Celestine has in this world, sir, and I *will* protect her from a *roué* and a cad." Her words sounded stilted and theatrical, even to her, but Justin appeared not to notice.

He circled her, his boots thudding on the flagstone floor. She could almost feel the anger radiating from him. He must have struggled to get through the miserable storm outside; anyone less in love would have sheltered at some house on the way and trusted to the morrow to find his intended. But still she would goad him.

"You will protect her right out of love, Emily." His voice was dangerously quiet, coming from behind her ear.

Emily whirled and faced him again. "Love? From the most determined flirt and breaker of hearts in all of England? Perhaps she is safer with the vicar."

He glared at her. "Where is she?" His voice cracked with emotion. He looked like a man at the end of his tether—a man ready to do violence.

"I'll not say."

Justin advanced on her again as she backed away. "The damned vicar doesn't love her. He just wants a wife who will work herself to the bone for the parish. She needs someone who really loves her, someone who can protect her. Would you deny your niece love and someone to care for her because of your own failure?"

He caught her unawares. "What do you mean?" Her voice echoed shrill against the bare walls.

"Are you so bitter from your own failed marriage that you would deny everyone else the opportunity to find love?"

Emily's backbone stiffened. "That was uncalled for!"

"Was it? Then tell me why you won't let me see her!" His angry stance lasted only a minute, then his voice broke and his manner changed. He flung himself down in a chair, his elbows on his knees, and hid his face in his hands. "Has she spoken to you? Told you she doesn't care for me? Is that it?"

Emily gazed down at him. The clock on the mantle chimed ten. It was love. Nothing else could turn Justin St. Claire, elegant, immaculate nobleman, into this wet, exhausted, heartbroken man. She couldn't toy with him any longer. She was about to open her mouth to say she would call Celestine down when Justin began to speak in a low voice. At the same moment she caught sight of movement on the stairs. Celestine had come down at the commotion and stood in the shadows of the staircase, her long hair down around her shoulders.

"Emily, I am thirty-two. I thought I knew everything about love. I thought it was a pretty game you played like any other, with winners and losers at the end. The one with the most hearts won. I thought love was seeing a pretty face across a room and falling into some mad infatuation." He sighed and rubbed his face, then stared into the fire.

Emily stayed silent. The step creaked again, but when Justin launched back into speech, Celestine stayed where she was.

"And then I met a poor, plain spinster governess, or so she would likely describe herself." He chuckled mirthlessly. "I always thought beauty was something people wore like a cloak, covering their outside, clothing it in a sparkling exterior. But Celestine . . . she is like . . ." He faltered.

"I don't know how to describe it, but it is how a minister I once heard described the angels. Beauty shines out of her eyes. It pierced me right to the core, like a bright bolt of lightning that shot through me. And when she sang, it was like heaven's gate opened and she was allowed out—was allowed to come down to me. *Me,* of all people.

"It is like she is turned inside out. Other people are beautiful on the outside while she is beautiful on the inside, and it just glows, Emily. It just glows." His voice was a whisper. "And now I can't believe I ever thought her plain. Oh, Emily, her eyes! They are so lovely. There are no words. And her skin and her hair . . ."

Emily let out a breath she didn't even know she had been holding. "You love her?" Her voice trembled. Never could she have imagined Justin St. Claire speaking like this.

"Love her? I can't live without her! I told her that, but I don't think she believed me. I was afraid I would scare her away if I was too demanding. I want to marry her. I want to take her away to Questmere and spend the rest of my life looking after her and . . . and our children, if we should be so lucky. I feel . . . different when I am with her. Stronger, better . . . like there is some purpose in my life. She makes me . . ." He paused. "She makes me whole."

Emily could not believe Justin St. Claire, rake of the *ton,* spoke of love and marriage and children. He was as Celestine had said, loving and giving and tenderhearted. But it seemed her modest niece wasn't aware that loving *her* had wrought the change. She glanced over at the shadow on the stairs. She put one finger to her lips, stole up the stairs past her niece and retreated to her room. Her job was done.

Celestine crept the rest of the way down the stairs and stood, her feet bare against the frigid floor. She had already changed into her nightrail, and her long hair was down and brushed over her shoulders. She stood gazing in wonder at the man huddled on the chair by the fire.

Her Justin. Her love. He was shivering, damp, and miserable. He was cold and unhappy. How had he found her? And how long had he ridden through the blizzard to come to her?

"I love her, Emily," he said suddenly, rubbing his hands

over his tired face. "I'll never love anyone else. Help me convince her of that. Please. Do you think . . . do you think she will have me?"

"Yes. Oh, yes, yes, yes!" Celestine whispered.

Justin's head shot up and he turned and stared at her. "Celestine?"

"Yes, Justin?"

"Did you . . . did you just agree to marry me?" His face held a mixture of hope and dread.

"Yes."

"Do you love me? Or can you learn to?"

"Oh, Justin, I've loved you since the moment in the carriage when you pressed your kerchief into my hand! How could I not? My heart reached out that night and touched yours. I lost it that very second. You have had it this whole time, in your keeping, though you didn't know it."

"Celestine!" He leaped to his feet and crossed the short distance to her. He noticed for the first time she was barefoot on the cold flagstone and in her nightrail.

"My love! What do you mean risking your health this way?" he scolded. Without warning he scooped her up and moved over to the hearth, cradling her on his lap as he pulled the chair closer to the fire.

He stroked her hair gently and cradled her head against his shoulder, kissing her forehead. "I love you," he murmured, his voice breaking with the wonder of it. "I love you more than words can ever say. You know, they say reformed rakes make the best husbands. I mean to make you a very good husband, indeed."

She blushed and giggled, a sound she had never thought herself capable of. She felt young and beautiful and cherished in his arms. She gazed up at him in wonder, at those blazing blue eyes and strong features. She stroked his chin, scuffing her fingers over the whiskers that had grown over the long day he had spent, and ran her fingers through his wet curls, smoothing them back off his forehead.

He turned her hand and kissed her palm, then lowered his lips to hers. For a moment she felt the scratchiness of his whiskers, but then the sensation of his warm lips on hers obliterated every other thought. She felt his powerful arms tighten and the kiss deepened.

Never had she experienced anything to compare to the wonder of that kiss. His tongue touched her lips. At her little gasp of astonishment, her lips parted and he touched her tongue with his. A surge of passion coursed through her veins, and she thrust one hand under his damp jacket, feeling the steady thud of his heart against her fingertips.

He pulled away with a groan and gazed down at her with fire in his blue eyes. "I don't think this is good for my sanity. I will want to anticipate the marriage vows if we continue."

She blushed and wriggled on his lap, trying to sit up more properly. Aware suddenly that she was very improperly clothed in just her nightrail, with nothing underneath, her body came alive to the sensations of her breasts brushing against his chest and her bottom against his hard-muscled legs. She had never thought of the marriage bed before, though she was aware of what occurred there. Now it seemed enticing and wonderfully mysterious that in just a few weeks, perhaps, she and Justin would be . . . her mind shied away, and she started talking to ease her shyness.

"How did you know where to find me?" she asked.

"A little bird left me a note," he chuckled, stroking her cheek with his fingertips. "I think it was that grim-faced companion of your aunt's. She said she knew I loved you, and to prove it I could follow you to this inn."

Celestine's brow furrowed. "How would Dodo . . ." Then a smile wreathed her face. She remembered Emily's insistence that they stop and spend the night at this particular inn. She nuzzled Justin's chin. "I think Aunt Emily has some explaining to do."

"What do you mean?"

Celestine told him and Justin chuckled. "Devious wench," he rasped.

Gazing at him with concern, Celestine squirmed to slide off his lap, but he held her fast.

"I . . . I should get some decent clothes on and get you something hot to drink and a blanket. You are frozen to the bone, and . . ."

"Stop," Justin said, placing one finger over her lips. "Stop trying to take care of me. Let me take care of you; give me that privilege."

He pulled her to him again, his strong arms holding her close, his fingers caressing her through the thin fabric. Loving hands skimmed her hips, her waist, her shoulders, and lightly touched her breasts. It was a tantalizing preview of what would follow after the sacred exchange of vows that would join them forever in the sight of God. She shivered, a swell of excitement coursing through her veins. She relaxed against him and closed her eyes, her deep sigh arrested by his warm lips closing over hers.

From the depths of despair she had been raised to the pinnacle of joy. Justin loved her and wanted to marry her. He didn't just pity her, he *loved* her and wanted her—*needed* her, even. Somewhere deep inside she had known it—had known the strong cord that stretched taut from his heart to her own was not woven of pity or compassion, but of love and desire, the sort of love that would last forever.

Twenty

Celestine gazed at herself in the cracked, scarred mirror over her dresser. It almost felt like the last twenty-four hours had been a dream. Yesterday morning she had set out from Ladymead, leaving behind for good the man she had fallen in love with, believing he could never really love her.

Now she was back at Ladymead, staring into her same mirror in her same small bedroom. And yet everything had changed—everything but her own reflection. She was still just Celestine Simons, spinster governess, even if there was a new glow to her skin and her eyes sparkled when she thought of a certain wickedly handsome nobleman.

They had set out this morning from the Fellswater Inn to return to Ladymead, after much discussion between Justin and Emily. Her betrothed had at first wanted to go on to Emily's home in Yorkshire so Celestine could marry him from there. He claimed he had no desire to see his brother and sister-in-law again, after the things they had said and the way they had sent her away.

But Emily had pointed out a number of reasons it was best if they returned and made an attempt to reconcile with Justin's family. When he asked her, Celestine had added her voice to that of her aunt's. She had no wish to see him divided from a family he loved so very much.

The miracle of his love for her must not separate him from his blood relatives.

And so they had traveled back, arriving at Ladymead just an hour earlier. They had been lucky to get there at all after the snowfall of the previous day, but a west wind had cleared the road somewhat, and they had slogged through. Justin had slyly held her hand the whole way, under cover of a lap robe, impatiently pulling off her glove and stroking her fingers until she tingled all over from the nearness of him. She was exhausted and yet invigorated. The night had been almost sleepless for her. She and Justin had sat for hours together on the chair, a blanket around them, talking in soft voices of the future and planning their lives.

A bubble of happiness welled up in her even now, as she glanced down at her serviceable lavender dress, when she remembered how he had talked about a lavish trousseau for her. They had had their first polite argument over it. Celestine called it clothing a pigeon in peacock feathers. He preferred to call it gilding the lily.

But he insisted, gazing at her with love in his bright blue eyes as he planned to dress her in gold silk and ivory lace, topaz jewels, and a diamond tiara. She had let him talk, loving to hear his voice, feeling it deep down in his chest where her body touched his as they rode side by side in the carriage. Dodo had snored part of the way, and Emily, probably wanting to give them some measure of privacy, had seemed lost in a book.

Celestine pinned her gold locket over her heart and then opened it, gazing down at the tiny painting of her father. "Oh, Papa, you would be so happy for me today," she whispered.

There was a light knock on the door and she ran to open it to find Justin, breathtakingly handsome in buff breeches and dark green jacket. He offered her his arm. "Shall we go down, my lady?"

Nervously, Celestine swallowed. Their arrival an hour before had been anticlimactic. No one had been about, so they had gone to their separate chambers to wash and dress after the long carriage ride, agreeing to meet back downstairs again.

But by now the marquess and marchioness would be aware of what had happened and would be awaiting them downstairs. Celestine was nervous. She gazed up into Justin's eyes.

"Don't worry, my love, I will not let the lions eat you up. That is my privilege." He chuckled and leaned over to nip her earlobe.

She gasped at the light caress and leaned her heated cheek against the cool cloth that covered his chest.

"Are you ready?" he said.

She felt the steady thump of his heart against her cheek and his strength flowing into her. "I . . . I think so."

"Then let us go."

They walked down the narrower stairs from the third to the second floor, then descended the wide, carpeted stairs to the main floor. Dobbs hovered, smiling, in the great hall.

"Where is the family, Dobbs, old man?" Justin asked.

"Everyone is assembled in the drawing room, my lord."

"Thank you." Justin started in that direction, guiding Celestine on his arm, when they heard Dobbs clear his throat. They stopped and turned back.

Dobbs's wide, pale face was split in a huge, uncharacteristic grin. "May I say, my lord and Miss Simons, that on behalf of the staff, I wish you felicitations on your betrothal. We . . . we could not be happier." His gaze rested on Celestine. "We mean that, Miss. We wish you well."

Celestine smiled and stood straighter. "Thank you, Dobbs. That means a lot to me. Please thank the others."

Justin covered her hand on his arm with his other hand. "Shall we go?"

She nodded, and they entered the drawing room together. The Stimson girls were at the pianoforte, their heads bent over a piece of music, but they looked up as

Justin and Celestine entered the room. Mr. and Mrs. Stimson were by the fire, and Lady van Hoffen was sitting with Emily and Dodo, probably trying to prod them for gossip. The look on the flamboyant redhead's face when she glanced up and saw Justin with Celestine on his arm was a caricature of shock. Her rouged mouth dropped open and her eyes widened.

"I would like everyone to congratulate me," Justin said. He glanced down at the woman at his side and smiled. He felt as though he had made a long journey, a journey of the soul, and had come through it exhausted, but with a sharper appreciation for simple things, like the light, flowery scent his betrothed wore, and the soft translucence of her skin. "I have been fortunate enough to convince Miss Celestine Simons to be my wife. She will be Lady Celestine St. Claire." He never took his eyes from hers, and felt the warmth glowing in their gray depths.

A babble broke out around him, and the Misses Stimson were the first to rush up and make their congratulations. He watched as Celestine was drawn away from his side by the two girls, who pulled her over to a settee and settled on either side of her, questioning her avidly. His fiancée glanced back at him once, and he grinned broadly at her.

Lady van Hoffen glided to his side and gazed up at him, licking her lips. "And what indiscretion are you paying for with your freedom, dear boy?" she murmured.

His eyes wide, he looked down at her. "Paying? I think you misunderstand." He watched Celestine and listened to her quiet, dignified responses to the two girls' prodding questions. Tenderness flooded his heart, as it did every time he looked at her. "My lady, whatever freedom I seemed to have was an illusion. It took me a long time to learn, but I'll share the lesson with you. Freedom comes when you give it up willingly, committing yourself to another. I'm free to love now and it's like . . . like a miracle to me."

Incredulity sparked in the lovely redhead's eyes. "I

wonder how long that'll last," she murmured, moving away from him and assuming a languid pose near the window.

A footman approached him and bowed. "The marquess and marchioness request your presence in the library, my lord."

Justin nodded. He started toward the door, but found Celestine at his side. He touched her arm, finding her skin cool to his touch. "I will go alone, my love. I will not have you offended by their plain speaking or Elizabeth's sharp tongue."

She gazed into his eyes and a smile, the tiniest lifting of the corners of her mouth, flitted across her lips. "I am not such a poor creature as that, Justin."

He started to deny he had meant that, but she lifted one finger and put it over his lips.

"We'll do this together." Her words held a note of finality as she squared her shoulders.

They walked together down the hall and into the library. August was sitting behind his massive desk, and Elizabeth stood at his shoulder.

"August, Elizabeth," Justin said, coolly. He drew Celestine's arm through his own and strolled to stand in front of the desk. "By now, I think you probably know my intentions. Celestine has agreed to marry me. It took some convincing, but I prevailed at last."

Elizabeth snorted, a burst of unladylike sound in the quiet library. "This is a farce," she started.

But August put his hand up and she fell instantly silent. Justin glanced from Elizabeth's frosty glare to August's troubled gaze. He felt Celestine's arm start to tremble and anger welled up in him—anger that they felt they had a right to tell him who was suitable for marriage and who was not.

"I think," he said, and his voice was hard, glancing off the walls of the library and echoing, "that congratulations to me and my chosen bride are in order."

August stood and circled the desk, standing in front of

the couple, towering above them both. Justin felt his lips compress and his free hand ball into a fist. So help him God, if his older brother had the slightest thing to say against Celestine, he would land him a facer and walk right out of there.

The older man's troubled expression smoothed. As his features relaxed, Justin felt the tension drain from him.

"Justin, I am glad you have found a woman to love, one who will put up with you. It must have taken some convincing for her to take on such a task as to make a respectable person out of you, and I wish her well of it." He turned to Celestine and his brows, thick like Justin's, rode down low over his blue eyes.

"My dear, you have taken on a formidable chore. I love my brother, but he is a rascal." He glanced at his brother affectionately. "But if you love him," he said, his voice softer, "I think you will both be fine. Welcome to the family, Miss Simons . . . Celestine." He took her hand and kissed it, holding it in his own for a long moment. "To you both I offer my most humble apologies. I never thought to see you in love, Justin, and that must be my only excuse for any ungraciousness on my part. Love was a long time coming, but I think it has been worth the wait for you both. Good luck and God bless you with long life and many children."

He released Celestine's hand and turned to Elizabeth. "Don't you have something you wish to add, my love?"

Elizabeth, with a stunned expression, heeded the subtle steel in her husband's voice. She came around the desk and, with a ghostly smile, said, "Welcome to the family. I hope you will both be very happy."

"Miss . . . er, my lady, er . . ."

Elise's anxious voice caught Celestine's attention as she drifted down the hall to her room to get ready for dinner. Several days had gone by in a flurry of skating and music and gossip. Celestine was still not used to her new role as Justin's betrothed, but was enjoying it more than she expected. She had been afraid it would be awkward, making the transition from member of the staff to member of the family. But where the marquess led, others followed, and he had gone out of his way to be kind to his brother's betrothed. This was Christmas Eve, and dinner was to be a huge family affair with all of the children, followed by presents in the drawing room.

"I am still Miss Simons, Elise," Celestine chuckled.

Elise bobbed a curtsy and thrust a parcel at her. "I know, but soon you will be Lady Celestine St. Claire!" She breathed a happy sigh. "It's like a fairy-tale, like your puppet play, Miss . . . my I . . . Miss Simons."

"What is this?" Celestine asked, gazing down at the bundle in her hands.

"Open it, if you please, Miss."

Celestine did, and found in the paper wrapping the two sets of dolls she had been making, their features finished in neat, perfect stitches. Tears welled in her eyes and she gazed up at the sweet, round face of the maid. "Oh, Elise!" She startled them both by putting her arms around Elise for a quick hug.

The girl turned bright pink and shyly looked down at her shoes. "I knowed you wanted to finish 'em so badly, but your hands bein' the way they were . . . an' you bin so kind to me, I thought I'd like to pay you back. So I stayed up last night an finished 'em. I decided to do it when you left. I was gonna give 'em to the little girls, telling them it was your gift to them, since you couldn't be here. But now you can give them to them yourself, 'specially now you're goin' to be family."

Celestine could only smile at her through the tears gathering in her eyes.

Dinner was a noisy, cheerful affair. Then in the drawing room they played silly games and sang Christmas songs in front of the crackling fire. Occasionally, when the doors opened, they could hear the strains of the fiddle from the servants' hall, where a party was in progress among the staff. The whole house rang with joy. At long last, when their excitement was at a fever pitch, the children were allowed to open their gifts.

Celestine had not expected, with the abundance of gifts they got, that Lottie and Gwen would take much note of hers, but they did, Gwen especially whispering that it was her 'fabrit' dolly. The little girls had been told she would no longer be their governess and would become their new aunt, but of course they did not really understand.

Gus did, though, and he politely thanked her for her work on the puppet play, his voice cracking under his uncle's gaze as he shyly admitted he had liked it more than he had expected. Playacting was not as babyish as he had thought, he said manfully. Celestine, holding a sleepy little Bertie on her lap at that moment, had to hide a smile as she saw the interaction between Justin, who was obviously coaching the young man through the steps of polite society, and Gus, who was desperate to please his uncle. What a good father Justin would make! She blushed at the turn her thoughts had taken and laid her flushed cheek against Bertie's fuzzy head.

She sighed tiredly. It had been a bewildering and exhausting few days, but in that time she had gained a husband and a family and a whole new life. The little boy on her lap gurgled happily, and contentment swept through her soul.

At last, after another hour of conversation, she felt she had stayed long enough and excused herself. Justin insisted on walking her upstairs. Slowly they mounted the wide staircase adorned with holly wound round the banister and big red bows attached every few feet.

"You did not have to come with me," she whispered in the hall, glad nonetheless for his strong arm to lean on. She started toward the door to the third floor, then remembered in chagrin she had been assigned a chamber on the second floor because of her new status as part of the family.

"Oh, but I wanted to come with you. I have my own wicked reasons." He tugged her into a dim alcove off the hall and pulled her into his arms.

"Justin! We might be seen!" She tried to resist, but the warmth of his arms around her and the feel of his lips on her forehead made her melt, as always, and she relaxed into his arms. How would she ever get used to having a man like Justin?

"Oh, look," he said, huskily. "A kissing bough!" His finger pushed her chin up and tilted her head back, and his lips closed over hers.

Warmth flooded her core and she sighed against his lips, responding eagerly when his darting tongue pressed the seam of her lips. She opened to him, shivering with desire as his arms tightened around her and his hands traveled over her back and up to the nape of her neck. His kisses trailed over her cheek and down to her throat, finding the pulse point at the base of her throat.

She opened her eyes. "There's no kissing bough here!" she cried, glancing around.

He made a deep sound in his throat and continued his kissing and nibbling. She giggled as his lips tickled her earlobes. "I see kissing boughs everywhere," he said, giving her one more big kiss on the lips.

"Justin," she sighed, clasping her arms around his neck, "oh, Justin, I love you. You bring my world to life. Your wicked laugh and your energy and your joy—they fill me with life!"

He laughed softly in the darkness. "What a wonderful, sweet thing to say, my love."

"It's true. Justin?" Her voice was wistful and soft, a whisper in the hush of the night, with just the faint murmur of voices from the drawing room downstairs breaking the silence.

"Yes, love?" he said. He bent his head and began again,

his kisses trailing up her throat to her chin, one long-fingered hand stealing up to her breast to cup it lovingly.

She gasped and covered his hand with her own, but did not pull away from him. She could never do that, not when the nearness of him was the very essence of the life force to her.

"What do I bring to you?"

"Mmmm?"

He was doing indescribably delicious things to her body. Even through the fabric of her dress, she could feel his hot breath over her breasts and the moist heat of his kisses. Her nipples were tightening almost painfully into pearly nubs as he caressed them with practiced, seductive fingers. It made her dizzy with desire as she tried to clear the fog in her brain. There was something important she needed to know. Now, what was it? Oh, yes.

"Justin, I need to know. What do I bring to you? How do I make your life better? It's important to me."

He sighed and straightened. "I think on our wedding night I shall have to teach you that some parts of love do not need the accompaniment of words."

He chuckled, though, and she could see his bright blue eyes glittering in the pale light from a branch of tapers on a small table in the hall. He looked down into her eyes and his expression grew serious.

"I apologize, my love. I get carried away with wanting you and forget myself. So I will answer your question, and then I have something to give you."

She rested her head against his chest, once again feeling the reassuring thump of his strong heart against her cheek.

"What do you give me? More than I can say in the brief moments we have right now. But I can tell you one thing—the most important. You have given me a life. For thirty-two years I have been walking and doing and playing and making love and functioning on the face of this earth, with no conception I was only half a man.

"When I found you, you made me whole, completed

me, gave me purpose and meaning and . . . and life. Oh, my darling," he whispered into her hair, his breath warm. He wrapped his arms around her more tightly, surrounding her with his love. "I was just a walking shell playing at being a human being until I gave you my heart and you breathed life into it. Once, in a dark church, I listened to an angel sing and wondered what I was on this earth for. Now I know. I was put here to love you and take care of you and make a life with you."

A sharp, soaring gladness flooded Celestine, the kind that roared through her blood when she sang. What he said matched the feelings in her heart, and she knew that it was forever, this love of theirs.

He pulled away from her and fished around in an inside pocket of his jacket. "This is my gift to you for Christmas, but more importantly to show everyone you are mine and we are going to be married—in no more than three weeks. Please say you will only make me wait as long as it takes to read the banns."

Celestine felt a ring being pressed into her hand. Tears welled up in her eyes. "I . . . I . . ." Her voice choked off, but through her tears she muttered, "I cannot wear it—it will not fit over my . . . my finger."

"I know, my love," he said, his voice gentle. "That is why it is on a gold chain. When the swelling goes down on your fingers, you can slip it on and use the chain for your locket. Until then, you will wear it around your neck, *outside* your dress, please, so everyone can see it. I want everyone to know I caught myself a Christmas angel."

His lips met hers as he clasped the chain around her neck, and she wound her arms around him. Her Justin, more gentle and thoughtful than any man she had ever known. Papa would be proud.

Emily and Grishelda van Hoffen moved quietly down the hallway toward their rooms, which were across the hall from each other. Both were arrested at the same moment by the sight of the two figures—or was it one?—in the alcove. In the dim light, they could just make out Celestine and Justin, their arms wound around each other, oblivious to the rest of the world.

"I do not understand it," the younger woman murmured. "He is pleasant enough, but she seems absolutely infatuated with him! And I thought she was such a sensible woman."

Emily watched the couple, knowing they were completely unaware they were being observed. A pang of happiness and sadness pierced her heart.

The happiness was for her beloved niece, Celestine, and the marital bliss sure to follow such a promising beginning. The sadness was for herself. So had her marriage begun, and yet look how it had ended! And she was denied finding love again by the fact that her marriage was still very much a legal entity and she could not bring herself to break the vows she had made fifteen years before.

She glanced over at the pale young woman beside her. Lady Grishelda's prim lips were pursed in a disapproving frown. The girl had so much to learn about life.

"My dear, no one understands love until you are in it. And even then, it is a beautiful mystery, and that is the way God intended it, I think. I hope someday you will discover that kind of joy." Emily smiled and urged her companion on, leaving the two still figures—two who were joined as one.

ABOUT THE AUTHOR

Donna Simpson lives with her family in Canada. *Lord St. Claire's Angel* is her first Regency romance. Donna loves to hear from readers, and you may write to her c/o Zebra Books. Please include a self-addressed stamped envelope if you wish a response.